The Three of Us

Vivien Brown

BLOODHOUND BOOKS

To my grandchildren: three pink and three blue

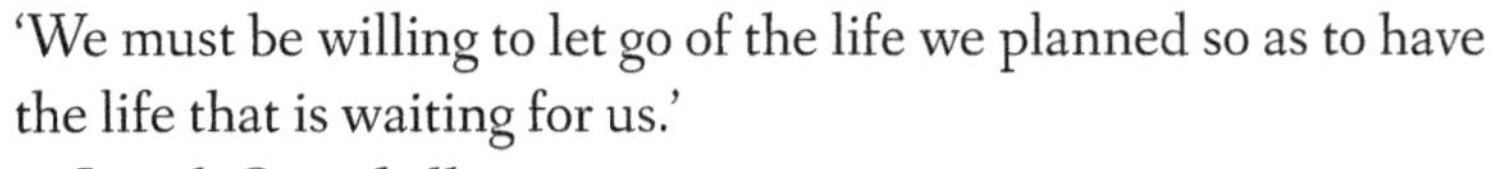

'We must be willing to let go of the life we planned so as to have the life that is waiting for us.'
— *Joseph Campbell*

Chapter 1

Carly

Thirty-one and still single. According to my mother, she of the 'nab him and marry him before you're twenty-five' generation, there must be something wrong with me. Either I'm trying too hard and putting men off, or I'm not really trying at all.

I'm sure, in another life, she would have made a very passable Mrs Bennet, desperate to marry off a string of eligible and not so eligible daughters before they ended up on the shelf. At least I'm the one and only daughter, but even so, Jane Austen has a lot to answer for!

If I would just get my head out of a book and pay more attention to my hair. Deal with the frizz and maybe add some highlights to my natural, and rather boring, mousey mop.

If I would just stay away from my usual pints of cider and sip at something smaller and more ladylike, preferably while gazing up all dewy-eyed at some man, leaving just a hint of cleavage on show so he can see what he's missing, although, of course, I must never give it to him. Not until I have the ring on my finger anyway.

If I could just be more... girly, then, in Mum-speak, I will have cracked it. I'd have a husband in the bag, and in my beautifully made Laura Ashley-clad bed, in no time at all.

If only it were ever that straightforward, or that simple.

Exes. There have been a few, I have to admit. Some who have got as far as the meet-the-parents milestone, some I would never have dreamed of taking anywhere near. The odd one-night stand too, whose names I'd struggle to remember the morning after, let alone now, but the less my mother knows about that side of my life the better. She may be only just turned sixty but there's something very old-fashioned and traditional about her. Gran was the same, so it must be in the blood, God help me. All jam-making and aprons and little lace doilies on the dressing table. Mum's a bit of a worrier too, and an even worse one in the last few years, since she lost Dad and has had to take on all the worrying for two.

Okay, she's right that my success rate with men has not been all it could be. But, in my defence, none of them have been what I would call husband material. But I let them all slip through my fingers, according to Mum. And now look at me. All her friends' daughters, and quite a few of their sons, are settled, spoken for – and there's me, like the last unwanted doll in the shop, still perched firmly on the shelf. It would never occur to her to lay the blame at the feet of any of the men I've had the misfortune to know, either biblically or otherwise. I'm just too critical, apparently. I expect too much.

He's too plain? 'Looks aren't the be all and end all, Carly,' she says. 'And looks soon fade anyway. After all, they can't all be Richard Gere, can they? A few wrinkles, a receding hairline, a bit of a belly are to be expected as time passes.' No, it's dependability I should be looking for, according to her. A good steady job. And if he's not already successful, then at least he should have prospects. Someone who'll work hard to build a career, pay the bills, and who'll keep his whatsit in his trousers when he's away from home. She wanders off into some tale about Auntie Sybil and Uncle Harold and how she should never have taken him back after all that business with his secretary, but I choose not to listen. Maybe he loved his secretary. Maybe he married the wrong woman. Who knows?

He's too boring? 'Your father could have bored for England,' my mother says. 'Especially once you got him started on mortgage rates or pest control or cricket, but he knew how to mow a good lawn, and look at how nicely he decorated the hall.' I know she doesn't mean it. The glint of tears in her eyes tell me that she would give anything to hear him talking about those pesky aphids, or even all that unintelligible leg before wicket stuff, again. She misses him a lot more than she's prepared to let on. As much as I do, and probably a whole lot more. She found her perfect man and she's trying her best to make sure I do the same. It's just that her idea of perfect isn't quite the same as mine.

So, I've set my sights too high, it would seem, turning away perfectly decent men just because they fail what she regards as my impossibly unrealistic compatibility test. But I know it's just that I don't actually fancy them. That's the real reason why. Because there's no chemistry, no spark.

Spark? When I try to explain, she stares at me in disbelief at the very mention of the word. 'What's a spark when it's at home? Wait too long for a spark and there'll be nothing left to burn,' she says, or words to that effect. I've left it all terribly late and I should now, it seems, despite me being too silly to realise it, be out there grabbing at any half-decent, run-of-the-mill bachelor who shows the faintest glimmer of interest in me, before someone else gets there first, before the pool is empty and all that's left for me to pick from are the ones every other girl has already rejected. The way-too-old, the mummy's boys, the pig-ugly or, God forbid, the divorcees, back for a second bite of the cherry, with kids and maintenance payments and vicious ex-wives and all sorts of other accompanying baggage.

To listen to my mother, I'm at the last chance saloon and have been ever since I turned thirty. The clock is ticking. Let's face it, she's desperate to be a grandmother, and who provides the sperm is hardly more than a detail.

Which is exactly why I decided, right from the start, not to tell her about Jack. *Never* to tell her about Jack.

Not to tell her that he was quite possibly the best-looking man I had ever seen and that, for the last five years, I have been secretly comparing every man I meet to him, and not one of them has come close.

Not to tell her that he comes from some out-of-the-way Norfolk village nobody's ever heard of and that he grew up on a farm. 'All those big boots and baggy overalls,' she would tut, 'and just think of the mucky fingernails and where they might have been!' How can she say that, with Dad always being so caught up in his beloved allotment and bringing clods of earth and the hint of manure into the kitchen on a pretty much daily basis? 'No, no, that's different,' she would say. 'Growing veg was a hobby for your father, not a job. He was a bank manager, Carly. Never forget that. Respected. Looked up to.'

I could tell her that Jack wore a suit these days and worked in an office, but I don't even know if that's true anymore. He went back there, didn't he? To the village, and a life I know nothing about. He could be spending his days knee-deep in mud or with his arm up a cow for all I know.

I certainly couldn't tell her that the sparks were flying so high the first time Jack touched my hand that I could have done with Dad's super-duper lawn sprinkler, just to cool myself back down. Or that there was more chemistry brewing in the back bar of the Rose and Crown that day than in all the test tubes in my brother Sam's favourite old toy chemistry set, multiplied ten times over. Light the touch paper and stand well back. Or is that what they say about fireworks? Come to think of it, there were a fair few of those flying about too.

If I close my eyes, I can still see Jack's face as clearly as ever, can still feel his fingers as they interlaced through my own, in that instant instinctive way that nobody else's ever have. Well, except Dad's perhaps. There was always something warm and safe and wonderful in my dad's big all-encompassing hands.

It's his voice I find hardest to recall. I don't mean Dad's, which I've spent a lifetime listening to and will never forget and, as Mum has never found the courage to delete it from the answerphone message, I can still hear anytime I need to. No, I mean Jack's. A voice I never had the chance to get to know that well, or to memorise forever. I have to think back, to something he actually said, bring the exact words into my mind first and then, if I'm lucky, the voice that spoke them will follow. I dread the day that doesn't happen, when I can't remember, when he becomes just a black-and-white photo of a man (not that I've actually got a photo of him, in colour or not, despite frantically searching through Facebook and Instagram and finding he's just not there) and I can't get him – the essence of him – back, if only for that wonderful fleeting moment.

Oh, Jack. How could you have done this to me? Started breaking my heart before I'd even given it to you? Before you even knew it was on offer?

It was all a case of bad timing. No, not just bad timing. It was bloody awful, couldn't-make-it-up, terrible timing. The worst. Because the one really big thing I definitely cannot tell my mother about Jack is that, just three months after that firework moment that changed my whole life, he got married. To somebody else. Rings, bells, pageboys, her probably in some huge dress like an over-whipped meringue, carnations in buttonholes, and a cake almost as tall as I am. The whole clichéd shebang. It was all already arranged, planned, paid for, before we'd even met. A girl from his village. Someone he had promised to go back to just as soon as his six months working in London were over. Someone he cared about and couldn't possibly hurt. And didn't want to. Well, why would he? It's like poor romantic Elinor Dashwood all over again, so heartbroken when she hears that her secret crush, Edward, has married his long-time fiancée Lucy Steele. Only that had been a total misunderstanding and he was still single, still hers, after all. What were the chances of that happening to me? Pretty much none, I reckon. Bloody Austen, with her false hopes and unrealistically happy endings.

Jack was the love of my life. We belonged together. I sensed it, felt it, just knew it, absolutely and instantly. Still do. If only he had felt it too.

Why was he taking such a huge step? He was young then, only twenty-four, just a couple of years younger than I was, and way too young to be tying himself down. There was time for all that, later, much later. Why couldn't he have seen that? That he could wait, put it all off for a few years, until he was sure, that he still had a choice. But it seemed he had made that choice and had no intention of changing his mind. The trouble was, apart from turning up at the church and making a complete fool of myself (which, to be honest, right up until the day of the ceremony, I hadn't completely ruled out), there was absolutely nothing I could do about it. So that was how it ended. How I lost Jack, *my* Jack, to the other woman, the woman who is now his wife.

But now, completely unexpectedly and right out of the blue, it looks like he might be back.

It's a Tuesday in early August, a sunny day, and I have no after-work plans except to relax and enjoy a couple of drinks in a pub garden with my friends Fran and Suze, sharing a big plate of chips with both ketchup and mayonnaise on the side because we never can agree on which is best, and a good old gossip. And most of that is about Rosie, once a stalwart member of the gang and now swallowed up in so-called domestic bliss, which roughly translates as being buried up to the eyeballs in crying babies, soggy nappies and never-ending piles of dirty washing. Living what my mother would regard as the dream life, but for me the jury's still out on that one.

From the moment Rosie had told us she was expecting twins, we'd lost her. All she could talk about was morning sickness and stretch marks and antenatal exercises and, as if that wasn't bad enough, when the time came, we had to hear all the gory details of the actual birth too. The gas and air, the pain, the stitches, her husband, Syd, turning a ghostly shade of white and almost hitting the floor.

That was three months ago, and since then... no booze, no sneaky fags, no girly shopping trips (unless ordering feeding bras and extra-large knickers online counts), no fun at all. It was like a perfectly normal girl who had spent the last fifteen years or so with a drink in one hand and a mascara wand in the other had suddenly been taken up into a flying saucer by aliens and returned looking pretty much like the same person but utterly, utterly changed. Like she'd had some kind of irreversible motherhood makeover. Maybe that's why those sci-fi films always seem to call it the mother ship.

'Projectile vomiting,' Suze is saying when I come back to the table with our second round of drinks balanced on a tray. 'It actually hit the wall, apparently. The far wall, you know, the one by the radiator, not the one by the sofa. Sprayed everywhere like someone had been pebble-dashing the place. Can you imagine?' I try really hard not to. 'I suppose she was lucky it was only *one* of the little buggers. Just think what it would be like if they were both at it at once.'

'Stereo sick.' Fran screws up her face. 'Yuck!'

'Must we talk about sick? It's enough to put me off my chips.' I slide back along the bench next to Fran, grab two lukewarm chips from the almost empty plate before anyone else can, and take a sip of my ice-cold cider to help swill them down.

'Yeah, you're right, Carls. We get enough of that from Rosie when she's here. At least let's spare ourselves the baby talk while she's not.'

'*Here?* She's never here.' Suze pinches the last chip, twirls it around in what's left of both the ketchup and the mayonnaise until it's bright pink and bites it in half.

'True. When was the last time either of you actually saw her, or spoke to her? Other than on Facebook, I mean.' Fran eyes the empty plate and reaches for her purse. She's going to go inside and buy more chips. No surprise there. It's what she always does.

'Dunno. Three weeks, maybe?' Suze shrugs her shoulders. 'It's all weighing clinics and mother and baby groups for our Rosie nowadays. Her idea of a social life. There's no time left for any of us.'

'Do you think we'll end up like that?' Somehow, I find the idea depressing, as if all my mother's dreams for me are one day going to culminate in me turning into another Rosie. 'All married and maternal and bored out of our brains?'

'Oh, God, I hope not.' Fran eases herself along the bench and stands up. I swear I can feel the seat tip in my direction as soon as her rather large bottom has vacated the other end. She and Suze are sisters but you'd never guess unless you were told. Fran's a redhead, while Suze seems to change her hair colour as often as her men. Fran's also two years younger but getting on double the size. She really shouldn't keep buying more chips, but I'm not going to be the one to tell her. I'm sure her working in a sweet shop doesn't help either. Far too many Crunchies and

Dairy Milks and nowhere near enough exercise. I thought my love life was bad enough but, since I started sharing a flat with her, I get to see at close hand when she goes out and who with, and I can guarantee that poor Fran's love life is currently non-existent. Not that she seems to care. She's actually the happiest and most laid-back person I know, so she must be doing something right.

'So, have you met the new IT consultant they've brought in at work yet?' Suze asks once Fran has gone inside. 'He was getting out of the lift this afternoon when I was on my way upstairs and I took the opportunity of saying hello. Drop-dead gorgeous, or what?'

Suze and I have worked together in the accounts department at Mandrake's Insurance for three years now. She was the one who told me there was a job going and put in a good word for me, so I know I should be grateful, but sometimes I do wonder if mixing up our social and business lives quite so closely is such a good idea. Here we are, for instance, supposedly out for a nice relaxing drink or two and the conversation still comes back to the office. A place I'd like to get away from and forget about once I've walked away every night. There are other downsides too. We burst into giggles at work just a little too often for a start, and sitting side by side all day makes it hard to have any sort of private life. She sees everyone I speak to in the office and can overhear every call I make. Still, that goes both ways, I suppose, and it is nice having a buddy to work with instead of some of the bitches I've had to put up with in the past.

Suze can be a bit of a flirt though, even when she's at work, and eyeing up any new male member of staff has long been a hobby of hers. She keeps a little not-so-secret star chart in her top drawer, just a jokey thing really, but it's divided up into sections for looks, charm, sense of humour, bum... and she marks them all out of ten. This new guy has clearly scored highly.

I laugh as she waves her hand about in front of her face as if fanning it furiously will calm the red-hot thoughts that are clearly in danger of making her self-combust.

'That good, eh?'

'Oh, yes. Sex on legs. Tall, dark, handsome. I wouldn't say no, believe me. He even smells divine!'

'I can't say I've had the pleasure. Well, not yet anyway. Maybe I'll take a stroll up there tomorrow and take a peek.'

'Well, he definitely smiled at me, so just you remember that I saw him first and don't you go muscling in. Not that he's exactly available, to be honest. I did just happen to notice he was wearing a wedding ring, but a girl can dream...'

'I don't know about dream. Looks more like drool to me! And haven't you forgotten you're meant to be going out with Sean Miller? He seems like a nice enough guy.'

'He's okay, I suppose. It's only been a couple of months though, Carly. We're hardly joined at the hip. I like to keep my options open.'

I laugh, because Suze has been keeping her options open for so long that I don't think she ever has any intention of closing them. No matter who she's seeing, she always seems to have one eye open for someone better. She's so scared of missing that elusive Mr Ten-Star who could walk into her life at any moment and sweep her off her feet, that she never lets any real-life ordinary man get close enough, however nice he might be. That's pretty much what my mother says about me, I suppose, but in Suze's case it's completely different. She's still waiting for her ideal man and I've already met mine.

'So, what's his name then? This new dream of a man I'm not allowed to snatch from under your nose? Not that I would anyway. Probably best we both steer clear, if he's married.'

'He said his name's Jack. Jack Doughty or Dockery, or something like that. I'm sure I'm going a bit deaf lately. I sometimes wish we all had to wear name badges, then I wouldn't have had to try and work out what he said. And a badge pinned in just the right place would be the perfect excuse to stare at his chest. Still, I suppose we'd get the men staring at ours too if we all had to wear them, so maybe it's not such a great idea.'

I've stopped listening. I'm sure my heart rate has suddenly shot up because the blood is thumping around my system and making my pulse race. There's heat rushing to my face and I think my hands are starting to sweat just a little bit. Jack? A gorgeous IT man called Jack, with a surname that sounds something like Dockery? That's what she said. But it can't be him, can it? Jack? Jack Doherty? *My* Jack Doherty? Back in London, after all this time? And working right here in the same part of town, in the same building, for the same company, as me?

Fran has come back from the bar and is settling down beside me, a chip from the plate she's just plonked on the table already halfway to her mouth. 'What have I missed?' she asks, chomping down on the chip and blowing frantically because it's too hot. 'Whatever it is you're talking about, our Carly's gone all pink.'

'Or *who*ever,' Suze says, suddenly noticing what Fran saw straight away. 'What is it, Carly? Is it Jack Whatever-his-name-is? Do you know the guy?'

I close my eyes for a moment and try to stay calm. 'If it's who I think it is, then yeah, I probably do. Or did, anyway. A long time ago.'

'Really? Come on then. You can't stop there. Don't keep us in suspense. Tell all. And we want all the juicy bits. When? Where? How? And, most of all, did you?'

The truth is that Suze and I just know each other so well.

Too well, maybe. If I had met Jack at any time in the last three years, she would have known about it, sensed it, squeezed every last detail out of me. Luckily, my Jack time was long before I came to work at Mandrake's, back when Rosie was my best friend and Suze and I would only see each other a couple of times a month at most, so he's managed to pass under her radar.

Nowadays, nothing gets past her, and now she's got Fran interested too.

Four curious eyes are staring at me, waiting.

I don't speak. I'm not sure I would know what to say if I did.

'Oh, my God, you did, didn't you?' Suze is getting all excited now. 'You dark horse, you! So, how come we don't know about this? I thought we told each other everything.' She reaches across the table and tilts my chin up with her finger, so she's looking right into my eyes, and then she just gently shakes her head. 'You and the gorgeous Jack. Carly Young, you lucky, lucky bugger.'

Chapter 2

Jack

'Oh, do stop moaning, Mol.' Jack looks in the hall mirror and fiddles with his tie. 'Yes, the flat's a bit on the small side, but I can't help it that London prices are so much higher than back home. It's all we can afford for now, but we'll get used to it. Enjoy it, even. This was too good an offer to turn down. I was stuck in a dead-end job in that dreary office. Moving here was the right thing to do. A no-brainer.'

'There was always the farm. Your dad would have loved it if you...'

'No. Farming's not for me, Molly. You know that. And nor is village life, not anymore. And what would have happened long-term? When Mum and Dad decide to retire? When they die? Two brothers can't both take it on, can they? End up trying to squeeze two families into one farmhouse? Let Richard have it, let him take it all on. The early mornings and the freezing cold winters, out in those muddy fields. It was okay when I was a teenager, glad of earning a few pounds after school, but a career? A way of life? No. This new IT job is what I've trained for, what I'm good at. And it's my big chance, *our* big chance, to spread our wings a bit, enjoy city living, have some fun, before we vegetate.'

'Vegetate?' Molly rolls her eyes. 'Living in Shelling wasn't that bad, and you know it. You make it sound like it's got nothing going for it at all.'

'Well, has it? One pub, a church we haven't set foot in since our wedding, a couple of shops and a bus that comes through twice a day. A population with an average age of... what? Sixty? It's hardly the centre of the universe, is it?'

'Of course not, but it's friendly, and it's quiet, and it's safe. It's home, Jack. Where our families are. Where we belong.'

'We belong wherever we choose to be, Mol. People move all the time, try out new things, new places. Look, I'm going to be late if I don't get going soon. Not the impression I want to make in my first week. And we've been through all this before, so many times...'

'I know. It's just... oh, I don't know. There's you going off to your exciting new job and I'm stuck here on my own, unpacking boxes. I don't know anybody, Jack, and I don't get the feeling it's the sort of neighbourhood where people pop in and out of each other's houses for tea and scones. What will I do with myself all day, every day?'

'You'll feel better when you find a job.'

'*If* I find a job. The only thing I know anything about is baking.'

'Then bake! Make us a nice flat-warming cake, one of your famous lemon drizzles, and then go out for a walk or something. You never know, there might be a lovely little bakery just round the corner, crying out for staff.'

'Yeah, right.'

'Or do what you should have done ages ago. Work from home. Set up a little business of your own. Making wedding cakes, birthday cakes, all those fiddly little overpriced cupcake things that everyone suddenly seems to want these days. Put cards in shop windows, the local paper, get something online. I could build you a little website to get things started, and you can add photos and things as you go along. You're good at cakes, Mol, just like I'm good at IT. And Londoners must want to eat cakes just as much as the people of Norfolk did. And they'll probably be prepared to pay a lot more for them here too. Now, I really do have to go.' He picks up the black leather briefcase his parents had insisted on buying for him as a leaving gift, even though there's nothing in it but a sandwich and the newspaper he's just lifted off the mat, kisses his wife on the cheek and closes the door behind him.

Jack Doherty loves London. He's lived here before, when his old company sent him to work on a short secondment five years ago, in their big fancy glass-fronted offices near the river. He hadn't quite done the full six months in the end. The company had secretly been in trouble before he'd arrived and, in the end, nothing he nor his colleagues could do was able to save it. He had managed to walk away with a small redundancy pay-out and a good reference, but having to skulk back home with his tail between his legs was not his finest hour. And although he'd found another job quickly, in an office in Norwich, it had only ever been a stopgap as far as he was concerned, a way of bringing in some money while he waited for his big break and a return to what he had been trained to do, and with a decent salary to match. There was only so much help he was willing to accept from his family, and Molly's, although he was glad that together the two sets of parents had footed the bill for the wedding. Not that he would have opted for the huge affair it had ballooned into if he had had to pay for it himself. A small register office do and a meal in the Brown Cow would have been enough for him, but that was not the traditional village way, and certainly not Molly's way.

Much as he will always have a soft spot for his childhood home, being away from Shelling at last feels strangely liberating, as if he is back in command of his own destiny. No more talk of taking over the farm, no more living in his in-laws' spare room while he and Molly save for a deposit on a place of their own, no more boring temporary job that he dreaded getting up for every morning. He knows he has more or less dragged Molly here against her will, but she will get used to it, he is sure. Well, she has to really, as the deed has been done now. They have packed up and moved. Escaped. He is happy and she will be too, given time. He passes a flower stall at the entrance to the Underground and tells himself, if it's still open later when he comes home, he'll buy her a bunch of something pretty. It's the least he can do.

It's his fourth day at Mandrake's Insurance and he's only just starting to figure out where everything is, and how it all works. It's a big old building, nothing like the place he was at when he worked in London before. There's a lot more wood than glass, for a start, with flaking paint on the walls, and box-like lifts, and tall oak doors, even just leading to the Gents, rather than the shiny escalators and stainless steel and sweeping Thames views he had begun to get used to and had found so impressive before everything had come to such an abrupt end. Still, he has a good feeling about his new job with the consultancy firm and his first placing here at Mandrake's. If all goes well, he will only be working here for three months, to see this new finance project through, and then on to something else. Variety, responsibility, security, and all right here in London, where he wants to be. Jack feels happier than he has ever been.

'Morning, Jack.' A girl he must have met at some point in the last few days but whose name he can't recall gives him a wide smile as he crosses the reception lobby and they both step into the lift. She is carrying a bundle of files and there's lipstick on her teeth, yet he chooses not to embarrass her by telling her. He nods and smiles back, then leaves her to carry on upwards as the lift shudders to a stop and he steps out at the second floor.

His desk is boxed off, as they all are, by moveable half-height partitions that break the large open-plan office into smaller cubes, offering only a pretence at privacy, but at least his own little cube is near the window. He has a view, even if it's only of the grimy buildings across the street. The desk is old and traditional, its top made of dark wood, dull and scratched and several inches thick, and it's already cluttered with a collection of paper and pens, and a black-skinned banana he brought in on Monday and still hasn't eaten. He sits down and immediately switches his computer screen on, opening up his emails before he's even slipped off his jacket or settled properly in his seat.

'Hi, Jack. Team meeting in Bob's office in five,' a voice calls from behind a partition somewhere to his left.

'Thanks, Jane.' He is slowly getting to know his colleagues' names and Jane has made her mark by bringing him a coffee and a doughnut on his first day and giving him the office version of the grand tour, so at least he now has a vague idea of the lie of the land.

He tucks his briefcase under his desk and unlocks the top drawer to find a notepad he'll probably need for the meeting. The photo is still in there too, a small square one in a cheap frame, a close-up of Molly, smiling into the camera, her straight blonde hair blowing in the wind, her suntanned arms wrapped around her parents' old dog, Flossy. She has given him the picture to put on display, but so far he hasn't done it. First, he needs to find out just what sort of place he's working for. He wants to figure out what the others do. Whether they have photos on their desks, of wives, partners, kids, pets. Whether they make personal calls in work time. Where they go at lunchtime, and whether they go there together. What's acceptable and what's frowned upon. What will go down well at a place like Mandrake's? Being seen as the kind of family man who goes home early on his anniversary and walks his dog at weekends, or a go-getter who stays till late to get things done and always puts the job first? He needs to work that out before he shows his hand, so for now the photo stays in the drawer.

Jack looks at his watch, the Omega his mum and dad gave him for his twenty-first, so reliable that he has never needed to replace it in the eight years it's been a permanent feature on his wrist. A quality thing, built to last, a bit like his shiny new briefcase. He stands up and closes the drawer and heads for the boss's office for the team meeting. He's part of a team now, and his number one priority is to be accepted, to learn all he can about the company and his place in it, to learn to fit in, even if he's only here for a while. Because nothing is going to drag him back to the farm or to some dead-end job he hates. Absolutely nothing.

Chapter 3

Molly

Molly pulls off the sticky tape, folds another empty cardboard box flat and stretches her aching back. She's sorted out everything in the kitchen and the bedroom now, plates and cutlery, a toaster, a kettle, far too many glasses, assorted towels and duvet sets, some of it still in its original wrappings and untouched since the wedding, having been stored in her parents' attic while it waited for a home to be absorbed into. And now she's made a start on the less important stuff. The old CDs, the paperback books, the ornaments she doesn't really like all that much but can't bear to part with. She takes a long look at the big glossy wedding photo in its ornate silver frame, the one where she and Jack are shrouded in a fluttering cloud of multicoloured confetti and the only one that managed to capture them both laughing at the same time, and places it on the small shelf above the fireplace, edging it along just a fraction to make sure it's exactly in the middle, and wiping it over with a duster.

'Time for a break,' she says out loud, although there's nobody listening.

They have been here precisely six days and there hasn't

been time yet to do a big shop but they've already had three takeaways, and there's a little shop called Rick's on the corner that never seems to close. She wonders when Rick actually gets to sleep as it's always him there by himself behind the counter. He sells a small selection of food and booze and sends his son out to deliver the newspapers every morning, and so far he's managed to provide most of whatever they've needed. Right now, what Molly needs are biscuits.

She opens a packet of chocolate digestives and nibbles at one, before she's even finished making the coffee to dunk it in. It's boredom, she tells herself. All this nibbling is her way of passing the time, comfort eating to help fill the void that leaving home, and her job at the little bakery-cum-café in the next village, and everything she knows, has created. So far, she's been living in jogging bottoms with elasticated waistbands and floppy oversized T-shirts, her long hair scrunched up into a messy ponytail. Not much need to dress up when all you're doing is pulling stuff out of crumpled boxes, scrubbing the bathroom, wiping dusty surfaces and running down to the corner shop to top up on snacks and pick out something for dinner. Good old Rick. What would she do without him? Still, she can tell the weight is starting to pile on. Perhaps, once she's had her coffee, she'll venture further afield, find a proper greengrocer or a butcher so they don't have to keep living out of packets and tins and polystyrene cartons.

They haven't brought a car with them, mainly as there is no parking near enough that wouldn't cost an arm and a leg and Jack has assured her that everywhere either of them is likely to want to go – his office, restaurants, pubs, theatres, perhaps an occasional bit of sightseeing – is easily accessible by public transport. And no drinking and driving to worry about either. Jack's brother, Richard, has bought their old banger from them. A car like that won't mind getting muddy, he says, so it will be useful around the country lanes. And Jack laughs, saying that the old car is still doing its bit and helping get him to work every day, as the money he got for it will pay for his travel card for a couple of months at least. To him, this is all one big adventure.

Still, Molly knows that if she's going to explore what's right here in their new neighbourhood, the real day-to-day stuff, she will have no real option but to walk. The exercise will do her good anyway. And the fresh air, if she can find any in London, where the air always feels so much more clogged with traffic fumes than she's used to. Oh, for a whiff of cow dung or a freshly cut field of hay!

Molly eats four biscuits before forcing herself to stop, tipping the rest of the packet into a tin and hiding it away in a cupboard. She pulls her hair loose and runs a comb through it, changing into a pair of jeans and struggling to do up the zip. The biscuits really will have to go. And if she does as Jack suggests and gets back into cake-making, God knows what all that recipe-testing and spoon-licking and picking at stray raisins will do to her waistline. No, if this move really is to be their brand-new start, then things will have to change. *She* will have to change. She can't allow herself to just sit here doing nothing but knit and bake, watch TV and get fat while Jack is out there meeting new people, making a career for himself. He is already slipping further and further away from her. She can feel it. He's moving in a different world, his ambition soaring, changing him in ways she can hardly understand, while she stays exactly the same. Go-getter and home-body, that's what they are. Town mouse and country mouse. Chalk and cheese. She knows she could lose him. Is probably already losing him.

She closes her eyes to try to stop a tear escaping. When did they last actually make love? Properly make love, not just go through the motions before rolling over and going to sleep, back to back? When did he last look into her eyes and tell her he loves her?

Leave him too long among all those career women in their pencil skirts and high heels and made-up faces and he will stop looking at her altogether, she's sure of it. He thrives on challenges and excitement and power, and she has none of those things. She no longer knows how to reach him, how to give him what he needs, how to hold on to him.

But they are here together, aren't they? He didn't come alone, didn't leave her behind. They are married and they come as a pair. Equal partners. A team. Team Doherty.

For the last few months everything has been about what Jack needs. A change of job, a new home in a new town, a change of scene. He had so badly needed something to stop him exploding with frustration, the chance to grab at something that had been out of reach for too long. He couldn't turn it down when it came. And she couldn't be the one to ask him to. So, here they are. Not quite so equal right now, but she can change that, can't she? He has what he wants and now she can concentrate on what she wants, what she needs, for a change. But what does Molly need? Has either of them even stopped to wonder?

She locks the door of the flat, its crumbling blue paint a stark reminder that this is not really a proper theirs-forever home. It's just a rented place, where someone else is responsible for the maintenance, for sweeping the communal stairs, for replacing the lightbulbs in the hall.

She walks down to the ground floor, steps out into the noisy street and looks both ways. Left or right? It hardly matters, as it's all new territory and she has no idea what she's going to find either way. She plasters a smile on her face and strides out, in the opposite direction to Rick's for a change, her shoulder bag swinging against her side. It's a sunny morning and after only five minutes she comes across a little park, tucked back from the main road. It has benches and rose bushes and is edged by trees. She sits for a while and lets the traffic noise subside, concentrating solely on the sound of the birds tweeting on a branch above her head. She can smell the grass, recently mown, and for a moment she can almost convince herself she is back home, in the countryside, where her heart belongs.

This is London and everything feels just a little bit scary and alien right now, but the truth is that it can't actually be so bad here. It's the same sun shining above her, after all, and the same birdsong she can hear, the same earthy smell oozing out from the grass. And the village is still there, just a few hours away. Home. It's not as if they've come halfway round the world. They haven't emigrated, crossed oceans, cut all ties. They can still visit, call, pop back for a weekend, anytime. The old life is not going anywhere. It's all still there. But the new life is here, and she has to give it a chance.

They will make a go of things. They have to. Jack's job will go well, they will settle and save, and then they will move onwards, upwards, own their own home one day. A proper home. Probably not the roses-round-the-door country cottage of her dreams, but at least they will be together. She has to let herself become a part of this new place, embrace this new life. Open her arms and her eyes to it. Move with him, not against him.

All Molly needs now is a purpose, something to restore her confidence in herself, something to *do*.

Chapter 4

Carly

It's been two days since Suze hit me with the bombshell that Jack is back and I still haven't summoned the courage to go up to the second floor and find out if it's true.

I remember the last time I saw him. He was wearing faded jeans and a dark-green jumper, his wavy brown hair a bit too long, but I didn't mind that because it suited him and made me yearn to reach across and push it slowly away from his beautiful deep-brown eyes. There was an uncharacteristic frown crinkling his forehead too, as he tried to take in what had happened. He'd just found out, as they all had, that the company he worked for was in serious trouble and he wasn't needed anymore. There was no real option for him but to pack up and head back home to Norfolk. He hadn't taken on a flat of his own, knowing all along that his time in London was limited. A lease, a deposit, all that rent payable up front. It didn't seem worth it, he'd said. The hassle, the cost, not just for a few months. And, besides, he was a farm boy, used to roughing it. There had been a few weeks in a cheap B & B hotel, then Rosie's Syd had helped out and let him sleep on the tatty old lumpy sofa in the even tattier flat Syd would be giving up in the next few months anyway, so he could move in with Rosie as soon as they were married. So, all in all, there wasn't a lot for Jack to sort out, not many possessions to pack, before he left.

We met in the pub that last evening, a whole gang of us. Most of them all worked at the same place as Jack, but there were a few other halves there too. There was an air of gloom, all of them moaning about the company closing, the loss of their jobs, with no real answer but to drown their sorrows. Syd was one of them, which is how Rosie had got herself included in the group. We were close back then, Rosie and me, before she had the babies to occupy her time, and I was between boyfriends, so it wasn't unusual for her to let me tag along. I remember how she just sat there that night with her worried face on. Syd losing his job just as they were about to get married did not bode well, but it meant she was all wrapped up in her own thoughts, not watching me, utterly oblivious to any connection that had been building between Jack and me, or to the way I was feeling knowing I was about to lose him.

We ate something tasteless that has made no impression on my memory at all, the men downing beers, the girls sharing too many bottles of wine. 'Might as well, while we can still afford it,' someone said, which just made the whole nightmare seem suddenly more real.

I sat as close to Jack as I could, my hand itching to wrap itself around his, my mind desperately telling me I should do something, anything, to make him stay, but it wasn't going to happen. We had had that one night, just a couple of weeks before, when we'd all gone straight to the pub after work, drunk too much, giggled and hugged outside on the pavement, and, when the others had all said their goodnights and wandered away, we'd walked by ourselves, Jack and I, our fingers entwined, through the dark streets and then along the riverbank, the lights twinkling on the water, stopping every now and then to gaze at each other beneath a lamp-post. That one time, when we had clung to each other and his lips, cold and still tasting of beer, had met mine, when we had come so close to taking things further that I had felt I was going to burst with love for him. But it hadn't happened. Honour, duty, I don't really know what it was that made him pull away, hold me at arm's length, remind me he was engaged, tell me how sorry he was...

But there had been tears in his eyes. Tears just as real as mine. He cared. I know he did. But there was nothing I could do.

We had carried on for a couple of weeks after that, still part of the same crowd, neither of us mentioning what we had so almost done, acting as if it had never been, not knowing what to say, and so saying nothing. I didn't know how long I could do it, keep my distance, keep on pretending. And then, without warning, it was over. The job, the future, the possibilities of this thing between us that had never even started. He would be gone in days. Back to where he had come from and had always intended to return to. And to a wedding he couldn't miss. *His* wedding.

There had been a last hug goodbye, a pulling back as his fingers slipped between mine for the last time and then out again, everyone crowding around, talking, crying, hugging too. And then Syd and Rosie had come to reclaim me so we could travel home together, and Jack had walked away, quickly and alone, into the dark, and I had never seen him nor heard from him again.

I stand in the small kitchen area now, my mind not on work at all, my memories as stirred up as my coffee, the spoon banging against the sides of the mug as I try to decide what to do. If he's here, I have to see him. I have to know why he's back, how long for, how being in the same building and likely to bump into him at any time is going to make me feel. But what I really need to know, of course, is how he feels. Does he still think of me? Does he even remember me? Does he know I'm working here too, just two floors down, and still as in love with him as ever I was? Of course he doesn't. How could he?

And what about her? This Molly woman? She'll be his wife now, assuming he went through with it. A part of me hopes beyond all hope that he didn't, that she's not here in London with him, or that the marriage has failed and he's free again. Or that she's been relegated to some kind of madwoman hidden in the attic and we can all pretend she doesn't exist. That's what comes of reading *Jane Eyre* so many times. My head is full of brooding heroes and lovelorn governesses and the eternal search for happy endings. *Reader, I married him.* I wish!

I close my eyes for a moment and take a deep breath, put my mug down by the sink and steel myself to face him. Because it has to be done.

I grab a pile of papers from my desk. Invoices, receipts, I don't know what. Anything to make it look as if I have a reason to go up there, to make it look like I'm just doing my job. I walk straight to the lifts, feeling more than a bit wobbly, press the button and wait.

I peer down at myself. My plain work trousers, my ordinary everyday shoes. Will I do? Is this the me I want him to see? I should have gone to the Ladies first, checked my hair and lipstick in the mirror, straightened my necklace and the collar on my oh-so-boring blouse. I still can, I suppose, only the lift's here and someone else has hopped in, is holding the door for me to follow, asking me which floor...

I travel up in silence, practising holding my stomach in, while also, strangely, holding my breath as well, to the point that I feel almost dizzy as I step out on the second floor.

I see him straight away. He's standing, stretching, at a desk by the window. What I can see of his back, above the partition, is half turned away from me as he looks out through the glass, a pen in his hand, a phone held to his ear.

Jack. It's him all right. No mistake. He looks the same as I remember him. Even with only a part of his face visible, I can see he's just as good-looking as ever, just as gorgeous as Suze has declared him to be, although his hair has been cut much shorter and I'm not sure I've ever seen him in quite so smart a suit. Just seeing him from a distance is scaring the hell out of me. I think about waiting for him to finish his call and then going over to his desk, trying to be all nonchalant, just saying hello, but I know I can't. Not here, not in front of all these people. I don't think I can trust myself not to say something stupid, do something stupid. I need time to get used to this, to think properly, to prepare. I need a plan. And so I turn away, as quickly as I can, and get straight back into the lift, still waiting with its doors open behind me. And I do exactly what Jack did the last time we were thrown together. I bottle it, and walk away.

Chapter 5

Jack

'You've done really well, Mol. It's only been a week but it looks like we've been here forever.' Jack moves her knitting bag onto the floor and settles back in a saggy floral-patterned armchair that came as part of the furnished flat deal and kicks off his shoes. It's been a hard week, trying to get used to a new job, and he's tired. 'I can't believe you've managed to unpack all those boxes and find a place for everything so quickly. And all that cleaning!'

'I didn't have much else to do, and I've enjoyed it in a funny sort of way,' Molly says, handing him a mug of coffee and taking her own with her as she plonks down in the matching chair on the other side of the fireplace. They haven't been here long enough yet to establish any kind of his-and-hers when it comes to chairs, but Jack knows they will soon settle into who sits where, just as they have when it comes to who sleeps on which side of the bed. That's how living together works.

Molly points at the row of mismatched ornaments lined up on the shelf between them. 'I know I probably brought too much tat with us, and there isn't really room for a lot of it, but I wanted it to feel like home.'

'That's good, isn't it? This place feeling like home, I mean. Because it will do, Mol, just you wait and see. With or without Aunt Freda's chipped spaniel.' He stands up and lifts the china dog from above the fireplace and studies it. 'Do you know, this is probably one of the earliest things I can remember. Standing there in Freda's dining room, with that old clock of hers ticking away too loudly, and this little dog watching me as I ate my fish fingers and beans! I can only have been about three. It's an ugly old thing but I'm glad you've hung on to it.'

'Well, we can't only love things because they're beautiful, can we?' Molly sips at her coffee. It looks as if she's about to add something else, but she doesn't.

'So, what shall we do with our first free weekend in London then? Fancy a bit of culture? Go to one of the galleries tomorrow, or a museum, maybe climb up into the dome at Saint Paul's or have a walk round the zoo or something? We might as well do all the touristy stuff while it's all still new and exciting. Before we get so used to living here that we stop noticing things.'

'Is that what happens? Once you get used to something you stop noticing? Take it all for granted?'

'What's up, Mol?' Usually, he can read her like a book, but not tonight. Something's bothering her but he has no idea what it is. 'Is that supposed to be a dig at me for some reason?'

'No.' She finishes her drink and stands up, heading for the tiny kitchen. She stops by his chair and runs her hand through his hair. 'Just feeling sorry for myself. Too much time on my own lately, with nothing but the hoover and the telly to break the silence, that's all. I'll be talking to myself next.'

'Well, we can put that right, now, can't we?' He looks at his watch. 'Come on, it's Friday night, and not even half past six. Why don't you go and get dolled up and we'll eat out somewhere, then catch a late film or something. Anything you like. You choose.'

'But I've already started on dinner.'

'What is it?'

'Just a lasagne. And I got us some nice fresh salad.'

'Can't you leave it?' He's not really in the mood for munching on lettuce leaves. 'We'll have it at the weekend.'

'I suppose.'

'Go on then. Bung it all back in the fridge and go get changed.'

She hovers for a moment as if she's thinking about it, then bustles away into the kitchen to deposit her empty cup and put a stop to whatever preparations she had been in the middle of.

Within half an hour they are on the crowded Tube, grabbing the last two seats as the train pulls away into the tunnel, she by the door, him three seats away on the other side. He watches her as she studies the map of the line up high on the wall, sees her lips twitch as she forms the silent words and counts the stations, like an excited child working out how long it will be until they are there. She looks down again and realises he is watching, gives him a smile as the woman next to her stands up ready to get off, and gestures for him to move, stretching her arm out to guard the empty seat until he is able to push his way through the people still standing and join her.

Her hand lands on his knee and stays there.

'Not long now,' he says. 'Three more stops. What do you fancy eating?'

Molly shakes her head. 'No idea. Let's just see what's around, shall we? Everywhere might be full on a Friday night. We haven't booked...'

'This is London, Mol. Tourists milling about, theatre-goers, kids. You can bet your life not a lot of them have booked! We'll get in somewhere, no trouble. And there's always McDonald's.'

'Well, you really know how to push the boat out, don't you?' She laughs.

'You love a burger and chips, and you know it!'

'True. And, honestly, I don't really mind what we have. Pizza, steak, Chinese. Anything but lasagne though, eh? It would be a terrible shame to have to pay for one when there's a perfectly good one sitting untouched at home.'

The stations slip by quickly and soon they are stepping out onto a crowded platform and heading for the escalators, Molly's hand looped through the crook of his arm.

Jack yawns. His working week is catching up with him, but they are in London and he wants to enjoy it, have some fun. What was the alternative? To slump in an armchair in front of the TV like a middle-aged man, picking at a plateful of pasta from a tray on his lap? Watching some soap opera or an old film he's seen before, and nodding off by eleven? He doesn't want that sort of a life. Not now. Not yet. Maybe never.

They emerge into a bustle of bodies crowding the pavement, people stopping to cross the road, work out their bearings, look up at some statue or other. There are big black taxis whizzing past, the constant noise of traffic, and the shops are still open, racks of curling postcards and tacky souvenirs, music and bright lights spilling out all around them. Molly looks at it all in wonder and slips her hand down his arm, gripping tightly at his hand as if she's afraid they might get separated in the crowd and she might get lost.

'Well, we did it, Mol.' He bends a little and speaks close to her ear. 'Like it or not, we're Londoners now.'

'I don't know about that.' She takes the opportunity to kiss him, aiming for his lips but just skimming his cheek as he straightens up again. 'But now we're here, we might as well make the most of it. Is that a cinema over there?'

'It's Leicester Square, Mol, so yeah, it definitely is. It's the one where they have all the big opening-night premieres, I think. Shall we go and see what's on and if we can get a ticket for later?'

'Do you think we might see anyone famous?'

'I doubt it. They may turn out in force for a premiere, but I don't suppose they hang about here on a normal night. But you never know. Even film stars and pop singers go out on the town, and they have to eat, don't they? And London's the place to be. We might find ourselves sitting next to Beyoncé!'

'Doesn't she live in America?'

'Well, someone British then. Ed Sheeran...'

'Who?'

Jack drops a kiss on the top of his wife's head. 'You do make me laugh sometimes.'

'So long as you're not laughing *at* me.'

'Of course not. I just love how unaware of things you are sometimes. As if you still live in a little village bubble that the big wide world can't touch. And I wouldn't change that – or you – for the world.'

'Good.' She squeezes his hand. 'I love you too.'

They walk on in silence, but Jack knows he didn't actually say that he loves her. He feels a little stab of guilt about that, but the moment has passed and it's too late to say it now. They stop outside the Odeon and look at the films on offer. He's lucky that she has agreed to move here with him, not put up a fight or make things difficult. She is doing her best to support him, let him have what he wants, even though he knows none of this is her dream. His stomach rumbles, and he realises just how hungry he is. There are restaurants everywhere, so much choice, so much life, and it's all here for the taking. He knows he owes Molly so much more than a burger and chips.

Chapter 6

Carly

'Got yourself a nice young man yet?' Mum looks up from her crossword as I let myself in through the back door, as I do most Saturday mornings, and head for the kettle.

'Mum! A hello first might be nice.'

'Hello, Carly. Got yourself a nice young man yet?' She puts her pen down and I can see that she's teasing me, but underneath the banter I'm pretty sure she means it. A single Carly is a disappointing Carly, as far as she's concerned.

'There's more to life than men, and you know it. Now, do you want tea or shall I just go straight out again?'

'Don't be silly, love. When have you ever known me to say no to a cuppa? And your brother will be back from the allotment soon. I know he'll want to see you.'

I drop teabags into two cups, add three sugars to hers and pour the water on. 'Got any biscuits?'

'Of course. Not that I should be encouraging you. We don't want you putting on too much weight, do we? All that sugar...'

'Says the woman who has three spoons of it in her tea.'

'Ah, but I don't have to think about my figure so much these days. Now that your father's gone... not that he was bothered by things like that. Had more interest in the size of his beetroots than the size of my waistline.' She forces a laugh but it doesn't hide the loss I can still see in her eyes, even now, almost six years after he died of cancer, in his mid-fifties. He was far too young to die, and she's far too young to be a widow, I think. They should be enjoying their life together now, going on cruises and holding hands on some foreign beach, now that the two of us are grown-up and can take care of ourselves, but instead she's diverting all her romantic aspirations in my direction. Nice young man, indeed!

I locate the biscuit tin, bypassing the Rich Teas and helping myself to two chocolate-chip cookies.

'How's work?' she says.

'Okay. The usual.' An image of Jack Doherty flashes into my mind, reminding me that things are suddenly far from usual, but I push it away.

'And the flat? Is Frances behaving herself?'

'Of course.'

'I'm not sure I'd want to share with a stranger.'

'Fran is hardly a stranger, Mum. She's Suze's sister.'

'Not family though. I still don't understand why you moved out, love. Your brother's happy enough to stop here.'

'Of course he is. He's twenty-three. You cook all his meals and do all his washing!' I smile to myself. What had I just been thinking about the two of us looking after ourselves these days? In my little brother Sam's case, that level of independent living only kicks in when Mum goes away somewhere for a day or two and he really has no other choice.

'And I'd happily do the same for you, if you'd let me. Your bedroom here is so much nicer than that pokey little flat, and you don't even have a garden.'

'When I want to sit outside, I go to the park. Or come here!'

'And all that rent you're paying! You could be saving it up, for your future. Your wedding...'

I laugh at that. 'What wedding?'

'Well, it will happen one day, and they don't come cheap, you know. If you came back home, you could be building up a nice little nest egg by now.'

'And if I did, I'd probably spend it on a nice little car, not a fancy wedding dress and a set of posh dinner plates,' I tease her, shaking my head. 'Anyway, what's with all the financial advice all of a sudden? I thought Dad was the bank manager in this family, not you!'

'Well, he's not here anymore, is he? And there's nothing wrong with thinking about money, Carly. Or the future. And, besides, I have no idea why you'd want to spend your money on a car when you can't even drive.'

'I'm thinking of learning.'

'I could teach you. I'm a bit out of practice, I admit, since we sold your dad's Rover, but it's not something you ever really forget, is it? Like riding a bike. And it would save you paying for all those expensive lessons. And, as for rent, I've only ever asked you for enough to cover your keep, you know that.'

'I've seen your driving, Mum! And I don't want to be *kept*. I like living closer to work, making my own meals, coming and going without you waiting up for me and looking at your watch if I'm not back by midnight. Anyone would think I'm going to turn into a pumpkin or something.'

'It's that Frances of yours who's turning into a pumpkin, Carly,' she says, giving up on the pleas for me to come home and changing the subject. 'The size of that girl! It's all very well looking after yourselves, but not if that means living on cream cakes and doughnuts.'

'Crunchies, actually.'

'What?'

'She works in a sweet shop, Mum, and she likes to sample the stock.'

'Well, thank God you work in an office then, and not the McVities factory, the way you're putting those cookies away. At least the only samples you're likely to take home from work are a few nicked pens from the stationery cupboard.'

She can be very blunt, my mum. And a bit too judgemental.

'Fran's all right. And she can eat what she likes. I'm not her keeper.'

'I can't imagine what her mother must think.'

'About what?'

'Letting herself go like that. She's got quite a pretty face too. But what man is going to look twice while she's so huge? It's such a shame...'

I try not to let her get to me, but she always does.

'I don't think she's particularly bothered. About catching a man, I mean. In fact, I suspect her interests might lie in the other direction.'

Mum tilts her head and peers at me inquisitively. 'What direction? I'm sure I have no idea what you mean.'

'Girls, Mum. She's never actually said it out loud, not to me anyway, but I think Fran likes girls.'

I watch her face contort as she lets this information slowly sink in. 'You mean she's... a lesbian?'

I nod and the room falls silent. Mum takes a sip of her tea and stares into the space in front of her. 'Well, I'm not sure she'll catch one of those either unless she loses a bit of weight. A lot of weight, in fact. Now, where's Sam? If he's managed to pick us a few nice tomatoes, we'll have them with our lunch. Help to counteract all those calories you've been stuffing.'

When my brother comes in his boots are covered in mud. He nods at me, says 'Hi, Carls. All right?' in his usual monosyllabic way, and then Mum makes a big fuss about him taking the boots off and leaving them on a sheet of old newspaper and scrubbing his hands clean before he's allowed to step across her clean floor or come anywhere near her, or me.

I like the fact that Sam has taken over Dad's old allotment. There's a kind of continuity about it somehow. The same routines, the same old moans about the mess from Mum, the same line-up of misshapen vegetables which, in Sam's less expert care, always seem to have a lot more nibble holes in them than in Dad's day.

'What have you two been chatting about then?' he asks, dropping a carrier bag of his latest crop onto the counter, clicking the kettle back on until it boils and making himself a mug of instant coffee.

'Nothing,' we both say in unison.

He laughs. 'Ah, it's like stereo in here. Or an echo! You two are so alike.'

I close my eyes and sigh. Alike? Me and Mum? God, I do hope not.

'I hope you're going to clean those, Sam,' she says, nodding towards whatever he's got in the bag. 'I don't want another caterpillar crawling across my plate. Especially as we have a guest for lunch.'

'I'm hardly a guest, Mum,' I say, grinning at Sam, who's inspecting a lettuce at close range and making little creepy-crawly movements with his fingers behind Mum's back.

'Oh, I don't mean you, Carly, love. I mean a proper guest. And he should be here any minute, so I'd go and run a comb through that messy hair of yours if I were you. First impressions are so important and we want you looking your best, don't we?'

'Who is it?' It will be one of her cronies from the bridge club probably, some elderly widower in need of a home-cooked meal. 'Anyone I know?'

'Not yet, Carly, but you'll like him, I'm sure.'

I'm just about to ask her who he is and where he's come from when the doorbell rings and she's up out of her chair, whipping her apron off and moving down the hall, pushing me towards the downstairs cloakroom with a hissed 'There's a comb in there. Sort out your hair, and then come and meet him. We'll be in the dining room. His name's Anthony. With an H that you're supposed to pronounce, apparently.'

That's when the penny drops. She's doing her best Emma Woodhouse impression and matchmaking again. Trying to fix me up with whoever it is she thinks is going to be good for me. Someone probably horribly unsuitable. Old, or ugly, or... well, not Jack, basically. Trapped behind her as she opens the front door, I am only too aware that, no matter how gruesome this Anthony with an H turns out to be, I'm going to have to grin and bear it. There is no escape.

Chapter 7

Molly

Jack rushes out of the door on Monday morning, slamming it behind him, a slice of toast in one hand and his briefcase in the other, still muttering under his breath about oversleeping because he didn't hear the alarm that she knows only too well he forgot to set. Molly laughs out loud as an image of the white rabbit from *Alice in Wonderland* pops into her head, the anxious creature late for a very important date, peering at its watch and scurrying away down a hole in the ground. Not that different from Jack really, worried about being late for work, checking his Omega every few seconds and dashing off to disappear down the steps into the Underground.

Molly rolls over in bed and stretches. Jack's side is still warm and smells slightly of sweat, the T-shirt he slept in lying tossed in a hurried heap across her feet. There is nowhere she has to be, no meeting she is in danger of missing, no boss waiting to tell her off. She should feel good about that, but somehow it just makes her feel aimless, a woman without purpose. They have only been here just over a week, and she knows there's no real hurry, but she needs something to do. A job, a hobby, a friend... something.

She stands under the shower until the water runs cold, not sure if that's because she has lingered too long with the new luxurious lotus blossom shampoo she found, quite unexpectedly, on the shelves at Rick's corner shop, or down to the inadequacies of the boiler. Still, she emerges refreshed and squeaky clean, from the ends of her hair to the tips of her toes and, slipping a robe on, she heads to the kitchen and makes herself a coffee and a bowl of porridge, slicing a banana over the top.

Over the last couple of days, she's been remembering what Jack said, about her having a go at making celebration cakes from home and selling them. It's tempting, but she doesn't know much about starting a business, and the kitchen is probably much too small. Wedding cakes take up a lot of room, and a lot of time, with their multi-tiers and their intricate decorations, and it's not as if she can just shove one out of the way mid-icing when it's time to make their own dinner. There isn't even enough cupboard space to store all the ingredients, let alone room in the tiny oven for more than a couple of shallow tins at once. She lets her mind drift. Small kitchen, small business, small cakes. There is a lot to be said for starting small. They don't have to be giant creations after all, do they? Maybe kids' birthday cakes, shaped like princesses or dragons. She'd enjoy making those, but parents of little children weren't known for being flush with money and could more than likely find what they want in the supermarkets a lot cheaper. Or cupcakes, as Jack had suggested. They were everywhere these days. In different colours and flavours, all beautifully piped with buttercream and decorated with edible flowers or butterflies, and each one selling for more than her mum would have paid for a whole box of six back when she was a kid and eating the plain old chocolate in a fluted paper-case kind. There had to be a market for something like that in London. People with money, wanting beautiful things and prepared to pay over the odds for them, not to mention all the offices where someone always wants something a bit more special than a packet of supermarket fairy cakes to share with their colleagues on their birthday or when they're leaving. But there would be a lot of competition, especially here in London. Other companies and home bakers with exactly the same idea. Bound to be.

She sits at the small table, with her coffee going cold in front of her, and starts making up names in her head. Names for a business that doesn't yet exist. Something suitably cakey but with her own mark stamped on it, that's what's needed. *Molly's Munchies*, maybe? Or *Molly's Miracles*? It would certainly be a miracle, her managing to start up a successful business! She toys with using just a string of M's in front of her name, as in *Mmmmolly's*, with *Mmm* meaning yummy, of course, but would anyone get it? Or know how to spell it? When she's exhausted the M's, she starts work on the D's. *Doherty's Dreams? Doherty's Delights?* Her surname would certainly work well enough if she was making doughnuts. *Doherty's Doughnuts* does have a certain ring to it. She smiles at her own unintended pun, thinking of doughnuts in the shape of a ring. But none of those names really bring luxury cakes to mind, do they?

She grabs a pen and a slip of paper and starts scribbling ideas down, the way she used to at school, in some sort of spider shape, all spilling out across the page without letting herself think too much about it. Random words that speak cake, loud and clear. *Sugar, sweet, sticky, sickly...* No, not sickly! She doesn't want to put people off! *Delicious, delectable, dainty, tasty...*

She puts the pen down and sits up, closing her eyes for a moment to clear her head. It's no good. She's no businesswoman, she's just a cook. No better and no worse than a hundred other cooks. Who is she kidding? There's a huge step, or a whole staircase of very steep steps, between coming up with some vague idea and actually making it work. Money and advertising and hygiene certificates, not to mention delivery, especially as they have no car. Not that she has ever learned to drive. The local bus between villages and a willing dad or reluctant husband to drop her at a friend's house when necessary had served her well enough until now. No, she should forget all about any sort of business of her own and get out there and look for a job. An ordinary job in a shop or a café somewhere nearby. Even thinking about anything more ambitious than that makes her feel sick.

Molly can't finish her breakfast. In fact, she suddenly realises, as a strong waft of the pungent vapour from her untouched coffee reaches her nostrils and her stomach starts to churn alarmingly, that she really is going to be sick.

She only just makes it back to the bathroom, kneeling on the floor with her head over the toilet bowl as clumps of undigested porridge force their way back up and the room takes on the smell of rotting banana. Her tummy really aches now, with all the strain of bringing everything up. Oh God, it must be something she's eaten. That lasagne she'd put aside half-cooked and then gone back to last night maybe? Two-day old mince was probably not such a good idea. Unless she's caught some sort of bug? But Jack seemed fine this morning, and she hasn't been near enough to anyone else she could possibly have caught it from. A glass of cold water should sort her out, then she really should go back to bed and sleep it off.

She flushes the toilet, gets up and rinses her mouth, then goes back into the kitchen. Maybe some paracetamol will help? She has only recently put them into the odds and ends drawer. Having only just moved in, she still knows exactly where everything is, right down to the last battery, reel of Sellotape and paperclip, and most of them are right here in this drawer. She takes two tablets out of their foil and swallows them, already feeling a bit better. She'll probably be okay again by lunchtime if she takes a little nap.

She drops the packet back in the drawer, pushing a few bits aside to make room. A tube of superglue. Spare keys. Her diary, the small pocket-sized one that she doesn't bother keeping in her bag anymore, now she has no appointments to worry about. And that's when it hits her. Why didn't she think of it before? She picks up the diary and flips to the page for this week. Jack's mum's birthday is coming up on Saturday. She must get a card, post a present or order flowers, remind him to ring. She turns the pages back, to their moving date last week, their anniversary the week before that. Five years already! And back again, and again, page after page until she finds it. The little tick she makes on period days. Always has, ever since she was thirteen and her first sight of bloodied knickers had almost frightened the life out of her. It's the first tick she's come to, and it's – what? Nine weeks ago? Ten? She turns the pages again, slowly, one by one, but there are no more recent ticks than that. How can she not have noticed? Realised? Or did she just forget to tick the last time, what with being so busy with all the stress of the move?

Molly slumps into a kitchen chair and puts her hand instinctively to her tummy. The tightening waistband, the craving for biscuits, and now the sickness? They all add up to something she hadn't expected at all. But she is, isn't she? Expecting? She has to be.

Oh, God, what will Jack say? This was never part of his plan. A new job, a new start, having fun in London. A new life, that's what he wanted, but nobody ever mentioned this sort of new life. The sort she feels almost sure is growing inside her.

She wonders if Rick sells pregnancy testing kits. He probably does. He seems to sell everything else. Because she has to be sure. It's the only way to convince herself this is real. She can't even begin to work out how she feels about any of it until she's sure it's real.

But, no, not Rick's. She'll go for a walk when she feels a bit better and find a pharmacy somewhere. She can't go to Rick's. It's too close to home, and he might say something to Jack. Pat him on the back or give him a cigar or something. She can't risk Jack finding out like that. Not yet. In fact, she's not sure how she's going to tell Jack at all. Or when. Or even if she should.

Chapter 8

Carly

As it happens, Anthony's not that bad. He must be at least mid-forties, if not a bit older, so no way is he of any romantic interest to me, but he made good conversation, even made me laugh once or twice, and he didn't slurp his soup or pick his teeth at the table. But he is not just the wrong age, he's also very much the wrong type. And he's shorter than me, by a good two inches, I'd say. The truth is, I just don't fancy him.

When Anthony had followed my mother into the kitchen after coffee, insisting on helping with the washing up, I'd huddled up close to Sam and asked him just who exactly Anthony was, where Mum had met him, and why on earth she had thought he might be a match for me. It turns out he's got the allotment next to theirs and they all sit and have a chat sometimes, if Mum pops down there with a flask of tea when it's sunny. Sam gives him the occasional cabbage and Anthony repays the favour with a bag of raspberries or a few gooseberries. It seems he's a fruit man rather than a veg one. He'd been there that morning, so Sam told me, doing some digging, but had told Sam he wanted to nip home to spruce himself up ready for their lunch engagement, otherwise they would have walked back to the house together. Nip, spruce... what sort of man talks like that? And engagement? I know he wasn't talking about diamond rings, but still, the less said about that word the better.

Sam said he'd seen the warning signs in Mum's eyes and had tried to tell her not to matchmake but she'd insisted she was doing no such thing, just being neighbourly, taking pity on a man who came across as a bit lonely, but I know her only too well, and it wouldn't be the first time. It's not that I blame Anthony. He probably walked into her trap just the same way I did. Oh, God, I wish she wouldn't do this to me. Or to him, poor man.

I take the scrap of folded paper out of my jeans pocket as I bend to put them into the washing machine, and open it out. Yes, he slipped me his number as we rather awkwardly said goodbye in the hallway on Saturday, on some pretext of wanting to talk to me about a car insurance quote. I've only just remembered it's there, but I have absolutely no intention of calling. If he really wants to talk about insurance, he can ring the office or visit the website like everyone else. I decide to treat our meal as a mercy mission and, whether the poor sod's lonely or not, I vow never to repeat it, and certainly not to phone him, for want of giving him, or Mum, the wrong idea.

I screw the paper up and lob it into the kitchen bin. Bye-bye, Anthony with an audible H. Beggars can't be choosers, so my mother keeps telling me, and there may not be many fish left in the sea, but I'm letting this one swim on by. I have my eye on a very different fish altogether. Jack's back, all tall, tanned and handsome, and today is the day I am going to walk right up to him, in my smartest dress and my highest heels, and try to stop shaking long enough to manage a friendly not-too-blatantly-sexy smile, and show him exactly what he's been missing all these years.

'Got room in there for a couple of pairs of pants, Carls?'

Fran has just come tumbling into the kitchen with an armful of laundry. 'Not worth doing a separate load.' And, before I can answer, she's stuffed her undies into the drum, closed the door and set the thing going on a full-length wash at forty degrees.

'Those were jeans in there, Fran. You'll end up turning all your knickers blue if you're not careful.'

'That's fine. Who cares what colour they end up, so long as they're clean? Not as if anyone's going to see them except me.' She laughs and dashes out again, grabs her bag and opens the door to the communal landing. 'Must go, I'm late. See you tonight.' The door slams behind her and I look at my watch. She's right. She is late, which means, if I don't get a shift on, I will be too. God, I do hate Mondays. I could have done the washing yesterday, instead of spending hours picking through my wardrobe for come-and-get-me clothes and scouring the make-up stands in Boots for blue eye shadow to match my eyes and just the right shade of lipstick to dazzle the man of my dreams. But here I am, as usual, leaving everything to the last possible minute and risking turning up in the office looking like I've just jumped off a horse in a gale-force wind.

I finish my coffee, dump the mug in the sink for later, take a final check in the hall mirror – front view, back view, close-up, touch-up – and I'm out of here, my ankle turning on the corner of the stairs as I try to remember how to hurry in heels.

I don't want to do this in front of a room full of curious colleagues and I can't think of any way of getting Jack on his own, so I have no option but to involve Suze. Since her questions in the pub garden, I have done my best to avoid giving her answers, but I can tell she's bursting to know everything there is to know about me and Jack, all the when and where stuff that, so far, I have managed to keep her in the dark about. So, I wait for a quiet moment and whisk her off to the Ladies where I check that all the cubicles are empty before giving her a brief potted history of what did and didn't happen between us five years ago.

'Oh, wow. Wow, wow, wow! So, what next?' she says, jumping up and down with so much excitement that she manages to bash her elbow on the washbasin. 'Will you hover by the lifts until he comes downstairs, or follow him outside at lunchtime, or just go right up to him at his desk and grab him? Oh, God, I do love a big dramatic moment. It's what romance is all about, like something out of *Romeo and Juliet*, all that held-back emotion just waiting to erupt at any minute. I would so love to see his face when he meets you again after all this time...'

'Yeah, okay, Suze. Hold your horses. A big dramatic moment is exactly what I don't want. It's just too... public, isn't it? And extremely embarrassing for me – well, for both of us really – in front of a bunch of other people if he doesn't want to know. Or doesn't recognise me.'

'Of course he'll recognise you, you dingbat! How could he forget all those sparks you say were flying about between you? But it doesn't have to be public, does it? We just need to get him on his own somewhere, that's all. Give you both a bit of privacy.'

'Which is exactly where you come in. To lure him out, away from his desk, distract him...'

'There's only one way I know to distract a man and I somehow don't think that's what you'd want me to do!' she says, lifting her hands and wiggling her boobs from side to side.

I look at Suze's ample chest and am glad to see she's wearing a high-neck top for a change.

'No, you keep those beauties to yourself, or you'll have his eye out! And I want him in one piece, please.'

'Spoilsport. What, then?'

'Something work-related. Look up his extension in the internal directory and call him, say you're having a problem with your software or something.'

She giggles and points to her breasts again. 'No problems with anything soft here,' she says. 'Oh, you mean on my computer! Okay, so let's say he takes the bait and comes down to take a look. Then what? You'll have just swapped one set of gawpers for another.'

'Not if we time it right. You just have to get everyone out somehow. Ask them all out for a lunchtime drink and troop them down to the pub. We don't have to empty the whole ground floor. Just our little corner. Make up something you're celebrating. They'll know it's not your birthday, but you could have won some money on the lottery or something and want to treat everybody.'

'It could work, I suppose. Most of them will do pretty much anything for a free drink. And you'll make some excuse to stay behind, I assume?'

'Yep. And when he comes down to fix the PC, it'll me sitting there, not you. What do you think?'

'The simple plans are often the best. It could work. How long will you need?'

'Who knows? Five minutes, fifteen, a whole hour if it works out and he feels the urge to catch up over lunch somewhere.'

'Enough about urges. I don't want to come back and find anything messy going on at my desk.'

'Nothing like that, I promise. So, you'll give it a try?'

'On one condition.'

'Which is?'

'Well, if I'm having to pay for a round of drinks, I expect full reimbursement. And all the gory details as soon as he's gone, of course.'

'That's two conditions.'

'I suppose it is. But you need me, so you can hardly say no, can you?'

'Okay. Thirty quid should cover it. Just don't make out you won a fortune or someone will expect to order champagne.'

'This all seems to rely on me having to tell a pretty big lie. It's not as if I usually even do the lottery. I won't be able to keep a straight face if they start quizzing me about what numbers I picked and how I'm going to spend my winnings. And, anyway, what if Jack's out to lunch himself or otherwise unavailable when we need him here? He might decide to pop down later, after we've all come back.'

'Better make it sound urgent then. Look, timing's everything here, and I'm counting on you, okay? Either that, or you all stay here and I lead Jack off down to the pub! Hey, maybe that's it. He comes down in the lift on his mission of mercy and I waylay him in reception and just lead him straight outside. Act now, explain later. What do you think?'

'Oh, for God's sake, Carly. I need a wee now,' she says, opening the nearest cubicle door and disappearing inside. 'So just make up your mind before I'm done, okay?'

In the end, it doesn't quite work out the way we planned. It turns out that Jack doesn't do the repairs side of things. He's more of a programmer or a project manager or something like that, and he immediately passes Suze's call on to someone else. Someone called Jess who turns up within minutes, has a fiddle with the mouse and declares nothing wrong at all, giving Suze a don't-waste-my-time look before hurrying back upstairs, luckily before Suze has had a chance to issue her lottery-winning invitation to everyone within a six-desk radius. The only good thing to come out of our failed mission is that I haven't had to fork out for a round, but I'm no nearer to getting Jack's undivided attention. Suze and I look at each other with a silent sigh as she shrugs her shoulders and actually gets down to doing some work, but I know I'm going to find it hard to concentrate until I've seen him and spoken to him. I just have to know, one way or the other, where Jack and I go from here, if anywhere at all, now that we've been thrown back together under the same roof.

I look at my watch. It's a couple of minutes past twelve and I don't usually take my lunch-break this early but I need some space, and some air, so I grab my jacket from the back of my chair and head for the door. Suze nods at me, as if she knows exactly how I'm feeling, and waves a little goodbye as I leave.

And that's when I walk right into him. Jack Doherty, rushing out of the lift and across the reception area, a big leather briefcase swinging from his right hand.

'Sorry,' he says. 'Wasn't looking where I was going.' And then he stops and looks up, straight into my eyes, and something registers. A sudden flash of recognition passes across his face. 'I know you,' he says, plonking the case down at his feet and slowly raising his hands until he's put them gently on my shoulders, so we are standing facing each other, just an arm's length apart. He pauses, as if to make sure he hasn't made a mistake. 'It is you, isn't it? Your hair's different but I'd know those eyes anywhere! My God, this is such a surprise. What are you doing here? Do you work here too?'

I nod.

'I'm here on a contract. Three months.'

Ah, so it's not forever then? I don't know quite what to feel about that.

'I never thought I'd see anyone I know,' he says. 'I had no idea you were...' And then he stops talking and just looks at me, and finally gives me one of his drop-dead gorgeous lop-sided smiles. 'Sorry. Ignore my rambling. What I mean is... Hello, Carly.'

'Hello, Jack.'

'It's been a long time.'

'Five years,' we both say together, and then we both laugh as he lowers his hands and picks up his briefcase again. I can't help noticing the wedding ring, but it comes as no surprise. Any ideas I might have had of him calling the whole thing off and still being single were a one-in-a-million chance, weren't they?

'I was just going out,' he says. 'A quick bite to eat before I have to dash back for a meeting later. I don't suppose you...'

'Fancy coming with you?'

He nods. 'I was going to read a report in the park, grab a quick sarnie, feed the crumbs to the pigeons...'

'I could do that. Well, not the report bit, but I'm happy to keep you company, if you like.'

'I would like, yes.' He hesitates, as if he's about to offer me his arm or hold my hand or something, but he thinks better of it and I follow him out, in single file, through the big double doors into the street.

'What flavour sandwich? Anything you like. Don't say I don't know how to treat a girl!' He laughs as we walk into the sandwich place on the corner and I pick some kind of soft bap out of the chill cabinet without really noticing, or caring, what's in it. I don't argue as he orders two coffees to go, pulls out his wallet and pays.

It's not far to the park, and within five minutes we've chosen a bench in the sun, down one of the smaller paths that run around the edge, and have settled ourselves side by side, looking out over the grass. A lot of people from our building come here at lunchtime, but we're very early and, so far, it looks like we're on our own.

'Carly,' he says. Nothing else, as though he's trying out the sound of my name after not having had to say it for so long. 'I didn't expect to ever see you again.'

'Me neither.'

'How have you been? And what have you been doing? Changing jobs, obviously. But what else? Are you with anyone? Married? Kids?'

I shake my head. 'No. Still the same old Carly. I've moved out of my mum's, sharing a flat with a mate, but otherwise I'm still living the same old life! Hanging out in pubs, reading a lot, seeing my mum at the weekends. No man, no kids. Still waiting to meet Mr Right. My own Mr Darcy! Not that I'm in any hurry.' I look away, for fear of blushing. It doesn't happen often, but this is one occasion when I'm afraid it just might.

'I'm surprised. I felt sure someone would have swept you off your feet by now, and whisked you down the aisle!'

'I'm not sure all that marriage and family stuff is all it's cracked up to be. You should see Rosie and Syd these days. Happy as Larry, but struggling a bit moneywise, I think. They never did get over to Oz to visit his parents. Other priorities got in the way. You heard they had twins?'

'No!'

'Yep! A boy and a girl, just a few months old, and yet to meet their Aussie grandparents.'

'To be honest, I haven't really stayed in touch with anyone from back then. I should have done, I know. Especially Syd, after he let me sleep on his sofa for weeks on end. Maybe I should have come down for their wedding, and invited them to mine, but it's a man thing, isn't it? We don't do friends the way you girls do. But twins, eh? Wow!'

'Yep. Hard work, and loud too. Very loud! But how about you? How's married life? Do you have any kids yourself?'

'God, no. Too soon for all that. We've only just moved here. New job, new flat, and still finding my feet. Well, *our* feet, I suppose I should say, although I don't think Molly's too keen on London life. Not yet, anyway.' He stops talking and turns his attention to opening his sandwich, a dollop of mayonnaise oozing out and just missing his trouser leg as he quickly holds the whole thing out over the side of the bench. A big fat pigeon swoops down instantly but soon waddles off again when it discovers nothing but a gloopy breadless splat on the path. 'Come on, eat up. Our little feathered friend here is looking most disgruntled.'

I laugh at his choice of vocabulary. 'Can a bird be disgruntled? More like just plain greedy, if you ask me.' I tear open the wrapping and take a bite of my roll. Cheese and pickle. I don't much like pickle, but I start to eat it anyway. We sip at our coffees, now they're not so hot, and I realise I have no idea what to say next. It's hardly the moment to pronounce my undying love, is it? And I really don't fancy hearing any more about his wife and how much she does or doesn't want to live in London. Let her leave if that's how she feels. And leave him here, for me.

He puts his coffee down on the ground by his feet and opens his briefcase, pulling out a heap of papers, but he doesn't make any attempt to start reading them.

'Do you ever think about that night?' he says, suddenly, as if he can read my thoughts.

'Which night's that?' He could be talking about something else entirely, for all I know, and I need to be sure before I make a complete fool of myself.

'Carly...' He turns to look at me, moving what's left of his sandwich over onto the wooden arm of the bench, so there's nothing in his hands, nothing between us. 'You can't have forgotten. I know you haven't. It was...'

'It was what? Special? Magical? A mistake?'

'Yes, all of those things.' He reaches for my hand but I pull it away, immediately wishing that I hadn't. I want to touch him so badly. 'But it couldn't happen, could it? We couldn't let it. Not with the wedding and everything. You do understand that?'

I nod. I can feel the tears starting to well up, the tears I have probably been holding in for the last five years, but I have to stop them. He mustn't see how I feel. He had been fair about it all back then, and totally honest. He hadn't made any promises. Well, not to me. Only to her.

'Wrong time, wrong place...'

'Wrong man?' he adds, peering at my face.

'No, Jack. The right man. Definitely the right man. But someone else got there first, didn't she? I'm sorry. I don't think I can do this.' I stand up, my food falling from my lap and signalling a mass pigeon stampede around my ankles.

I'm making a spectacle of myself, I know I am. Stumbling about and saying the first thing that comes into my head. I've already said too much, and it's time to cut my losses and leave. Only, he should know, shouldn't he? This could be my last chance, my only chance, to tell him how it was for me.

And so I do.

'That night was very special to me, one of the most important of my life, ridiculous though that probably sounds to you, as nothing really happened, did it?' I find myself staring at my shoes, and at the last of the pigeons still pecking determinedly at the remains of my bap, now little more than a pile of mangled crumbs. My voice drops almost to a whisper. 'But I think it's best, in the circumstances, that we just keep our distance again now. We've managed it for years, but we'll just have to try a bit harder now we work in the same place, won't we? I don't have a lot of reasons to come up to the second floor...'

'You know where I'm working?'

'Not too tricky to work out, as you're in IT. That's where they're based.' I swallow hard. The last thing I want is for him to think I've been stalking him, that I've already been up and found out exactly where his desk is. 'Anyway, I should go. I'm sure the last thing your wife would want is you having lunch with another woman, especially one from the past, who she knows nothing about. I assume she doesn't...'

'Of course not. There was no reason to tell her. Not that there was anything much to tell.'

'No, you're right. Nothing at all. Okay then. I'm going back to work now. It's been nice seeing you again, Jack. I'm glad you're happy.' Has he actually said he's happy? He has to be, he has to have left me for the right reasons, made the right decision, or the last five years without him have all been for nothing. I lost; she won. It's as simple as that. What was I thinking, trying to engineer some sort of secret meeting, working out some crazy plan to get him back? It's not going to happen. It can't. He's married, and I don't get mixed up with married men, especially happily married men. I have to back off, stay away, let him go, once and for all.

I start to walk back along the path, forcing my feet to take me away from him and, when I turn, he's just sitting there, staring after me. 'You'd best read that report now, before your meeting,' I say, my voice as level and businesslike as I can make it, as my heart pounds away, nineteen to the dozen. 'And thanks for lunch.'

Chapter 9

Jack

Jack had never expected to see Carly Young again. In fact, wrapping up the memory of that time they had briefly shared together and shoving it away in a box somewhere at the back of his brain has worked pretty well up until now. He has to admit that the lid has eased itself off from time to time, allowing just a glimpse of a memory of that night down by the river, but the feelings that come with it are best pushed aside.

He made his choice, went home to Molly and married her, and that was that. Of course, he has wondered sometimes what might have happened if he had not been made so suddenly and unexpectedly redundant, if he had stayed in London for longer, if their paths had carried on crossing...

He can't deny that he had fancied her rotten, from the moment he had first seen her. Carly was so unlike other girls he had known – the country types, all ruddy-faced and wellie-boot practical, or the few he briefly dated or bedded, all let loose from home for the first time and hell-bent on drinking themselves stupid, while he was away at uni. He can't define what it was, but something about Carly had jumped up and grabbed him by the throat, taking him by surprise, sending the sort of shockwaves through him that had scared the life out of him.

He still doesn't know how he managed to hold himself back when they had taken that moonlit stroll by the river, how he had stopped that long lingering kiss from developing into so much more, how he had kept his hands under control and stopped them doing what he longed for them to do, exploring every inch of her. But a quickie in some dark alley, or sneaking her into Syd's, or finding a cheap hotel for a few hours, none of that had felt like the right thing to do. She deserved better, and so did Molly.

He watches her walk away from him and out through the park gates, never taking his eyes off her, the remains of his lunch uneaten at his side and the work report lying unread in his lap. What next? Meeting again is far more than just a possibility now. It's unavoidable, inevitable. They are working in the same building and he could run into her again at any moment. The thought should worry him but it doesn't. It excites him. In more ways than one, he realises, adjusting the pile of papers spread across his lap so no passer-by will notice the erection that is suddenly pressing hard against his trousers. It is only the second one he can ever remember experiencing while wearing an office suit. And the first? That had been down to Carly too. That night by the river.

Oh God, what is this woman doing to him? He hardly knows her, but he wants to. He wants to, so much.

'Good day?' Molly is bustling around in the tiny kitchen when he gets home. She has obviously been baking because the whole flat smells so strongly of cake mixture that he feels a sudden urge to grab the mixing bowl and start licking it, the way he always did when he was a kid.

'It was okay,' he says, preferring not to talk, or even think, about the office now he's away from it. 'Something smells good.'

'It's cherry and sultana. Your favourite.'

He's surprised to hear that he has a favourite. Cake is cake, as far as he's concerned, and he'll eat it. Whatever flavour it happens to be.

'You know me so well,' he says, his gaze scouring the worktops for the bowl and failing to find it. She's so super-efficient, his wife, that she's already washed everything up and put it away. 'So, why the cake? Are we celebrating something?'

'No. I was just in a baking mood, that's all. But talking of celebrations reminds me, it's your mum's birthday coming up. I thought maybe we could go home for the weekend and see her? Well, see everyone, I mean. I'd like to see my mum and dad too.'

'We could, I suppose. But without a car...'

'The train's easy enough. Not as if we need to take a lot with us, is it? Although I would like to take her a birthday cake.'

'Ah, I get it now. This one's a trial run, right? But you do know she's not a fan of sultanas?'

'Of course I do. No, I was thinking of something a bit fancier than this. Something lemony, maybe with a hint of ginger, with royal icing and some roses on the top. If I'm going to try selling posh cakes from home, I need to start experimenting, getting plenty of practice.'

'You're really going to do it? The cakes thing? It's nice to know you listen to my ideas sometimes!'

'Maybe. I'm not sure yet. There's a lot to think about.' She leans over and plants a kiss on his cheek. 'But it beats having to find a proper job. Now, go and get out of that suit and I'll make you a cup of tea to go with the cake. I haven't started on any dinner yet.'

'Too busy cake-making to think about proper food, eh?'

'Something like that,' she says.

'You all right, Mol? You look a bit pale.'

'Fine. A bit of a headache, that's all.'

'We'll get a takeaway then,' he says, going into the bedroom and stepping out of his trousers. They lie on the carpet, the striped cloth a puddle of crumpled grey, zip open like a gaping mouth, and he can't help but think about lunchtime, the park, Carly...

'That'll be nice,' Molly says, following him into the room and flopping onto the bed, watching him as he undoes his tie. 'I really don't feel like cooking. Something light though, eh? I don't fancy a pile of greasy chips tonight.'

He slips out of his shirt and lies down next to her on top of the covers. 'So, what do you fancy?' he mutters, his nose burrowing into her hair, his lips grazing her ear. She likes that. Well, usually she does. But this evening she pushes him away.

'I told you. I've got a headache,' she says. 'The kettle's on. Go and have your cake and I'll be out in a minute. I'm going to ring Mum and tell her we're coming down. Friday night okay with you? I know the trains will be busy but we'll get an extra night that way, won't we?'

'Yeah. Sure. Whatever you think best.'

Jack pulls on a pair of old jeans and a T-shirt and goes back to the kitchen and makes himself a cup of tea. It's gone very quiet in the bedroom. He thought Molly was meant to be ringing her mum, but he can't hear her voice. He cuts a big slice of cake and stirs the teabag around in his tea, then pops his head round the door to ask if she wants a cuppa too, but she's not on the phone. She's lying on her side, her mouth slightly open, her hair falling over one eye, and she's fast asleep.

🐾

Jack is half disappointed and half relieved not to run into Carly again over the next few days. He likes the thought of her being around but he needs time to get used to the idea and, luckily, he's too busy at work to stop and think about it, or her, too much.

He pulls the photo of Molly out of his drawer, wipes the dusty glass on his sleeve, and puts it on display on his desk. Not that he needs reminding that he's married, but he does it anyway. Steady, reliable, honest. That's what he wants to be, and the way he wants others to see him. It's the right image, he decides. The version of Jack Doherty that fits in a place like this.

All he has to do now is put Carly Young back where she belongs – back into that box in his head – and leave her there, just as he has done, mostly successfully, ever since he last saw her five years ago. He's a different man now – a married man – and even though sometimes it feels like he's just going through the motions, doing all the grown-up responsible stuff that's expected of him, waiting for some kind of real, exciting life to begin, he refuses to forget that one simple undeniable fact. He made a choice, and he's sticking by it. Carly's in the past, and she has to stay there. He doesn't want to do anything stupid, anything he knows he will only come to regret. Well, okay, maybe he does want to, but he's not going to. He shakes his head as if that will somehow shake her out of his thoughts, turns his attention back to the screen in front of him and puts himself firmly back into work mode.

Friday comes around quickly and he does something he hasn't dared do before, not while he's still settling in and learning the lie of the land. He sneaks off early. Molly has booked them reserved seats on the six fifteen train and he needs to get home, get changed, and get them both onto the Tube and to Liverpool Street in time. If anyone notices or wants to make a fuss about it, it will have to wait until Monday, but it doesn't look as if anyone cares. Half the office is empty by four, so he's probably not the only one wanting to start the weekend early.

Molly's waiting for him, a weekend bag packed and ready by the door, one of her special plastic cake carriers loaded up with the special lemon cake she's so proud of. She's wearing a thin floaty dress in a flowery pattern that skims her ankles, and a bright-pink jacket he can't remember seeing before.

'I went shopping,' she says. 'Do you like it?'

He nods, looking her up and down. 'You'll do nicely. As long as it didn't cost too much. We are living on only one wage, remember,' he jokes, flicking at her hair as he rushes into the bedroom to get changed.

'It didn't,' she says as he emerges into the small hallway, and grabs his keys, ready to go.

'What didn't what?'

'It didn't cost too much. Not that I know how much too much is. I just wanted something new, that's all. Something nice.'

'Okay, okay. I didn't mean anything by it. If you like it, that's fine.'

He can't help feeling, as they hurry towards the station, that he's said something wrong. She's walking with her head down, saying very little, and it's impossible to grab for her hand while she's concentrating on balancing the cake and he's trying to manoeuvre a case with a wonky wheel along the busy pavement without rapping it into someone's ankles.

'You okay, Mol?' he says, as he stows their bags on the train and they finally settle into their aisle seats, facing each other across a table. So far, nobody has turned up to claim the seats beside them, so there's room to spread his legs out a bit. The big cake in its plastic container dominates the table in front of them.

'Fine,' she says, laying her head back against the headrest and closing her eyes. 'Just tired.'

'Did you bring anything to eat? Make any sandwiches or anything?'

She gives a quiet sigh. 'We'll be there in time for dinner. Mum's making a roast.'

'Oh, right.' He feels his insides rumble. Norfolk feels like a long way away on an empty stomach, and seeing that cake on the table and knowing he's not allowed to touch it doesn't help. 'That's going to be pretty late though, isn't it? I'll just go along to the refreshment place and grab a quick coffee and a muffin or something. Or a beer, if they've got any. Want anything?'

She shakes her head. 'I'm okay, thanks. Maybe just a tea?'

'Right. Won't be long.'

He has to wait a few minutes for the coffee place to open, and there are already three people in front of him in the queue. He places his feet apart, allowing his body to sway with the motion of the train and watches through the window as the grubby London buildings pass by.

He hasn't given a lot of thought to home since they've been away, but now he finds he's looking forward to getting back to the village, seeing their families, breathing a bit of good old country air. He has no regrets about leaving but something in him still craves the familiarity, the safety of a place he knows like the back of his hand. Seeing his mum and dad, and that easy comfortable way they have with each other. Loyal, trusting. He could never imagine them wanting anyone else, doing anything to hurt each other, or ever being apart. It's the sort of relationship he's grown up around, the sort he just naturally expected to find for himself one day. Is there passion there? Who knows? It's not something anyone wants to think about, their parents having sex. But theirs is an uncomplicated, deep and steady, forever kind of love, the kind that's just there, always, unspoken but ingrained, right through to their bones. He knows, without ever having to ask, that there have been no Carly moments in his dad's life, and that there never will be.

Molly is asleep when he gets back to their seats. He puts her tea down on the table and tries to decide whether to wake her up or just let it go cold. She's a pretty sleeper. Not one of those whose tongue lolls out or who dribbles down her chin. Not a snorer. He likes watching her sleep, wondering if she's dreaming, and what about. He knows he's lucky. That she is a good wife, a loving and loyal wife, just as steady and capable as his mum, and hers, in it for the long haul.

He doesn't deserve her. What man gets horny sitting in the park with a woman he hardly knows? Wonders, every time he gets out of the lift at work, if he's going to bump into her, and hopes he might? Wonders why he can't quite get her out of his head? He remembers their conversation, what Carly had said about him being the right man at the wrong time. She was right, of course. It had been a mistake, and one he could not let himself repeat. For that one evening though, down by the river, there had been magic in the air, something new and exciting in his life, something he had never felt quite so intensely before. But, just as in all the best fairy tales, magic rarely lasts. Reality comes back with a bump. This isn't Cinderella, and he is no Prince Charming. Molly is his life, his reality.

'Oh, sorry, did I nod off?' She opens her eyes and pushes her messy blonde hair back behind her ears, reaching for her cardboard cup of tea and taking a sip. 'Can't have been for long. It's still warm!'

He rests his elbows on the table and reaches out, finding her fingers and rolling her rings around. 'Looking forward to being back?' he asks.

'God, yes! Seeing our mums and dads, and Flossy, of course. The fresh eggs, the pub, the lumpy bed...'

'Not so sure about the bed. That mattress will be the death

of me. But the pub sounds good. I could just eat one of their famous pies right now.'

'Tomorrow maybe. I expect we'll be going out to eat for your mum's birthday. Your dad won't want her to have to cook. But we've got the roast tonight, remember.'

'With Yorkshire puddings? And roast potatoes? And parsnips?'

'Jack! I can see you drooling already. Of course. When did my mum ever do a roast any other way?'

'I must say, Maureen's gravy alone is almost worth the long journey home for.'

She kicks him playfully under the table. 'It's not a long journey, Jack. We'll be there before you know it. We should make sure we do it often. There's nowhere quite like home, is there?'

He smiles, takes his hand away from hers and reaches for his beer. Home's fine, he thinks. In small doses. But home – that home – is not somewhere he wants to live again. He's moved on now, and taken Molly with him. The last thing he wants is to be sucked back into that dead-end life. They've only been out of London for half an hour but already he's thinking about Sunday, and itching to go back.

Chapter 10

Carly

It's one of those dull drizzly Saturdays when all I feel like doing is lazing around with a huge bar of Cadbury's Fruit and Nut and a can or two, in front of the telly. Well, preferably Mum's telly, so I don't have to think about the washing or what to make for dinner, or Jack.

She has a habit of talking too much, my mum. It's quite comforting, in its way, that feeling of not being on my own, of family life going on around me, and I've learned how to tune her out over the years, only really hearing the bits I want to hear, so it doesn't bother me when she keeps coming into the room and chattering away about nothing in particular. I can always press the rewind button if I miss a good bit of the film I'm only half-watching anyway.

'If I'd known you were planning on hanging around, I'd have bought extra meat,' she's saying now. 'It's okay when it's a joint but you can't really divide pork chops up, can you? It has to be one each.'

'Mum, it's okay. I don't want a chop. You and Sam go ahead and eat them. I'll grab something out of the freezer or the cupboard, if that's okay? You must have some fish fingers or a can of beans. That'll do me. Or I'll get a takeaway delivered.'

'Carly, you're very welcome to stay, you know that, but I can't have you eating baked beans, or chips out of a paper bag, while the rest of us have a proper meal. It will look...'

'Look what? And who exactly is doing the looking?' I sit up from my curled-up position on the sofa and drop my legs back down to the carpet. 'Hang on, am I missing something here? What do you mean by the rest of us? Have you got someone coming over for dinner?'

'I thought I told you.'

'I don't think you did.'

'Well, it's no big deal. I ran into Anthony during the week. You remember Anthony? From the allotments? He gave me a bag of plums, and they look delicious. I've made a pie. I thought it might be nice to ask him over to share it, that's all. And for a bit of dinner too, of course. A man can't live on plums alone.'

'Oh, Mum. I told you to stop the matchmaking. He's really not my type, and I have no interest in his plums!'

She doesn't laugh at my joke. In fact, I'm not sure she realises I've made one. 'I have no idea what you mean, Carly. I didn't even know you'd be here for the evening, did I? I thought you'd drop by for lunch and a chat and be gone again, like you usually are on a Saturday. I would have got an extra chop otherwise...'

'Right. Okay.' I'm confused now. Maybe she really is just being kind to this Anthony, knowing he's in need of company. Maybe she was never actually lining him up for me at all. 'I'm sure Anthony won't really care what I'm eating. You can tell him I'm not having the pork because I'm vegetarian or something! Or would you rather I go? Or I could pop out and buy another chop if it will help?'

She stops twisting the tea towel she's holding and perches

next to me on the sofa. 'Whatever you want. I think you might be a bit bored though, if you stay. Once Anthony and Sam get together, the talk does tend to revolve around allotment business, you know. Pesticides and the Autumn Show and who's going to tell old Mr Barton to get rid of his weeds before they infect everyone else's plots. It can get a bit...'

'Boring?'

'Yes, I suppose so. If it's not your thing.'

'It's not. So, I'll go then, shall I? What time's he coming?'

'About seven. Oh, but I don't want to push you out. It's just that...'

'It will be boring and you don't have enough chops? I get it, Mum, honestly. I expect Fran will be home. We can get a takeaway together.'

'No date tonight then? No nice young man to take you out somewhere?'

'You know there isn't.'

'Shame,' she says, under her breath, as she leaves me to curl back up on the sofa and heads back into the kitchen.

I look at my watch. It's only just gone five, so I have time to finish the chocolate and the film, and crack open a second can of lager, before I'm bundled back out into the night. And I'd like to see Sam before I go. He'll probably be back from his football match soon. It's only a little local team. They play in a bumpy field tucked away behind the playground in the park, and Sam plays in goal, but he likes to tell me how they got on and talk me through the highlights. Mum doesn't know the first thing about football and, since we lost Dad, I think Sam likes still having someone to brag to when he comes home, especially if he's managed a particularly impressive save. Although, to listen to him, they're all impressive.

The season's only just begun, but I must try to get down there and watch a match soon. I have a sudden vision of being there with Jack, like a proper boyfriend and girlfriend, wearing matching scarfs, holding gloved hands on the touchline and only letting go when our team scores and we raise our arms and cheer like loons. It's never going to happen though, is it?

As it happens, Sam's late and Anthony's early, and they arrive together. I hear the back door bang as they come clomping in to the kitchen, and Mum squealing as they've caught her unawares, still in her dirty apron and with her hair a mess.

She rushes up the stairs to sort herself out and Sam brings Anthony into the living room.

'Did you win?' I say, crinkling up my purple wrapper and stuffing it into my pocket and edging the empty lager cans round to the side of the sofa with my toe. Who wants to admit they've been drinking, and have eaten a whole giant-size bar of chocolate, all by themselves?

'Three–nil,' Sam says, with an air of triumph.

'Well done. I wish I'd been there. You can tell me all about it tomorrow. I'll call you, okay?' I get up then and hold my hand out to Anthony. 'Nice to see you again, Anthony, but I'll be off now. Have a nice evening.'

'Oh, you're going?' I hope I'm wrong but he looks really disappointed.

'Yes, I've been here far too long already. Things to do, you know how it is.'

He nods, hesitantly. 'I hope I'm not pushing you out, Carly. I'm sure Joyce wouldn't want that. I know how much she likes having you around.'

'Of course not. I raise my eyes to the ceiling, and wonder how long Mum is likely to be and if I should just slip away or wait to say goodbye.

Sam leaves the room, kicking off his shoes in the hall. I hear the water splashing into the kettle and the rattle of mugs. He's obviously decided not to wait for Mum and to make them all some tea. I almost wish he hadn't as that leaves me alone with Anthony.

'Did you manage to get your car insurance sorted?' I say, not being able to think of anything else to talk about. I'm still standing and so is Anthony.

'Yes, thanks. Not your company, I'm afraid. Got a better deal somewhere else.'

I laugh. 'There goes my Christmas bonus then!'

Anthony looks uncertain, as if he's not sure if I'm being serious.

'Joke! I think the company profits will survive. Please, Anthony, sit down. I can recommend the sofa. It's very comfy, and I've been on it a while so it's still warm!'

He smiles then and, I have to admit, he's not so bad-looking really. Not in Jack's league, obviously, but he'll do for someone.

'Anyway... I'll say bye now. Enjoy your dinner, and your plums. Maybe Mum will save me a slice of the pie, if the plums are as good as she says they are.'

'They are. Very plump and juicy,' he says, and I manage to hold my laughter back just long enough to get me safely out into the hall and out of sight.

'Bye, Mum,' I call up the stairs, and I make my escape before she tries to talk me into staying and the chop situation rears its ugly head again.

The rain has managed to hold off, although the sky is heavy with dark clouds. It's a bit of a walk to the station and then two trains to get back to the flat, and I'm starting to worry that I don't have a coat. I'm hurrying along, head down, when I hear a voice calling my name. A car has slowed down beside me and I recognise the head that's sticking out through the open window.

'Syd! What are you doing around here?'

'Just dropped Rosie and the little ones off at her mum's.

Some sort of baby-shower thing for her cousin. Do you want a lift?'

'Are you sure? I can get the Tube.'

'It's fine. I'm going near your place anyway. Come on, hop in!'

I flick a few crumbs off the passenger seat and sit, dragging the seat belt across and clicking it into place. My foot hits something on the floor and I reach down to pick it up. A dummy, covered in dirt.

'Oh, don't worry about that,' he says, taking it from my hand and throwing it over his shoulder onto the back seat. 'This is Rosie's car, and we've given up trying to keep it clean and hoovered! There are dummies all over the place. She bought a job lot. It's easier to chuck them away than bother with all that sterilising lark, when you can get them so cheap. Thank God for Poundland, eh? To be honest, if it's just a bit of fluff I just give them a suck and swish them under the tap sometimes. Doesn't seem to have done the kids any harm.'

Really? Doesn't he worry about the germs? Still, what do I know about babies and how to look after them? And the twins always look in perfect health to me.

'So, how are they?'

'The kids? Fine. Noisy, messy, never bloody sleep, but wouldn't be without them, you know? Rosie's thinking of going back to work soon, but there's a lot to sort out. Childcare-wise.'

'There must be.'

'I've got my own business now, see. Gave up on the IT stuff. Not sure it was ever really my thing. Well, Rosie's probably told you. I give driving lessons now. Got a new posh car with dual controls and everything, so I can pick and choose my hours, which works out well. Evenings, weekends... I can be out when she's in, and vice versa. Means we hardly see each other sometimes though, and we're still going to need help to make it work on any sort of permanent basis. Nurseries cost the earth. There's only so much free childcare you can expect from the in-laws. Financially, I'm not sure it's worth it, Rosie going back. We could end up paying out more than she earns. But I think she misses it, you know. Mixing with people, feeling useful, getting back into the real world...'

Rosie's a teacher. A good one, too. Secondary level, English. All the GCSE and A-level stuff she thrives on. I can imagine how much she must be missing the classroom, and the kids.

'The new term starts soon.'

'I know, but she doesn't have to go back just yet. She's spoken to the head teacher and they're looking at after Christmas. There's a locum, supply teacher or whatever they call her, holding the fort until then.'

The rain is hitting the windscreen now and Syd puts the wipers on. The rhythm of them, swishing backwards and forwards, almost sends me to sleep. Must be the lager.

'So, how about you, Carly? How's work?'

'Okay.' Should I tell him? About Jack? They were mates once, and he'll want to know how he is, won't he? They might even decide to meet up for a drink or something, once Syd finds out he's back. Besides, I want to talk about Jack, to think about Jack, and here's my chance. 'There's been a bit of a development actually.'

'Oh, yeah?' He looks at me quizzically as we wait at traffic lights, the rain thundering down on the car like someone banging a hammer on a shed roof, the wipers struggling to cope with the deluge.

'Do you remember Jack Doherty?'

'Of course. Slept on my sofa for long enough to leave an imprint! What about him?'

'He's back in London. Working at Mandrake's, by some weird coincidence. I ran into him last week.'

'Oh, that's great. I always liked old Jacky Boy. How is he?'

'Fine, I think. He hasn't changed much. Still doing well in his career, still smarter than the rest of us put together!'

'I'll have you know I've been known to scrub up pretty well in my best suit, when I can get the baby sick off the collar! Or did you mean smart as in clever clogs? I can't claim to outdo him on that score, that's for sure.'

The car is moving again, and I realise we're only about ten minutes from home. Thank God for Syd, or I'd have been drenched.

'You had a bit of a thing for our Jack, didn't you?'

I'm shocked into silence. Syd had noticed that? And if he had, maybe the others had too.

'Oh, don't worry. I never said anything. Not to him, or to Rosie. Not my business, after all. And you were both single back then. Well, maybe not for much longer in Jack's case, but he wasn't actually hitched, was he? I did wonder, for a while there, if he might call the whole thing off. I take it he didn't though?'

I shake my head, feeling the threat of tears. 'No. He went back to Norfolk and got married, just as he'd planned. Probably never gave me another thought.'

'Any kids?'

'No, he says not.'

'If he's telling the truth. Be careful, Carly. Men can be... well, shall we say economical with the truth, when they want to be. And, if you felt he was out of bounds back then, then he still is now. Even more so, now he's actually married, eh?'

'Yeah, you're right. Girl code – not that you'd know a lot about that – says that we never take another woman's man. It's just that I never really forgot about him, and it's been a shock, seeing him again. He's still so...'

'What? Handsome? Irresistible? The one who got away?' He shakes his head. 'Don't go there, Carly. You're a pretty girl.

A catch. Don't let my Rosie hear me say that! You can have any man you want.'

'But what if the man I want is Jack?'

'Out of bounds. That ship has sailed. You said it yourself, so don't do it, Carly. Don't even think about doing it. Just because he's back in London doesn't have to mean he's back in your life. It didn't work before, when he was still free to let it, so why should it now? Going after him...'

'Who said I was going to go after him?'

'Okay, maybe not, but if you're thinking about it... well, it can only lead to trouble, you do know that? Somebody will get their heart broken, and I don't want it to be you, okay?'

I nod. 'There's just nobody I can talk to about it, Syd. Suze thinks it's all a bit of a laugh, and Fran's got more interest in her next doughnut than in my love life.'

'Harsh, but probably true. So, why don't you come round to ours one day soon? Rosie sees so little of her girlfriends these days. I know the baby talk can be a bit off-putting if you don't have any of your own, but they do go to bed sometimes, despite the impression I may have given before! And she knew Jack. She'll be happy to listen. Give advice, even if you don't want to hear it.'

'I might just do that.'

'Now, are you sure you want to be dropped off at home? I've got no learners booked in, so I'm free for the evening. We could grab a drink somewhere? Talk some more?'

'Syd! After all you said about me steering clear of married men!'

'Oh, I don't count. Too knackered and too much in love with my wife to be any danger.'

'Thanks, but not tonight.'

'Not even to share a bag of chips and a saveloy? I'll be

getting some anyway. I love a bit of unhealthy stodge. When the cat's away and all that.'

'Very tempting, but who knows where a chip could lead? Greasy fingers today, full-blown affair tomorrow!' I laugh, and Syd joins in, pulling up outside my flat and putting his hand over mine.

'Good decision. We men are so easily led! But seriously, Carly, I would like to catch up with Jack, if that's all right with you. We could get some of the old crowd together. Once the company went bust, we all went our separate ways but I still see quite a few of them. And Rosie does let me out occasionally. You wouldn't have to come along yourself. Unless you wanted to, of course.'

'You know I'd want to. There's just something about him, Syd.'

'Let it go, Carly. Honestly, after all this time, let it go. He's not available, and life is too short.'

'I never had you down as such a philosopher.'

'Just a realist, that's all. It might feel like he's the only man for you, but there are millions of us, you know. Plenty of good guys who could make you happy. Marriage, kids, domestic bliss. You should give it a try.'

I give a shrug, lean over and kiss him on the cheek. 'Thanks. I don't have Jack's number or address or anything, but if you want to talk to him, just call the office and they'll put you through. He's in the IT department, obviously. Best not tell me where you're meeting up though. I can't give in to temptation and turn up if I don't have the details, can I?'

'Good decision. And he's not that special, you know. Believe me, as a man who's shared a flat with him, I know these things. That guy farts in his sleep, just like the rest of us. And his feet smell.'

I get out of the car, laughing, and run up the path through

the rain, waving over my shoulder as the car moves away. Fran's home, and I can detect the unmistakeable aroma of a Chinese takeaway as soon as I reach the top of the stairs and open the door to our flat. Suddenly, I feel really hungry and hope there's enough going spare. A girl can't live on chocolate alone, and I was starting to regret turning down that meal at Mum's. To be honest, I've never been that keen on pork chops, and all the allotment talk would probably have been a real turn-off. And chips with my best friend's husband didn't feel right either, no matter how innocent the invitation.

'Just in time,' Fran says, as she spoons a dollop of chicken chop suey onto her plate and hands me what's left in the carton. 'Grab a fork, and stop me eating the lot!'

Chapter 11

Molly

Molly settles into a cosy corner in the Brown Cow village pub and slips off her shoes. Is it a pregnancy thing, she wonders, feet swelling up and aching like they've been walking for miles when she's hardly done a thing all morning? And how is she going to explain saying no to her usual vodka and orange when her father-in-law starts taking orders for their drinks?

Jack's mum, Brenda, plonks down beside her and pushes her handbag down under the table. 'Won't be needing my purse today,' she jokes. 'Steve's paying for everything. Birthday girl privileges.'

'Quite right.' Molly smiles at her. 'I hope he bought you something nice.'

'Oh, he's not much of a one for presents. I got a nice bunch of flowers, and there's this meal to look forward to. I don't need anything else.'

'You'll not be wanting this then.' Molly nods over to Jack, sitting opposite, and he pulls a small wrapped package from his inside pocket.

'Happy birthday, Mum.'

'Oh, you shouldn't have.'

'I'll take it back then, shall I?' Jack pretends to pocket the present as his mum's hand whips out across the gap between them and grabs for it.

'Don't you dare!'

Molly watches her pulling off the paper and ribbons and cooing over the expensive bottle of perfume inside.

'It's lovely. Thank you both. But I don't know when I'll ever wear it. It's not as if we ever go out anywhere posh.'

'You mean this doesn't count?' Her husband is laughing beside her, still standing as he tries to memorise the round of drinks he's about to go and buy. 'The Brown Cow's as posh as it gets around these parts. Come on, love, give us a squirt so we can all see what it smells like.'

'You can't see a smell, Dad.' Jack's brother Richard always has been a stickler for facts, but he's first to lean forward and take a sniff as his mum liberally sprays the perfume onto her wrists. 'Mmm. Very nice. But we're here to eat, and I'm so hungry I could eat a horse.'

'I don't think horse is an option, love. They do a very nice chicken pie though.'

'Well, let's order, and then you can have our present. Call it a gift horse!' He laughs and touches his mum's arm. 'Just don't look in its mouth.'

His wife, Jennifer, raises her eyebrows and places their gift on the table. 'Forgive him, he thinks he's funny,' she says, a hint of sarcasm in her voice. 'Happy birthday, Bren.'

'Now, now, children. First things first.' Steve looks around at his family and silently mouths the list of drinks he's already tried to memorise. 'Let's all get a drink and toast the beautiful birthday girl. I'll grab us a couple of menus from the bar, but our Maureen and Bill aren't here yet, so we can't eat just yet.' Molly had left her dad sorting out food for the dog while her mum dithered over which coat to wear and whether to bother bringing her mobile when anyone likely to call would be here for the meal anyway, but she knows they won't be long.

Steve looks towards the door as it creaks open. 'Ah, speak of the devils! Come on over and find yourselves a couple of chairs.'

Molly gets up and kisses her mum as her dad shakes hands with the other men around the table.

'Now, what will you two have to drink, and who else haven't I asked?' Steve carries on, wallet in hand. 'Jack, what will you have? And Molly? Usual?'

Jack stands up. 'I'll come with you to the bar.'

Molly tries to say something. To ask for just the orange juice, without the vodka, but she can't think of a decent excuse, so she says nothing. Nobody will notice if she just sips at it, uses it for the toast and then leaves the rest. She knows it will be easier than having to explain.

It's quite busy today. Saturday afternoons in the rain, with nowhere else to go, tend to bring half the village out for a drink and a meal they don't have to cook for themselves, and the horse racing being shown on the giant TV screen is the clincher, here in the heart of East Anglia where racing seems to be in the blood.

The general noise of so many conversations going on around her makes it hard for Molly to join in, so she takes the opportunity to sit back and just think. She knows she has decisions to make. Not about keeping this baby, because she absolutely will, whatever Jack might say. That, at least, is non-negotiable. But there's also who to tell, and when. Her parents will be thrilled, and so will his. A first grandchild. And while they are all here together, already in a celebratory mood, she could so easily tell them here, right now, today... but she has to tell Jack first, and that's the bit she worries about. She's known for five days, but she just keeps chickening out. It's not what he wants. She knows that. Not part of the plan.

Of course, the test had been positive. There had never been much doubt about that, really. She had wrapped the test stick up tightly in the pages of an old newspaper so Jack wouldn't find it, and had been just about to dump it in the bin outside when she'd realised paper is recyclable and pregnancy tests are not. Which bin to choose? The last thing she wanted was for some busybody to start moving the screwed-up bundle from one bin to another and her secret tumbling out onto the pavement. In the end, she had taken it around the corner and, when she was sure nobody was looking, had separated the test from the newspaper and deposited them both in someone else's bins. She knew it was ridiculous. Jack was hardly likely to go rummaging in the rubbish, at home or anywhere else, but why take the risk?

Steve comes back from the bar, balancing a tray, and plonks her drink down in front of her. She can almost smell the vodka from here. He must have got her a double. She nods her thanks and wonders how she is going to avoid drinking it. Because she may not know a lot about pregnancy but she does know that babies and booze don't mix.

'You okay, Mol?' Jack has squeezed in beside her and has already downed a couple of mouthfuls of his pint on the way back from the bar. 'Are you coming down with a cold or something? You're looking a bit peaky again.'

She smiles at him and puts her hand on his knee. 'Fine. A bit tired, that's all. Must have been the travelling yesterday. And the effects of that huge dinner at Mum's last night. I have no idea where I'm going to find room for another one already.'

'Do your best. I'm more than happy to finish up what you leave.'

'I swear you've got hollow legs!'

Richard and Jennifer are handing over their present now, and Jack's mum is happily tearing at the paper. It's a hairdryer, which she seems really pleased with, although Molly is fairly sure she has at least two already.

Everyone is reading menus and moving discarded wrapping paper about to make room for their drinks, and the two dads are half-turned towards the TV screen, waiting for the first race to start. Molly feels happy, safe, surrounded by the familiar, so glad to be back home. But, as she rests her hand over her invisible bump, she's scared too. This is not a secret she can keep for long.

❧

Pouring an unwanted drink into a plant pot is an old trick, but not one she's ever had to try before. If the little spider plant on the windowsill beside her ends up dying an alcohol-induced death, then she's sorry, but it had to be done.

'Your glass empty already, love?' Jack turns as she sits back down from her visit to the Ladies and spots the glass she has tried to hide behind her menu. 'Want another?'

'No, one's enough. I don't think my stomach could stand it. I must be getting old!' she jokes, pushing the remains of her dessert away, only to see Jack's spoon swoop down into the bowl and scoop up the last chunk of apple pie and the scrapings of cream. 'I feel like I could just curl up and sleep for a week after all that food.'

'Well, maybe not a week, but you can have a lazy evening and a lie-in tomorrow if you want. Our train's not until the afternoon.'

'I know, but I'd quite like to get out and see a few people while we're here. Maybe take a walk with Flossy in the morning and pop in on Sian?'

'Your mate who married the vet? Yeah, sure, you do that if you like. I'm sure you've missed having a dog to walk, and seeing your own friends. Not sure all that girly gossip's for me though, so I'll give it a miss, if you don't mind.'

Molly nods. 'That's fine.'

Everyone's getting up to go now. Brenda is stuffing her presents into a carrier bag that has mysteriously appeared from her coat pocket, Richard is jiggling his car keys in an irritatingly impatient way, and a barmaid is clearing away the last of the plates.

'You coming straight back with us?' Molly's mum asks. 'Or going back to Brenda and Steve's for a while?'

Molly looks to Jack for the answer, but he just shrugs his shoulders. 'I'm easy,' he says, leaving it up to her.

'With you,' Molly says, linking her arm through her mum's. 'I fancy an evening in front of the telly. Is there a film on?'

'Bound to be if we hunt through the channels,' her mum replies. 'Something all Hollywood glamorous, I hope. If only I had somewhere to go where I could unleash my inner Marilyn and wear posh dresses and make-up and six-inch heels!'

Molly laughs. She can't imagine her practical country-girl mum in anything but brown tweed or a plain pleated skirt and home-knitted jumper, with perhaps the occasional horse-patterned scarf around her neck. But everyone has their dreams...

They say their goodbyes to Jack's family and head back along the lanes towards home.

'So, how is big city living?' her mum asks, when they have managed to put a good few yards between themselves and the menfolk coming along behind. 'All you hoped it would be?'

'If you mean what Jack hoped it would be, then yes. I'm still making up my mind.'

'Oh, love. It will take time. It's bound to feel different. A bit overwhelming. You've lived here in Shelling all your life. But you're young, you'll soon adapt.'

Molly is not at all sure she will. Or even that she wants to.

&

Sian opens the door to the cottage that she and Ralph have only recently moved into, and flings her arms around Molly's neck. 'Oh, wow. It's so good to see you. And Flossy too!'

'I've only been gone a couple of weeks!'

'Oh, I know, but... well, come on in, both of you. Mind the boxes though. We haven't quite finished unpacking yet, and the bloody things are everywhere.'

'It must be lovely to finally own your own home.' Molly stops in the doorway to the small lounge and looks around. 'Much as I love my parents, I didn't want to live with them forever.'

'Oh, us too. Ralph's dad's a sweetie, but I was always a bit wary of treading on his toes, you know. Taking over his kitchen, wanting to redecorate but not daring to suggest it, being careful not to let the bedsprings squeak too loudly!'

Molly settles down on one of two big fat armchairs, Flossy curling up instantly at her feet, and kicks off her shoes.

'Make yourself at home, why don't you?' Sian laughs, dropping into the matching chair on the other side of the old-fashioned fireplace. 'Talking of which, how's yours? The new home, I mean.'

'Okay, I suppose. But it's just a little box of a flat, and we're only renting. I just have to view it as a stepping stone to something bigger and better...'

'Not exactly the home of your dreams then?'

'Oh, Sian, I'm not complaining. Really, I'm not. It's just that it's all a bit drab, and you can hear people through the walls, and it's got no garden...'

Sian laughs. 'I get the picture. Look, this little house is far from perfect but we'll make it what we want it to be. And you'll do the same, in time. Now, let me get you a drink. And, you're in luck, I have cake. Not up to your standard, just a cherry and coconut from the shop, but it's passable.'

They sit for a while, catching up on village gossip, until Molly hears Ralph's key in the door.

'Working on a Sunday?' she says, watching him dump his medical bag in a corner and shrug off his coat.

'Hi, Molly. Good to see you. No surgery this morning, but I'm always on call, Sundays included. Animals don't much care what day it is! I had a difficult delivery out at one of the farms. Puppies. A litter of five. Mother and babies all safe and well, I'm pleased to say.'

'Ah, I must go out and see them,' Sian says. 'I'm a sucker for a newborn puppy.'

Flossy gets up from the carpet and sniffs curiously at Ralph's muddy trousers. 'I think she can smell them, bless her! A dog can always sniff out another dog. Territory marking and all that. But don't you go getting any ideas, Sian. We can't take in every homeless animal or cute puppy, or we'll end up with a whole menagerie.'

Molly gets up to leave. 'Well, I've kept you long enough and I'm sure Ralph will want his armchair back... and his lunch!'

'No need to go, honestly.'

'No, I must. Mum will have food ready soon, and I still have a few bits to pack before we head back. Stuff I left behind when we moved, but have realised I can't live without!'

'Oh, God, tell me about it! Moving's no joke, is it?' Sian leads her out into the hall, just as Flossy decides to stop and investigate an interesting-looking box propped against the wall. Molly is not looking where she's going and she doesn't stop quickly enough. She trips over the dog, loses her balance and swings an arm out to try to save herself from falling. There is a sickening crunch as her hand hits the door frame and she crumples to the floor, landing heavily and hard.

Ralph is there in a flash, on his knees beside her. 'Oh, Molly, that sounded bad. Are you hurt?'

Molly is stunned into silence. Tears have flooded into her eyes and she takes big breaths, trying to calm herself, trying to cope with the pain that is throbbing through her fingers and into her wrist, and the awful twisting feeling of fear that flutters through her tummy. Flossy pushes against her legs and starts to lick at her left hand as she moves it across and gingerly cushions the injured right one in her palm.

'Come on, lie still and let me take a look at that wrist. I know I'm only a vet, but bones are bones, and I'm afraid you might have just broken one.'

Chapter 12

Jack

'There's been some sort of accident.' Maureen comes into the room where Jack is reading the Sunday paper, the telephone still in her hand. 'Molly's hurt her hand round at Sian's. Quite badly, they think. Ralph is driving her to the hospital.'

'What? What sort of accident?'

'Here, talk to Sian, she'll tell you.' She hands him the phone and he listens as Sian rushes through what's happened and explains that she would have gone with them if it was not for poor Flossy who she couldn't leave alone.

'I'll come and get Flossy first then, shall I? Or do you think I should go straight to the hospital?' For once, Jack wishes he still had a car, but his mum is signalling that she will walk round for the dog and that he's welcome to borrow their car if he needs it.

He hangs up, and takes a breath. 'Sounds like she's broken a bone in her wrist, or maybe more than one.'

'Oh dear.' Maureen perches on the arm of the sofa, a tea towel slung over her shoulder. She is a straight-talking practical country woman and not the sort to panic. 'I didn't even know a wrist had more than one bone. Probably best that you go up there to the hospital and find out what's what. They can make you wait for hours sometimes in these casualty places, and our Molly will need someone there with her. We can't expect Ralph to stay, can we?' She gets up and turns towards the kitchen. 'It's nearly lunchtime. I'll make you a sandwich to take with you. And a flask. It's nasty stuff in those hospital coffee machines. Now, I'll just tell Bill what's going on and then I'll pop down for the dog. Come on, Jack, hop to it! If you're lucky, Molly might get treated quickly and you can still catch your train.'

The car park is a nightmare. It must be all the Sunday visitors, heading up to the wards with their get well cards and bags of grapes. He drives round twice before spotting a space and quickly claims it before walking back to the machine to pay.

The girl at the A & E reception desk directs him through a door into a large square area with curtained cubicles around all four sides. He can hear Molly before he sees her.

'But is it safe?' she's asking, her voice sounding more agitated than usual. Jack can't make out the reply, but within moments a nurse emerges, shoes squeaking on the shiny floor, and walks over to the central desk where she talks to a porter holding a wheelchair and points back towards Molly's cubicle, shaking her head.

'Excuse me.' Jack approaches the desk. 'I'm here for Molly Doherty. I'm her husband. Can I go in?'

'Of course. Just in time, as it happens. Maybe you can talk some sense into her. I've tried explaining that X-rays are perfectly safe. It's only her hand, after all, not her abdomen, and we do need to see exactly what she's broken. We deal with women in your wife's condition all the time, and the radiologist will take every precaution.'

Jack stops. 'Pardon me? What do you mean? In her condition?' A fear flashes through his mind. Molly is sick. She has cancer or a tumour or something, and she hasn't told him. Or maybe she's only just found out. Suddenly he feels pretty sick himself. 'What exactly is wrong? She's not ill, is she?'

'Oh no, clumsy of me, and not very professional. I'm sorry. I meant at her stage of pregnancy, that's all. Nothing to worry about, but it's only natural that mums worry, isn't it? But the baby will be well protected, I can assure you.'

Jack just nods. He can't speak. This can't be true, surely? The baby? What baby? No, she can't be. He would have known, he would have noticed something, she would have said...

He turns away from the desk and takes a moment to think but, in all honesty, he has no idea what to think. Molly is going to have a baby. *They* are going to have a baby. How long has she known? And why has she kept it to herself? Or has she only just found out, here, today? He wants to feel angry, he ought to feel excited, but all he feels is confusion, and a strange stopped-in-his-tracks sort of numbness. He can't take it in. Surely this can't be happening to him. Not again. His mind flashes back to the last time. To Katie, and a pregnancy he hadn't wanted, hadn't expected, had no idea how to deal with. It was so long ago now, but it was still etched into his memory as the absolute worst time of his entire life. No. It couldn't be happening again. He couldn't let it. Not here. Not now. There must be some mistake. Just stay calm, just breathe, and Molly will tell him it's all a mistake...

Slowly, he pulls back the curtain. Molly is on a narrow bed, wearing a hospital gown, her clothes piled up on a chair beside her. Her right arm is in a sling and there's a needle poking out of the back of her left hand, attached to a drip. There is no sign of Ralph.

'Hello, you,' she says, looking up at him with tears in her

eyes. How much did she hear when he was talking to the nurse outside? Does she know that he knows?

He wants to reach out and hold her but he can't. There is a huge unspoken lie hovering in the room between them. Is she going to tell him? Was she ever going to tell him?

'They want me to stay for some more tests. It's almost definitely a clean break, but they need to make sure. And to check me over... generally. You don't have to hang around, Jack. I've already sent Ralph home for his lunch. I'll be fine on my own. And if things... well, if they don't think I'm ready to go, or to travel, then you can still get the train back to London this afternoon as planned, in time for work tomorrow. I'll stay on here at Mum's and catch you up when I can.'

'Check you over generally? What exactly do you mean by that, Mol?' He stares at her, willing her to stop lying, to just be straight with him. 'It was only your wrist you hurt, wasn't it? Nothing else? A bit of plaster of Paris and a few painkillers and you'll be good to go, surely?'

He waits but she takes her time to answer.

'Who knows? These doctors are a law unto themselves. It's all tests, isn't it? To be on the safe side. Nothing to worry about, I'm sure.'

'Any luck?' The nurse has appeared again. She's looking straight at Jack, not at Molly.

'Luck? What are you talking about?' Molly turns her face from one to the other.

'I asked your husband to have a word, Molly, that's all. To try to persuade you to let us X-ray that hand. I'm sure he's just as concerned about the baby as you are, but...'

Jack stays just long enough to see the look on Molly's face. She has gone very pale. Surprise, shame, guilt, it's all there in that look. She shakes her head slowly. 'I'm sorry, Jack. I...'

He doesn't hang around to hear her excuses.

Chapter 13

Molly

She had not expected to have a scan quite so soon but the fall has worried her, and the doctors, so here she is, lying on a narrow bed with her hospital gown open and her belly exposed as a girl in a white uniform squeezes cold jelly onto her skin.

'How many weeks do you think you are, Molly?'

'I'm not sure. I hadn't actually been to see a doctor yet, or a midwife or anybody. I only realised I might be pregnant very recently, so it's just been a home test...'

'That's fine. And your last period was...?'

She wouldn't normally remember the date but this time, ever since she'd found that diary and started counting, it's been imprinted on her brain.

'The tenth of June.'

The girl is holding a thing in her hand. It looks like some sort of computer mouse, and she is moving it around in the stickiness, rolling it back and forth over Molly's slightly rounded belly – when had that happened? – and the pressure is making her want to wee. 'Yes, that sounds about right! Do you want to take a look?'

Molly turns her head towards the screen and there it is. A baby. Small, grey, hardly more than a blob, but it is moving, and it has a shape, a head. The girl is twiddling with her equipment, bringing up different images and close-ups on the screen, almost as if she's editing a photo, looking for the best angle or adjusting the light. For a few moments she says nothing, just concentrates on doing her job.

'Is everything all right?'

'Well, from these measurements, I would say you are around eleven weeks. First trimester almost done already. And everything looks fine, honestly. I don't think your fall has done any harm at all. Babies can be very resilient, and of course, he or she is very well protected in there!'

Molly nods. She doesn't know what to say, it's all so unexpected, so unreal. Eleven weeks! How can she not have known, not even suspected, for so long?

'You will need to check in with your own GP and get yourself into the system. There will be midwife appointments, some antenatal classes, and you'll be given all the paperwork so you can have free prescriptions and dental care.' She is handing Molly a big piece of paper, like a chunk of thick kitchen roll. 'There. All done. You can give yourself a wipe clean and pull your gown back round now.'

Molly sits up and adjusts her clothing. 'Thank you.'

'All in a day's work. And I'm sure you'll be back here for more scans, scheduled ones, including the twenty-week one, of course, where we will be better able to tell you the sex... if you want to know, of course.'

'That may have to be at a different hospital actually. I've recently moved, to London. I was just here visiting when I had the fall.'

'That's fine. Just make sure you register somewhere. And, in the meantime, congratulations, Molly. It's lovely to meet your baby for the first time, isn't it? Would you like a picture?'

Molly stands on the steps outside and takes in a big breath of fresh air. There's always that strange chemical smell in hospitals, like someone has tipped a big bottle of bleach over everything, which they probably have. She had given in and allowed them to X-ray her, with all precautions in place, and it is a simple break, one they have assured her will heal well, and quickly. Her wrist has been plastered and her arm is in a sling but that hardly seems to matter anymore. It doesn't hurt, even though she has refused any sort of pain relief. She may not be able to write or clean her teeth, or even wipe her own bottom, without learning to use her left hand, but it's temporary and it could have been so much worse. All she can really think about now is the baby. The baby is okay, healthy, unharmed.

The first person she wants to tell is Jack, but the look on his face when he stormed out has made it pretty clear he's not in the mood for celebrating. But he will come round, won't he? They've been married for five years. They are not teenagers anymore. They have a home, an income. It's not unusual to start a family at this stage of life, is it? So, okay, it wasn't planned, they hadn't talked about it, and she should have told him the minute she suspected, but none of that can be changed now. What's done is done.

She looks at her watch. It's already half past two. Their train back to London leaves soon. She wonders if he has gone already, grabbed his stuff and left without her. Or would he have put it off, waited to switch to a later train so they can go together?

She takes out her phone and hesitates. Will he even answer?

Possibly not. So she dials home instead. Well, her parents' home, technically, although it will always feel like home to her.

Her mum answers on the second ring. 'Molly! How are you, love? We've been so worried.'

'I'm all right. It's broken, but not too badly, and I'm all plastered up and ready to come back. Is Jack there?'

'No, love. We assumed he was with you. He took the car and headed off to the hospital a couple of hours ago. Didn't he turn up?'

'Yeah, he did, but he didn't stop long.'

'Really? Well, where can he be then?' Her mother sounds puzzled. 'Can't you call him and get him to come back for you? You'll be needing a lift home.'

'I'll do that. Don't worry. I'll see you soon. And get the kettle on. The stuff they give out here is awful!'

She hangs up and walks across to a bench, perching on the end and turning her back to avoid the smoker in a dressing gown and slippers who is occupying the other end. She could call a taxi, or Ralph, but she has to speak to Jack at some point, and if he's got her dad's car, he will have to go back to the house anyway.

It takes him a while to pick up, but he doesn't speak. 'Jack? Are you there?'

'Yes.' His voice, when it comes, is clipped, abrupt. 'So? Are you done? Both of you okay?'

She doesn't like the way he emphasises the word *both*. There is something grudging about it. Cold. There is a lot of noise in the background and it's hard to hear him at all, but she hears that.

'Yes. The wrist's broken. Baby's all right. I'm ready to leave. Jack, where are you?'

'Just out. Having a drink. Taking in the news. Wetting the baby's head.' Sarcasm hangs heavily in every word.

'A drink? Is that a good idea? When you're driving?'

'I can do without a lecture from you, thanks very much. And it seems to me you're the one who shouldn't be drinking. The size of that vodka yesterday...'

'I didn't drink it. I just... well, I hadn't told you yet, or anyone, and it would have seemed too obvious to refuse a drink, so I just got rid of it. It's in the plant pot.'

'Ha! Poor plant. Didn't see that coming, I bet. Its roots have probably shrivelled up by now. All a bit sneaky. It seems you're pretty good at deceit though, doesn't it? Keeping secrets, telling lies...'

'That's a bit harsh, Jack. I didn't lie to you. I just hadn't quite found the right time to tell you, that's all. But I was going to.'

'Well, I know now, don't I?'

'Yes, and I'm sorry.'

'What for? Not telling me, or for letting me find out like that, from a stranger, or for getting pregnant in the first place?'

'I think you'll find it took two of us to do that, Jack.'

There is silence, until she hears him slam his glass down, presumably on some bar somewhere.

'I suppose I'd better come and get you then?'

'Yes, please. If you haven't had too much to drink. We have to be more careful now...'

'I've only had one pint,' he huffs, and then the call is cut off.

He turns up ten minutes later. She climbs in beside him but he stares straight ahead as he drives. His hands, white and tense, grip the steering wheel.

'What about our train?' she asks.

'Missed it, obviously. There's another in an hour. I have to get back for work, but you don't. Maybe it would be best if you stay down here for now. It doesn't look like you'll be able to do much for a week or two. I should think even having a shower or washing your hair will be tricky. You certainly won't be out looking for a job, or doing your baking, and I'll be at work all day. At least down here you'll have your mum to help you. And some company.'

Molly nods. She has no idea if he is being kind and thoughtful or just wants to be rid of her for a while.

Within minutes of getting home, her mum guiding her on to the sofa and fussing over her with tea and cake, and Flossy flopping like a big warm furball at her feet, Jack has packed his bag, kissed her briefly on the cheek, called a taxi, and gone. She hasn't even shown him the picture from the scan.

Chapter 14

Carly

It's time I did what I've been telling myself I'll do for ages. I'm going to learn to drive. Running into Syd the other night reminded me it was time to steer away from Jack – excuse the pun! – and find myself something else to concentrate on. And who better to teach me than Syd himself?

I have invited myself round for the evening, partly to make the arrangements about the lessons, but mainly to catch up with Rosie who, I have to admit, I've missed seeing regularly these last few months.

Rosie is so pleased to see me it makes me feel guilty for leaving it so long. Both babies are asleep upstairs and, for once, the living room is tidy, if you don't count the teetering pile of washed baby clothes on a chair, waiting to be put away, and the basket of dirty ones on the carpet, waiting to take their place in the machine.

'Oh, it's a never-ending operation.' She laughs, noticing what I'm looking at. 'Like painting the Forth Bridge!' She points me towards the sofa and takes the bottle of wine I hold out to her. 'I really shouldn't,' she says, 'but a little one won't hurt, will it? And I can't leave you to drink the whole bottle by yourself.'

'How about Syd?'

'He'll be back soon, but he's out teaching again later, so he won't drink. More than his job's worth to even think of risking it.'

'Very sensible. And good to know, if he's going to take me on. More than enough risk there, with me let loose on the roads, without adding alcohol to the mix.'

'Oh, don't be daft. You'll be great. You'll take to it like a duck to water, I bet.'

I don't remind her that water and me are not all that compatible either and that I can only just about manage one width of the pool, doggy-paddle style, before I collapse, breathless, at the side. The only things ducks and me have in common are big feet and a liking for bread!

'So,' she says, once she's been out to the kitchen to find glasses and a corkscrew and then realises it's a screw-top bottle. 'Syd tells me Jack's back on the scene after all this time.' She pours me a glass of wine so full it's in danger of slopping over the brim, and then does the same for herself. So much for a little one won't hurt! I know she and Syd are not ones for keeping secrets from each other, but he did promise he wouldn't say anything, so I'm really hoping she has no idea about Jack and me, or how I feel about him.

'Good-looking bloke, was Jack. She's a lucky lady, that little country wife of his.'

I laugh. 'Rosie! And you a married mother of two. You're not meant to notice good-looking blokes anymore.' I take a big sip from my glass so I don't have to say anything else.

'Ah, but I wasn't married back then, when I was noticing him, was I? He could be all wrinkled and gone to seed by now, for all I know.'

'I've seen him, and he isn't.'

'He would have made a good match for you, you know,

Carly. Up-and-coming professional type, smart suits, nice bum... Still, all water under the bridge now he's been snapped up by someone else. God knows it's time we found you somebody though, before the old ovaries dry up.'

I splutter my wine and put the glass down on the coffee table before I risk spilling it all over the furniture. 'Ovaries? And *old* ovaries, at that! You sound just like my mother. There's more to life than having babies, you know.'

'Is there? I've forgotten.'

There's a crackling on the baby monitor, propped up on the mantlepiece to my left, closely followed by a loud wailing. Talk about timing!

'Oh, no peace for the wicked,' Rosie says, standing up and heading for the stairs. 'At least it's only Jamie. Let's hope I get to him before he wakes Becca up as well.'

'You can tell which is which? Just from one cry?'

She gives me a strange look, as if I've just asked the most ridiculous question. 'Of course I can. I'm their mum.'

By the time Syd comes home, I have been collared into holding Jamie while Rosie goes back up for Becca who has woken up crying within minutes of her brother. I have managed to dodge changing a nappy, although I had no choice but to watch at close range while Rosie did it, and it was not a simple wet one, believe me. How can one tiny baby make such a mess? And now I am cradling a baby in one arm and a feeding bottle in the other hand and wondering how I'm supposed to move my legs into a more comfortable position without disturbing the flow of milk and before cramp sets in.

Syd leans against the open door and watches me, smiling. 'We'll make a mother out of you yet, Carly,' he says. He sees my expression and backtracks. 'Well, a babysitter at least.'

I have to admit that this particular baby is quite cute, when he's being quiet anyway. 'Is that a hint? Because I could, I suppose. Babysit sometimes, I mean. If you were really stuck, obviously, because I know I'm not first choice material. But as your family are so far away, and you can't keep asking Rosie's mum...' I have no idea why I just said that. Me, alone with two babies, for a whole evening? I just don't have the experience, or the confidence, to know what on earth I'm doing. I should think before I speak sometimes, and there's no way I should have made such a stupid offer. I hope they can see it's stupid too and don't take me up on it.

'We can give lessons, if necessary,' Rosie says, instantly attuned to what I'm thinking. I think my face might just have given it away. 'Nappy changing, bottle warming, burping...'

'I think maybe I should just start with the driving lessons, if that's okay with you?'

'Not a lot of difference really,' Syd says. 'Once you get the hang of the basics, it will all just fall into place. Mirror, signal, manoeuvre is pretty much like sniff, grab a nappy and wipe, when you come to think about it. Just a procedure to follow. Talking of which...' He goes to a table in the corner and picks up his diary. 'When did you want to start? The driving? I've got a slot spare tomorrow if you're up for it? Seven o'clock, at yours? And I've got a copy of the Highway Code here somewhere. Never too soon to start working on the theory.'

We talk about the fees, which are horrifyingly higher than I'd realised, despite Syd giving me a mates-rates discount, and he checks that I've got my provisional licence, which I've actually had for ages although I never quite took the next scary step. A chicken, that's what I am. Then he writes my name in the diary before he swigs down a big mug of coffee, grabs his car keys and leaves again. So, there's no going back now. I am officially a learner.

Jamie opens his eyes and looks startled as he lets out an enormous burp, even though I haven't put him up on my shoulder or done any of that back-patting stuff I thought you had to do. He's only little and I guess he's still learning about how things are meant to be done too.

I can do this! Babysitting, driving, maybe even swimming if I was to put my mind to it. And, as for getting over Jack Doherty... well, I can do that too. In fact, I'm doing it already. I just need my head to tell it to my heart, and job done!

When I next run into Jack, I have my coat on and two bulging carrier bags of lunchtime food shopping in my hands. It's half past five and I'm about to head for home. As he comes out of the lift at ground level, I'm struggling with the main door and he rushes forward to hold it open for me. I get a delicious whiff of his aftershave as he squeezes through next to me and we stand together, a bit awkwardly, on the pavement outside.

'Off home?' he says.

'Yep.' I nod towards my bags. 'Got a fridge to fill. You?'

'Thought I might go for a drink first, actually. I don't suppose you fancy keeping me company?'

My insides do a little jig, but I try to ignore it. Fancy it? Fancy *him*? Of course I do, but even as my head starts to nod all by itself, I remember that he's married and I know I'm making a stupid mistake, so I immediately start to backtrack, looking for an excuse to turn him down. 'I'd love to, Jack, but...'

'But you have other plans? A date? But maybe just a quick one, eh? Only half an hour. For old times' sake?'

A quick one? I know he only means a drink, but I wish he wouldn't say things like that, putting naughty ideas into my head. I feel myself hesitate. There is nothing I would rather do than spend time with Jack, but...

'You'd be doing me a favour, rescuing me from an evening in

front of *Coronation Street*.' He has that look in his eyes that I just know I'm not going to be able to resist. Sort of pleading but cheeky at the same time. Oh, God, Jack, stop it. Don't you know how much I want you?

'I don't believe for a minute that you're a soap fan! But won't you be expected home straight after work? Your wife...?'

'She's away at the moment. At her parents' place. So, I'm not in any hurry to get back to an empty flat, despite my undying love for Deirdre Barlow and her sexy glasses.'

'I think you'll find she's not in it anymore.'

'Ah, well, the other one then. The old woman with the hairnet. Ena, or Elsie. Something like that. Come on, it's just a drink, Carly. I'm not asking you to run away with me!' He laughs, and suddenly my refusal seems churlish, childish, ridiculous. He's right. It is just a drink.

'Okay then. Why not?'

Jack takes one of my bags from me. He probably would have done the full-on gentleman thing and carried both if he didn't already have his briefcase in one hand. 'The Clarion all right with you?'

The Clarion is more of a posh wine bar than the pub I'd been expecting, but I don't argue as we walk the five minutes or so to get there. It's almost empty as we step into the calm, plush red-and-silver interior, quiet music playing in the background, and Jack leads me to a velvet-lined booth in the far corner.

'What can I get you?' he says, plonking my shopping down beside me and getting his wallet out of his jacket pocket.

I want a cider but I'm not sure they'd even have it in a place like this, so I ask for a small glass of Merlot, and Jack strolls over to the bar to get it. While he's gone, I take the opportunity to adjust my belongings and myself, whipping out a mirror from my bag and quickly rearranging my hair and slicking on a dab of lip gloss, and piling both shopping bags onto the chair on the other side of the table so, when Jack gets back, he has no option but to sit beside me on the plush bench seat.

He comes back carrying two large empty glasses and a whole bottle of red. 'I thought we were only stopping for one,' I say. 'I don't want to get tiddly. I need a clear head. I've got things to do.'

'Like put your beans away in the kitchen cupboard? What's the problem with a bit of alcohol, Carly? Loosen up. I know you're not driving tonight.'

'You've spoken to Syd, haven't you? You know about the driving lessons.'

'I have, as it happens.' He's concentrating on pouring the wine, and carefully places an almost full glass down in front of me. 'And I hear it's down to you that he tracked me down, so thanks for that. It was good to hear from him, especially the blow-by-blow account of your first three-point turn.' He's smiling so much he's bordering on actually laughing at me.

'He didn't tell you about that, did he?' I can feel my face redden as I remember the mess I made of it, the bump as the front wheels slammed into the kerb. 'Whatever happened to client confidentiality?'

Jack's been holding the laugh back but he lets it escape now. 'Just a little bit of banter between mates. It's not going any further. It's not as if he took photos and sold them to *The Sun*.' He takes a big slug of his wine and looks at me. 'I'm sorry. You know I'm only teasing. We've all had to learn, all made mistakes. I think it's pretty brave of you actually, starting at your age.'

'My age? I'm thirty-one, not bloody ninety!'

'Yeah, but you know what I mean. I had my first lesson the minute I was seventeen. All over-confident and cocky. And did all my practising on little quiet country roads, but it still didn't stop me hitting a fence post or running over a pheasant.'

'You didn't! The poor thing.'

'Oh, it was already dead before I got there. It happens a lot, in the country. But still not a nice feeling squishing what was left of it into the road. Not as if I could have picked it up and taken it home for Mum to cook. It was too far gone for that.'

'Yuk!'

We sit in silence for a few minutes. In my head, the image of the dead bird seems to merge with the redness of the wine, which suddenly looks a lot like blood. It's good wine though, far better than the cheap plonk the pubs sell. It must have cost a fair bit.

'So, are you meeting up with Syd? He said he'd quite like to get some of your old workmates together for a catch-up.'

'Yeah, Saturday.'

I am not going to ask for the details. I promised Syd I'd stay away from Jack and I've already broken that one, even though I hadn't meant to. Besides, he could be taking his wife along, for all I know, if she's back by then. And I really don't want to meet her. I don't even want to know what she looks like. It's best she remains shadowy, if that's the right word. Faceless. I don't want to think of her as an enemy, a rival. Not even as a real person. In fact, I don't want to have to think about her at all.

'Molly will probably still be away, so I'll be footloose and fancy free.' It's as if he's read my mind. 'Boys' night out.'

'Well, behave yourself, or make sure Syd does anyway. He's a father now, remember. A responsible family man.'

Something passes over Jack's face, but I can't quite pinpoint what it is.

'It's just a drink, Carly.' The same words he said to me just minutes ago. 'Well, a few, probably. But no funny business. When men get together it's not all strip clubs and trying to get off with the barmaid, you know. I like to think we've grown out of all that. Well, I know I have.'

'Sorry.'

He gives me one of those killer smiles of his and touches my hand. The briefest of touches but I swear I can still feel it, all warm and tingly, after he takes it away.

'Nothing to be sorry for. I'm just not the same man I was when you knew me before. I'm...'

'Married?' I wish I hadn't jumped right in with that, but it just slipped out. Anyone would think I was jealous.

'Well, yes, that, obviously. But I meant that I'm older, more settled, at work as well as at home. And I want to do well, make something of my life. I have... ambition, I suppose.'

'Me too. That's why I changed jobs, and moved out of Mum's, and why I'm learning to drive. Having a go at being a proper grown-up!'

'And how's that going?'

I pick up my wine, lift it to my lips and blow a stream of noisy bubbles into it. 'It's a work in progress,' I say, giggling until a spurt of wine erupts out of the corner of my mouth and runs down my chin, and we both laugh so much that Jack nearly knocks his glass over, makes a grab for it and wobbles the table, making one of my tins of beans leap out of its carrier bag and roll away like a bowling ball, hurtling across the floor towards the bar.

I stumble forward, bend down and make a grab for it, my hand grasping at Jack's ankle to stop myself landing flat on my face. He hauls me to my feet and pulls me back down beside him, our bodies now suddenly much closer than they were before. I can feel the heat from his thigh, and all sorts of delicious thoughts come rushing into my head. Oh dear! Drinking may not be such a good idea, for either of us, but as he lifts the bottle and tops up my glass I don't try to stop him.

Chapter 15

Jack

Jack wants to kiss her. She's so damn beautiful when she laughs like that, her eyes sparkling under the chandeliers. What sort of a bar has chandeliers in this day and age, anyway? He knows it's corny and a bit over the top but, still, he's glad he chose this place. None of the massive TVs and sticky tables and noisy crowds of office workers most of the ordinary pubs have to offer. He sits closer and wraps his hand around the back of hers, her warm fingers still clutching her glass.

'Carly...'

She turns her head to look at him, and her face is just inches away. He can almost feel the electricity between them, the pull that was always there, from the first time he'd met her all those years ago. If he hadn't lost his job, hadn't gone back home, hadn't married Molly...

It's wrong to think like that. He knows it is. Nobody made him do those things. It was the life he chose, and he can't go back. He loves Molly; he always has. It's just that, right now, he can't think about her, about what's about to happen in their lives, the changes a baby is going to bring. These things are supposed to be talked about, considered, planned. He's not ready. Just like the last time, when he was a naive seventeen-year-old, acting like Jack the Lad, thinking with his dick instead of his brain, taking stupid chances. If it hadn't been for his parents, discreetly sorting things out with Katie's, paying for the abortion, allowing him to go away to uni without the worry and the responsibility hanging over his head, where would he be now?

He can't believe it's happening again. He's older now, more sensible, and he thought Molly was too, but that doesn't stop him being angry, confused, and – yes – scared. If babies were ever going to be a part of their lives, he always thought it would be by agreement, something discussed and planned. How can this be happening? Isn't she meant to be on the pill? Of course, she might have done it on purpose, stopped taking the damn things, tricked him...

He doesn't want to think about it, to have to even consider that his wife could do such a thing. He just wants to blot it all out, enjoy something uncomplicated, fun, even if only for one evening, one night. While the cat's away...

Carly's lips are so close. If he's going to do it, now is the time.

There is a moment, a long tingling moment, when they both stop and just look at each other, but neither makes the all-important move.

'Jack, I can't.' Carly pulls back and he lets her hand break free from his.

He closes his eyes for a second or two and, when he opens them again, she is sitting upright, the distance back between them, and she's looking away from him, down at the table. 'Me neither. I'm sorry.'

'I think maybe I should go, don't you? I don't do this sort of thing, get involved with married men... Not that we are... involved, I mean.'

'I know. It would be so easy though, wouldn't it?' So easy, so tempting. He still wants to, but the moment is lost.

She turns her back and stands up, slipping her arms into her coat and picking up her shopping. 'I really do have things to do. Thanks for the drink, but this really isn't a good idea, is it?'

'Probably not.'

'I just don't want to end up falling into something I shouldn't, and ending up as the other woman, you know. Because that's what could happen if we let it.'

He doesn't answer, but he knows she's right.

'And we both know that men in this situation don't leave their wives, they just juggle, have a go at having their cake and eating it, don't they? I'm sorry. I know I'm jumping several steps ahead here, but I don't want to be anyone's dirty secret, Jack. You know, three of us in this marriage, as Princess Diana said once.' She shrugs. 'I can't see myself as Camilla somehow.'

He stands up too, leaning over and planting a short, chaste kiss on her cheek. 'Me neither. Not that Molly's much of a Diana, to be honest. And I don't have the ears to be Charles! But I get what you're saying. Stop it before it starts, yeah?'

She nods.

'See you at work then?'

'Yeah, see you. Friends though?'

'I hope so.'

And then she walks out, quickly, without looking back, and he's left with two half-full wine glasses and the rest of the bottle, and he has every intention of drinking it all. In fact, he might even order another.

When he gets back to the flat it feels cold and empty. Mad though he is with Molly, he misses her being here. The smell of her latest batch of baking, the sound of her singing along to the ads on the TV, her warmth in the bed.

He has known Molly since school, although she was two years below him and their paths didn't really cross until he came back from uni, living on the farm and working in town. Molly was doing a few shifts in a pub he used to visit two villages away, having blossomed from shy schoolgirl with a ponytail and knee-length socks to the quiet understated beauty she is today. He couldn't fail to notice her, be drawn to her.

They have been together as a couple for eight years now, and married for five, only ever apart for those few months he worked in London, but even then they were always in touch, phoning, texting, him nipping between home and here whenever he could. But this time feels different. He hasn't spoken to her in days, has ignored her texts and voicemails, and the missed call from his mum which would inevitably have led to all the obvious questions. Why was Molly still there in the village, she'd want to know? So, she'd hurt her hand, but surely that didn't have to mean she couldn't have gone back to London with him? Or followed him the next day? He's pretty sure Molly won't have said anything about the pregnancy, won't have told his parents, or even her own, until they are ready to do it together, but in his parents' world, couples stick together, travel together, look after each other. Without the facts, his mum is going to be drawing all sorts of conclusions about this sudden and unexpected separation, anything from some minor domestic tiff to full-on divorce, either of which she is bound to blame on Molly, and sooner or later he is going to have to put the record straight.

He is being a coward, he knows that. Avoiding Molly, ignoring his mum, even making some sort of ill-advised pass at another woman, brushing it all under an imaginary carpet as if it might just go away. But he knows it won't. Molly is having a baby, no matter how much he wishes she wasn't. Ready or not, it's happening.

He makes himself a strong coffee to try to counteract the alcohol and drinks it too quickly, burning the top of his mouth, so he has to follow it with a huge glass of cold water. Then he lies down, fully clothed, on top of the covers on his half of the bed. He should ring Molly, try to talk about it at least. Not that he knows what to say. He's not sure he will be able to pretend he's happy about any of it, but there will be practical things to work out. He doesn't even know when this baby is due, when she will be having midwife appointments or scans, what it will all mean when it comes to money and the need for an extra bedroom and whether this will put an end to Molly's plans to start a business or find a job. In the end, he decides there's too much to think about all at once, and that, with a brain befuddled by booze, this may not be the best time to do it.

It's getting late anyway. She's probably asleep. He remembers how tired she has been lately, nodding off in the evenings and on the train. Does being pregnant do that to a woman? He is only too aware just how little he knows about the whole process. The whole being a prospective parent thing.

He turns out the light and, one arm draped loosely around Molly's pillow, he wriggles under the duvet and lets himself drift into sleep. The last question to flutter randomly through his mixed-up thoughts is whether this baby will be a boy or a girl, and which he might prefer. His sober self would already know the answer to that. Neither. He doesn't want to be a father at all. Not yet. Not now.

Maybe things will feel different in the morning.

They don't.

Jack wakes up as confused as ever. He has an important meeting this morning. They are working on a whole new software package that is costing thousands to develop, and the last thing he wants is to mess it up. He can't let what's happening at home distract him.

At least while Molly is away, he doesn't have to deal with things. Pretending nothing is happening is not the finest of strategies but, for now, it's the only one he has.

He stands under the shower for a long time with his eyes closed, letting the soothing water wash over him, then puts on his best suit and gives his shoes a quick polish. He doesn't leave himself enough time to eat breakfast, but it will be easy enough to grab a cereal bar or a banana or something on the way and eat it on the train. Being good at his job, making a success of it, matters. And, if there is going to be another mouth to feed, an added responsibility he hadn't seen coming but was going to have to accept sooner or later, then hanging on to this job suddenly matters even more.

Chapter 16

Carly

I'm sitting in the pub garden again with Suze and Fran, after work. We're into September now and it's not so warm these days, but I'm not prepared to let summer go just yet. A woolly cardigan over my fancy top, and a pair of thick jeans, are enough to stave off the effects of the cool breeze that's rustling the serviette tucked under our almost empty plate of chips and blowing a wisp of Fran's curly hair straight into her mouth and dousing it in ketchup.

'You did what?' Suze has got it out of me about my visit to the Clarion with Jack and my near-miss kiss, and she's going for the jugular. 'Carly Young, I despair of you. What did we say about married men?' If she wasn't sitting down, she'd have her elbows stuck out and her hands on her hips by now, her face is looking so stern.

'Not to go anywhere near them?'

'Exactly. So, what did you do the minute my back was turned? You not only went out drinking with the man, you damn near sucked his face off!'

'But I didn't actually go through with it. I might have

wanted to. Well, yes, I admit I definitely did want to, but I didn't, okay?'

'No, it's not okay. He's got a wife, for God's sake.'

An image of her pops into my head. Faceless, naturally, as I still have no idea what she looks like. She hovers in my peripheral vision, like a wishy-washy painting, all pale and mysterious, and much as I try to brush her away, I just can't do it.

'I know he has a wife. I know it only too well, but she's away at the moment.' As soon as I say it, I know I've only gone and dug myself into a deeper hole.

'And that makes it all right, does it? Look, I know he's gorgeous and you fancy him rotten, and I can't blame you for that. He is a very good-looking bloke, but he's off-limits. Carly, watch my lips. Do... not... go... there.'

'I won't. Not again. I promise.'

'Good. Now, let's change the subject, shall we? Romance, sex, men... I'm sick of all of it. Let's have a man-free evening, okay?'

'Things not going well with what's-his-name then?' Fran says. That's the thing about sisters. Brothers too, come to think of it. They know how to push each other's buttons.

'I said let's change the subject. And his name's Sean, as you very well know.' Suze does that face of hers, the one that says enough is enough. She rolls her eyes and lifts her chin so her nose is stuck up in the air. 'Is it just me or is it getting a bit cold? Shall we go inside?'

I'm actually quite enjoying the breeze, but I know Suze well enough to realise there's something gone wrong in her already rather rocky fledgling relationship with Sean that she doesn't want to talk about, and not to argue when she's got a strop on, so we all pick up what's left of our drinks and walk through into the pub.

Somehow, shifting position has given us the chance to start again when it comes to conversation and both Jack and Sean have been instantly wiped out of our invisible list of topics.

'I like that top,' Fran says, leaning forward to have a feel of my hem, rubbing the fabric between her fingers and thumb. 'Is it silk?'

'Only the cheap fake kind. I got it in the market, would you believe?'

'I don't suppose they do it in my size,' Fran says with a sigh. 'All the fashionable stuff seems to stop at a sixteen, if it even goes that far. Do you know, there's one place in town that calls a size twelve extra large!'

We make sympathetic noises, but she does have a point. There are plenty of women who weigh in at the heavier end of the scales but still want to look good.

'You could always have a go at making your own clothes,' Suze says, a bit unhelpfully as she knows as well as I do that Fran is no needlewoman. She tried to knit a bobble hat once and it came out with so many holes it could have doubled up as a tea cosy, with the handle and the spout free to stick out just about anywhere they needed to.

Fran shakes her head and turns her attention to the bag of crisps she has just bought at the bar, ripping it open and offering it round before diving in.

'So, how are the driving lessons going?' Suze is digging for something to laugh at and I'm not going to be the one to give it to her.

'Very well, according to Syd. I've only been out three times but I haven't hit anything yet – well, not since the infamous three-point turn in lesson one. And I did what he called a textbook reverse around the corner the other night. And I'm working on the Highway Code. It's not quite as riveting as reading the latest Milly Johnson, not much in the way of plot, but I'm persevering. Road signs, stopping distances and all that. You can test me if you like!'

'Okay, what's that sign that looks like a pair of 48 double H cups lying down in the road?' Suze has the light back in her eyes now, and has switched back to naughty mode.

'You mean Fran when she's had one too many vodkas?'

Fran bashes me on the arm in indignation, but she's laughing along with us, and I know she doesn't mind. She makes enough jokes about her own size, after all. 'I'm only a 42E, I'll have you know,' she says, as if to prove my point. 'And I can never have too many vodkas!'

'I know we're not talking about men tonight...' Suze says, looking pointedly at her sister, 'but that doesn't stop us talking about your love life, does it?'

Fran stares straight back at her. 'What love life?'

'My point exactly. Look, Frannie, I can't pretend to know much about gay romance...'

'No, you can't, so don't ask, okay?'

'Nobody on the scene then?' Suze never seems to know when to stop.

'I have met someone, actually.' I don't often see Fran blush but her cheeks are looking a lot redder than they did a moment ago. I wouldn't be at all surprised if she's making it up, just to get Suze off her case. 'But it's early days, and none of your business, so can we just leave it, please?'

'Suit yourself, but come on, Fran. You're one of the first to stick your ears up whenever there's even a hint of gossip. And if Carly and I are fair game, I don't see why you shouldn't be. And, besides, what are sisters for, if not to share a bit of the intimate stuff from time to time? You know, marks out of ten, and have you kissed her yet?'

'You never know when to just leave it, do you? Some things are private, okay?'

Suze looks at me and does a ridiculous exaggerated wink. 'That means she hasn't!' she says, dodging out of the way as Fran swipes at her with her hand.

'Well, I don't see you spilling all the latest on that Sean of yours.'

'Not mine, as it happens.' Suze clutches at her glass so hard I think it's going to break in her hand, and takes a long swig. 'Seems he's been seeing some girl he met on a bus.'

'Oops, sorry. Sore point?' Fran's anger subsides in an instant and she shuffles up closer to Suze and puts an arm across her shoulders.

'He's lucky he didn't end up with a sore point of his own when I found out. There was a very tempting rolling pin nearby at the time, but I resisted. Very good of me, I thought, considering. And it doesn't matter, not really. She's welcome to him.'

'Plenty more fish in the sea, eh?'

'Okay, that's enough of the clichés, Fran. Seeing someone else behind my back? No, there's no way I'm going to put up with that, or forgive him. He's denying it all, of course, but you know I can't tolerate cheats.' I'm sure she's looking straight at me as she says that. 'At least it means I'm free again, ready for when the right man does come along. Assuming someone else hasn't claimed him first, of course.' Now I know she's definitely aiming her comments at me. And she's right. I know she is. Right man, wrong time and all that. I have to stop obsessing over Jack Doherty and move on with my life.

We don't stay long after that. Somehow the fun has leached out of the evening, and by eight o'clock we've called it a day. I decide to call in on Mum on my way home. A third of a plate of chips and one of Fran's cheese-and-onion crisps – there was no way she was letting either of us take more than one – haven't quite managed to fill the hole and I'm hoping Mum's cooked one of her fabulous big family dinners, knowing that Sam is usually starving after football practice, and there might be some left for me.

I let myself in at the back door as usual but there's nobody in the kitchen, and sadly no sign of any cooking going on either, unless it's already been washed up and cleared away.

'Hello! Anyone home?' Well, I know there must be because the back door wasn't locked and Mum would never go out without at least double-checking that.

I walk through into the hall. There are voices coming from the dining room, and some music which sounds too loud to be the background noise from the TV.

I pop my head round the door and there they are. Mum and that man from the allotments. Anthony. And no sign of my brother. There's a pile of takeaway containers in the middle of the table, two mucky plates, not three, and an open bottle of something that looks decidedly fizzy. And they're dancing. Oh, not all lovey-dovey cheek to cheek, but they do have their arms hooked around each other, in a jiggy-jiggy sort of way, and they're flinging themselves around the room and laughing fit to burst.

They don't spot me for a minute or two, but then Mum skips around and is suddenly facing me. I see the laughter drop from her face, and it's replaced by a mixture of shock and what looks suspiciously like embarrassment. 'Oh, Carly,' she says, her feet grinding to a halt and her hand reaching out to turn the music down. 'You should have said you were coming. Anthony and I were just…'

'Dancing. Yes, Mum, I can see that. Don't let me stop you.'

'Oh, I think we were probably about ready to take a breather anyway.' She flops into a high-backed dining chair and wipes the back of her hand over her brow. Is that sweat? 'Come on, Anthony, sit back down for a while and I'll go and make some coffee.'

'That would be lovely, Joyce.' Anthony flops down and makes himself look far too comfortable for my liking.

'Fancy one, Carly?'

I nod wordlessly and sit down in what was always Dad's chair at the head of the table. At least she hasn't suggested Anthony sit there. 'No Sam tonight?'

'Off out with some mates. He said he might be late.'

'Right. Mind if I help myself to some food?'

'Of course not, love. Anthony always buys too much.'

Always? Did she say always? Just how often do they share these cosy little get-togethers?

I dip a serving spoon into what looks like chicken korma. It's already a little congealed and not quite hot enough, but I eat a spoonful anyway, straight from the carton. Going in search of another plate would mean following Mum into the kitchen and I'm not sure I'd know exactly what to say to her just yet. Anthony sits there smiling, almost shyly, but he doesn't speak. Does he feel as awkward as I do? There was me thinking Mum was doing her best to match me up with him, as unlikely as that seems now, and all the time she's been seeing him herself. I can't quite get my head around it. The age difference, for one thing. He must be, what? Ten or fifteen years younger than her. Still, he was a good ten or fifteen older than me and that hadn't stopped her feeble attempts at matchmaking, had it?

'You remember Anthony, don't you?' Mum says, as she comes back, carrying a tray of coffees and a plate of chocolate biscuits. What is this? Let's-pretend-we've-never-met time?

'Of course I do.'

She pushes a few foil cartons aside and places the tray on

the table before sitting down in an empty seat between us. I wait for her to say more, to tell me why he's here, but she doesn't. She just hands the mugs round, the milk and sugars already taken care of, so she clearly knows just how he takes it.

The CD comes to an end and all I can hear is Dad's old clock ticking on the wall and Anthony blowing vigorously and noisily across the surface of his coffee to cool it before taking a tentative but equally noisy sip.

'Go on, love,' she says, smiling at me. 'Tuck in before the rest of that curry gets cold. Or is it already? I can always microwave it for you.'

'No, it's fine, Mum. All fine.' And I eat what quite possibly warrants as one of the most awkward meals of my life as the two of them sit there comfortably, chatting about parsnips and dahlias and plain versus milk chocolate digestives and whether they prefer Cliff or Elvis, almost as if I'm not there.

Chapter 17

Molly

Jack's been back in London for eleven days now and they've only spoken twice. At first, Molly was upset, but gradually that's been overtaken by anger. How dare he cut her off like this? As if it's her who's done something wrong? She's as surprised by this pregnancy as he is, but he's acting like a spoilt child who can't get his own way, throwing his toys out of the pram. Which isn't a bad comparison really, considering it's all about a baby he clearly doesn't want.

Molly can feel the tears brimming up as she takes out her feelings on the cake mix, turning the mixer on to full speed and battering it so hard she's likely to break the bowl.

'Calm down, love,' her dad says as he strolls into the kitchen with an empty mug in his hand. 'What's that cake ever done to you?'

'Sorry, Dad. Just feeling a bit stressed.' She doesn't turn round, not wanting him to see her on the verge of crying. 'Can I make you another cup of tea?'

He goes over to the sink and refills the kettle. 'It's fine. I can manage. Better than you can probably, with that wrist of yours. But I'd like to know what's bugging you, and I think it's more than just a broken bone, isn't it? You know you can tell me anything, don't you?'

She nods, still not turning to face him.

'Is it painful still? You're looking so pale lately, and you were sick again earlier, weren't you? Sorry, but those bathroom walls are thin, you know that.'

'No. It's a pain, but not painful, if you know what I mean. Just feeling a bit down. A headache and a bit of a dodgy tummy, that's all.'

'Is that all? Really? Not Jack then? Something he's done. Or not done?'

She switches the mixer off and turns round. Her dad's pouring the boiling water into the teapot, not looking at her. She knows that's deliberate. He wants her to talk.

'Because I can't help wondering why you're still here and he's not,' he says, easing himself down into a chair and tapping the one next to him, inviting her to join him at the table. 'Well, he has work, obviously, but why didn't you go back with him? You've never explained, and it's been, what? Getting on two weeks and you're still here. Not that we don't love having you, of course, and you know I don't like to pry, but shouldn't you be at home, with your husband?'

Molly lifts the mixing bowl off its stand and tips the creamy yellow mixture into two baking tins, then puts it down again and runs a spoon round the bowl to scrape out the bits left behind. Once they are safely in the oven, she takes two mugs to the table and sits, pouring tea from the big old brown teapot that's so much a part of this kitchen it's probably older than she is.

'I don't know where to start.'

'The beginning's usually a pretty good place.'

'A kitchen drawer, that's where it began.' It sounds silly, but it's true. 'And a diary with nothing written in it...'

'Well, now I am intrigued.'

She looks into his eyes and sees real concern there, and she knows this isn't fair. They deserve to know. If she's going to tell all, it's going to need to be with both of them here. Mum and Dad, together. The way married couples are meant to be.

'Where's Mum?'

'Upstairs, changing the beds, I think. Shall I fetch her?'

'Yes, please. I know you're both worried and I don't want you to be. And I'm sick of keeping secrets.'

⁊

Her dad looks so relieved now she's told them. 'There was me thinking all sorts – divorce, money worries, even cancer, would you believe? And it was a baby all along! My little girl having a child of her own. Wow! We really should be celebrating, Maureen, and a mug of cold tea doesn't really cut it, does it? Where's that bottle of champagne we tucked away from our anniversary?'

'Dad! You do know I'm not supposed to drink?'

'Oh, it's not for you, love. This is a special occasion for your mother and me too, you know. Our first grandchild!'

Maureen is dabbing at the corners of her eyes with a screwed-up hankie. 'Oh, Molly, I'm so pleased. Why ever didn't you tell us? All this time you've known. Three months already! I should be knitting bootees by now, and ordering you a pram. The grandparents always pay for the pram! And your dad and me will be opening a little savings account for him just as soon as he's born.'

'Or she!'

'Well, yes, of course, but it will be a boy. I have a feeling, and you know my feelings are never wrong.'

Molly stands up and moves to behind her mum's chair,

122

throwing her arms around her neck and kissing the top of her permed head, and in seconds her dad is up on his feet too, sandwiching Molly between them in a really strange kind of group hug.

'And Jack? Where does he fit into all this?' her dad asks quietly, as he goes back to his chair, his gaze not leaving her face. Molly can almost hear his thought processes gearing up. 'Why isn't he here?'

'He's... well, let's just say it came as a bit of a shock. I don't think he feels ready. We hadn't actually planned on this happening just yet.'

'Babies come when they're good and ready. A gift from God.' Maureen doesn't often bring religion into things but she is a Christian, and family means everything to her. 'He should be thrilled. Just like your father was when we first found out you were on the way.'

'Oh, yes, I downed a few pints that night, I can tell you. And bought one for everyone in the pub. It's not every day...'

'I'm amazed you can remember,' Maureen says, cutting his memories off with a shake of her head, but she's smiling, so no matter how drunk he must have been she's clearly long since forgiven him.

'He'll come round. Your Jack.' Her dad hesitates for a moment. 'But it's not going to happen while you're miles apart, now, is it? You're going to be a mummy, and he's going to be a daddy, in six months, whether he's ready or not, so it's time he stepped up. And manned up. I think the sooner we get you on a train back to London the better, my love. If the mountain won't come to Mohammed...'

'I think I'm more of a mountain these days than he is. Have you seen the size of my tummy?' Molly lifts up her baggy jumper and lays her hands – one of them encased in plaster – on the little rounded mound of bare flesh.

'No, because you've been hiding it away, Molly, love.' Maureen smiles wistfully. 'But it's time you showed it off with pride. May I?' She waits for the nod, then reaches out and touches her daughter's skin, gently stroking it. 'Fancy a bit of shopping later? Your first maternity clothes? My treat. We might as well send you home looking the part.'

'Shopping would be lovely. I just need to rescue this cake from the oven before it burns.'

Her dad produces the champagne from the back of the enormous fridge and pops the cork, showering them all with sticky bubbles.

'To baby Doherty,' he says, raising the bottle in the air as if he's about to swing it at the side of a ship. 'And all who sail in her.'

'Him!' Maureen says, very firmly. 'I told you, Bill. It's going to be a boy, I just know it. When it comes to a mother's intuition, I am never wrong.'

Molly laughs, for the first time in a while.

'No champers for me,' she says, shaking her head, her hand still cradling her bump. 'Booze is off the menu. From now on, this little one comes first.'

Chapter 18

Jack

Molly's back. When Jack gets in from work on Friday evening, she's already there, in the flat, unpacking her case in the bedroom.

'Mol, why didn't you tell me you were coming home? I could have met you at the station.'

'No need. I managed to find my way back on the Tube. And I'm sure you were probably much too busy anyway. Like you've obviously been too busy to call me or answer my messages.'

'There's no need to be like...'

'Oh, yes, there is. There's every need. I'm your wife, Jack, the mother of your future child. I deserve better.' She turns away from him, still standing in the bedroom doorway, and bends to remove the last of her things from her luggage, using her one good hand, struggling to slip what looks like a new dress onto a hanger before hooking it over the wardrobe door handle.

'You've been treating yourself.'

'Mum bought it for me. And new clothes – maternity clothes – are hardly a treat, more of a necessity, I would have thought.'

'Oh. You've told her then? Your mum? And your dad too, I

guess?' He's not sure why, but he wishes she hadn't. It just makes the whole thing more real, no longer something they can stop. Molly nods, and he knows, deep down, that it's far too late to stop it now anyway.

'I had to, Jack. I was sick a couple of times, and not feeling great, and they couldn't figure out why you'd gone and I hadn't. I could only use the excuse of a broken wrist for so long. They were asking questions.'

He takes a few steps into the room and fingers the dress. It's soft and loose, a nice shade of blue. 'Do you actually need maternity clothes already?'

'What did you think, Jack? That I'd still be squeezing into a size twelve right up to the day I deliver? Babies grow. Mothers grow. Not that you'd know that as I haven't seen you for getting on a fortnight. Did you know our baby is the size of a lemon now? That's how they do it these days, by fruit sizes. Helps you to picture it in a real way, I suppose. The last time I saw you, it was only a fig. Not that you probably have any idea how big a fig is. It's hardly your normal diet, is it?'

'Okay, I get it, all right? The baby is getting bigger every day and it's not going to go away. I know that. I just have to get my head round it, that's all. Because it's not actually a lemon, is it? Or a pineapple or a watermelon or whatever it's going to expand into over the next few months. It's a proper little person. With arms and legs, and all that puke and poo and all the rest of it to look forward to.'

Molly slumps down onto the edge of the bed and he risks sitting down next to her, although he's not quite brave enough to touch her just yet.

'Look, don't bite my head off, okay? What do I know about babies? They're noisy and messy and cost a fortune, everyone knows that much. I want to be positive about it, to feel excited about it, but it's not easy. We didn't plan any of this, did we?

And I'm assuming it's been as big a shock to you as it has to me.'

'Of course it has. Why wouldn't it?'

'I just need to know how this happened, that's all. You're taking the pill, right? Or you were anyway. So, how come...?'

'You know I was. Oh, Jack, don't tell me you think I did this on purpose. Stopped taking it to trick you? Surely you know me better than that by now.'

'I thought I did.'

He doesn't think he's ever seen her looking so hurt.

'Just to be absolutely clear, and I won't be saying this again, I did no such thing. I don't know why the pill let us down. Stress, moving house, that tummy bug I had a while back, just bad bloody luck... I have no idea. I don't suppose any method of birth control is one hundred per cent foolproof, except abstinence, and I can't see you agreeing to that. But what's done is done, okay? He or she is real. Look.' She lifts her T-shirt and grabs for his hand, flattening his palm against her bare skin. He's surprised to see how rounded her belly is already, that her tummy button seems to have changed shape or angle or something. Her body looks different.

'What does it feel like, Mol? Knowing there's someone in there?'

'Odd, good, exciting, frightening... So many things. But I've had time now to get used to it, to be happy about it. There's no way I'm getting rid of it.'

He is shocked. 'Who said anything about getting rid of it?'

'Well, it's very clear you don't want it. Or that you're still not sure anyway. But I do want it. With or without you, Jack, I'm keeping this baby.' She stands up and leaves the room, and soon he hears the water running in the bath. At least she didn't slam the door behind her. She's not angry, just upset. But there is a new determination about her that he doesn't recognise.

He changes out of his work suit and into a pair of old jeans and a rugby shirt. One of those with a Guinness toucan on it, a present from his brother, and probably only passed on because for Richard, all muscle and bulging biceps, it was way too small. Not that Jack's ever been a Guinness drinker, but he would down one now if he had one. Or anything alcoholic, to be honest.

He walks out to the kitchen and checks the fridge. There's one can of lager and an unopened bottle of white wine. He drinks the lager first, quickly, not bothering to pour it into a glass, then twists open the cap on the wine. Well, Molly won't be drinking now, will she? She can hardly complain if he knocks it all back by himself. Then he rummages in the kitchen drawer for the takeaway menus. He can't imagine either of them is going to feel much like cooking tonight. There's a lot to talk about, a lot to think about, and he can't put it off any longer.

'I'm going to order some food. Chinese or Indian?' he calls, but Molly has turned the radio on, very loud, and he's not sure whether she can't hear him or has decided to ignore him, because she doesn't answer. It's only the rhythmic sound of vigorous sloshing that reassures him she is okay, and that she's washing, not drowning. He wonders how she's managing, with the plaster cast, and if he should go in and offer to help, but she's coped without him these last two weeks, so he's probably best to leave her to it, and hope that the warm water and a bit of alone time will help to calm her down.

❦

They sit at opposite sides of the small table later, the food spread out in front of them. Somehow, he had expected her to pick at it, to say something about not being hungry or feeling sick, to slope off alone to bed, but he's wrong. She is eating like a demon.

She looks up, realises he's watching and stares back at him, defiantly. 'What?' she says. 'Never seen a woman eat before? It was a long journey home, and it's not easy lugging a case and a handbag and a couple of shopping bags with only one working hand. I could hardly manage to carry a packed lunch as well. Not that Mum didn't try. And, besides, I'm eating for two now, aren't I? Not so important to work at keeping my weight down anymore.'

'I didn't say a word!'

'You didn't need to.'

'Look, Mol. Can we start again? Try and put all this animosity behind us? I have no problem with you eating. And I have never for one moment thought you had to worry about watching your weight, before or since you got yourself pregnant.'

'Got *myself* pregnant?'

He holds his hands up in surrender. 'Sorry, sorry, bad choice of words! I know I had a hand in it too. Well, more than a hand.'

They look at each other in silence, and then Molly laughs. She puts her fork down and reaches for his hand across the table, her face suddenly serious again. 'Can you love this baby, do you think?'

'I won't know until I try, will I?'

'And you're willing to do that? To try?'

'If it pops out looking like you, I won't be able to help myself, will I?'

'If it's a girl, fine, but a boy that looks like me? Let's hope not.'

'With long blonde hair and boobs to die for? Maybe not!'

She stands up and fetches her handbag, digging into a side pocket and pulling out the little black-and-white picture they gave her at the hospital, the one taken from the scan. 'I can't actually see any hair or boobs just yet, but do you want to meet our baby?' She sits back down, smiles encouragingly and hands him the picture. He stares at it for a long time. No, he can't tell if it's a boy or a girl, who it looks like, even which bit is supposed to be which. But this is their child, and it's real. Just as real as the last time. More so. Because there was no picture then, no guessing the sex, no plans to be made. Except to be rid of it as soon as humanly possible.

This time will be different. It has to be.

They lie side by side in bed later, and he runs his fingers over her skin, tracing little circles over her breasts and her belly. Already, her body feels different, as if it's getting tighter, before stretching to accommodate what's going on inside. She gives a little moan and he takes his hand lower.

'Jack...' she says, wriggling into position, closer, trying to slither underneath him.

'Should we?' He wants to. Of course he does, but something is holding him back. He has never made love to a pregnant woman before. Not knowingly anyway. 'What if it hurts the baby? You know, the pressure, the movement, the weight of me...'

'Just be gentle then. Or I can go on top. We don't have to go into full-on heavy bonking mode, do we? We can take it slowly. But it's been a long time, Jack, and I've missed you, missed this.' She slides her good hand around him and guides him towards her. His hand is still between her legs, and she is soft, damp, eager.

'Something about it doesn't feel right. I can't explain it.' He pulls away. It's dark in the bedroom and he can't see her face very well, but he hears her sigh.

'You don't want to? That's a first. What's wrong, Jack? Don't fancy me now that I'm pregnant? What is it? My size? My shape? Or is it still about there being a baby at all? That you can't forgive me for being pregnant in the first place? You said you were willing to try to love the baby. I hadn't realised whether or not you loved me was in question too.'

'It's not. I do. You know I do. But it feels odd, weird, I don't know, poking about inside you when there's someone else in there.'

'Poking about? Oh, Jack, you are such an idiot.' She laughs, but he can tell she's not really amused, just exasperated. She edges away, her head close to his on the pillow, but her body distant again. 'Yes, there's someone else in there, but we put her there. Or him. This baby is part of us. What do you think's going to happen? That the baby is going to be disgusted with us, be traumatised for life because her parents had sex?'

'Well, no, not when you put it like that.'

They lie silently for a while and then he feels her hand slide back onto him and start to move, rhythmically, up and down.

'Is this okay? Less dangerous? Less weird? Or is this banned too?'

A great swell of need rises up in him. What the hell is going on in his head? He has no idea, but he knows what's going on in his body.

'This is very okay.'

He snuggles closer and touches her, in all the places he knows she likes to be touched, until her body shudders in that old familiar way that makes him feel wanted, needed, that he's finally doing something right. And then he lets her do the same to him. Touch, pull, caress, release. No penetration, no knocking his penis against some unseen fig or lemon or whatever fruit it's supposed to be by now, this growing thing that is going to one day be his child.

And, for now, as he lies there on his back in the dampness of the sheets, waiting for his breathing to recover its normal rhythm, with his wife beside him, his life feels a little more normal too.

'Do you have any preference?' she says, sleepily, pulling the duvet up around their necks, her warm feet slipping between his own as he rolls to face her. 'For a boy or a girl?'

'I hadn't thought really.' And he hasn't, because he hasn't wanted to, hasn't dared to. 'Just the old cliché, I suppose. Not minding, so long as it's healthy.' He runs his fingers through her tousled hair. He can smell her on his hands. 'You?'

'Same. Mum's convinced it's a boy though. One of her feelings!'

'Yeah, like when she was totally sure the village kids' football team were going to win that cup, remember? And what happened? They lost five–nil, and young Donny scored an own goal, the poor lad. No, I don't think we should rely too much on her little prophecies and go too heavily on buying blue. Which reminds me, we still have to tell my parents too, don't we? About the baby, I mean. Before the village rumour mill does it for us. You do know we won't get a moment's peace once they know? Once everybody knows?'

'We'll do it tomorrow.' She lifts his other hand, the one not looped through her hair, and lays it on her belly. 'Tonight, let's just go to sleep. Together. And enjoy it being just the three of us.'

Chapter 19

Carly

'You're doing great.'

Syd and I are sitting at traffic lights and I have one eye on the red light in front of me and the other on the rear-view mirror, aware of the car behind, the sound system blaring out, the driver with one elbow half out of the window, fingers tapping impatiently on the steering wheel, and revving his engine as if he can't wait to overtake.

'Am I? It still worries me when there's some idiot like that on the road. How am I meant to know what he's going to do next?'

Syd touches my arm. 'Just chill, Carly. You can't do anything about other drivers or how they behave. Just concentrate on what *you're* doing. You can try to anticipate any problems but that's it. Just because someone else is speeding or getting angry or driving up your rear end, don't rise to it. What's the speed limit here?'

I look at the road, for signs and cameras, and note the rows of street lights. 'Thirty?'

'Spot on. So, drive at thirty. If the bloke behind you doesn't like it, that's his problem, not yours.'

I like Syd. I like his hint-of-an-accent and that laid-back attitude all Aussies seem to have. I feel comfortable with him, and safe. I have picked a time for my lesson, straight after work, when, even though there's more traffic about, at least I know there'll still be daylight. I know I'm going to have to face it sooner or later but for now I feel a bit wary of being out on the roads once it starts to get dark.

The lights change and the car behind swerves out and roars past. We both laugh, five minutes later, when we pass the driver at the side of the road, out of his car and talking to two police officers.

'See?' Syd says. 'You didn't have to do anything. He did that all by himself. Arrogant, impatient, thinks he's king of the road. Look where that got him. I call that karma, don't you?'

When we get back to my place, I ask him in for a coffee.

'I shouldn't really. You were my last lesson for today and I promised I'd get back to help with the kids. Rosie fancied a night out but we couldn't get a babysitter, so the least I can do is get home and cook something, so she can put her feet up. Give her a break.'

'I don't have any plans.' I've said it before I've had time to think what I'm doing.

'Well, I know Rosie would probably love to see you, but I was thinking more of dinner for two, if you know what I mean. Date nights are few and far between these days.'

I laugh. 'I didn't mean me turning up and being a gooseberry. I meant me turning up and being your babysitter. If you still want to go out.'

'You mean it?'

'Of course I do. You'd have to give me a bit of a crash course in what to do, but you're a good teacher. The driving has shown me that.'

'Not so much of the crash talk when it comes to driving

though, eh?' Syd laughs at his own joke. 'But, honest, Carly, that would be great, if you're up for it. There's not a lot to nappy changing and bottles once you give it a go. I couldn't have been more of a novice myself when they were first born, and we wouldn't be asking you to do anything much except just be there. They'll be in bed asleep most of the time. I hope!'

'Right, you're on. What time do you want me?'

'Come now if you like. I can drive you, save messing about on public transport later. And it's already half past six. I'm happy to pay for a pizza delivery for your tea, or you can raid our fridge. There's cider and lager, and plenty of biscuits if you fancy a snack later. We won't stay out too late, I promise. Ten thirty? Eleven? We never make it awake until midnight these days. Too scared of turning back into Cinderella! And the little buggers get us up so early in the mornings.'

'Okay, why not? Pop up for quarter of an hour while I get changed and grab a book or something?'

We get out of the car and head up the stairs to the flat. Fran is sitting cross-legged on the carpet in the living room, surrounded by a tumbling pile of old socks and rolled-up tights. She looks up and grins. 'Just having a sort-out,' she says. 'Knicker drawer next, so you're lucky you came in when you did. Not a sight for male eyes!'

'Oh, I don't know,' Syd says. 'I like a pair of big old Bridget Jones bloomers. They're great for washing the wheels of the car, and for wiping the windscreen when it snows. Better than the cloths you can buy for the job. And bigger. Let me have any you're going to chuck.'

I can see from Fran's face that she isn't sure if he's joking or not. He winks at me and follows me into the kitchen. 'You go and get sorted. I can make my own coffee,' he says, reaching for the kettle. 'Shall I do one for Fran too?'

'She's never been one to say no. Especially if you throw in a chocolate biscuit.'

When we walk into Syd and Rosie's, she is nowhere to be seen.

'I called her, gave her a bit of warning,' he says. 'So, she's either frantically hiding all the piles of dirty washing or she's upstairs getting changed.'

'I heard that!' Rosie comes down the stairs, unusually without a baby in her arms, and greets me with a hug. 'They're both in their cots, just while I'm getting sorted, but it's a bit early to expect them to go to sleep. Still, you'll want to see them properly before we go out, won't you? If you want to have a go at nappy practice or whatever.'

'It's the whatever that bothers me. You do realise that I have never looked after a baby before, don't you? Let alone two at once.'

'You sure you want to do it?'

I see the flash of disappointment cross her face.

'Well, I'm not going to let you down now, am I? Not when you've already got your glad rags on.'

Rosie looks down at her sick-stained top and baggy jogging bottoms and we both laugh. 'I will be getting changed, honestly. Now that you're actually here and I know Syd wasn't just getting my hopes up.'

'As if I'd do that to you.' Syd plonks himself down on the sofa and checks his phone before switching it off. 'Right. I am officially not working tonight. No calls, no messages, no appointments. Rosie, my love, I am all yours.'

I settle myself down and open my battered old childhood copy of *Mary Poppins* while my friends disappear up to their bedroom to get ready for their date. Something about this evening has put me in the mood for a bit of magic, with beautifully behaved children and everything going like clockwork, spoonfuls of sugar and all. I know that, later, when the twins are downstairs, I'm unlikely to get much time to myself. Hot drinks could be risky, and is it even possible to eat pizza with two crying babies balanced on your lap? Oh, well, there's only one way to find out. And, really, what's the worst that can happen? A wonky nappy or a bit of spilt milk never killed anyone, and we can't all be the perfect Mary Poppins, can we? If I have to get by without a cup of tea, or go home hungry, so what? It's just one evening, and I had nothing else planned. In a funny kind of a way, I'm looking forward to it.

As it turns out, I quite enjoy myself. I watch as Rosie does both nappies just before they leave, and unless some awful pooey accident occurs she assures me they shouldn't need another change until morning. I am given two bottles of milk, colour-coded and already warmed, a cloth to sling over my shoulder, and vague instructions about when to take them up to bed, which I take to mean it could be at any time, whenever their little eyes close, and basically just to play it by ear. She lies them down on the sofa, one each side of me, and promises me they won't roll off so long as I keep an eye, or a hand, on them, and then she and Syd go out and I'm on my own. Well, not quite!

Jamie is a sweetheart, all smiley face and squishy little grabbing fingers. I lift him into my lap and he's got his fist looped into my necklace within minutes. The only way to get it away from him and stop myself from being strangled seems to be to take it off and drop it into my bag. He takes his milk easily and slowly slips into sleep, so I carry him across the room and lie him down in one of the Moses baskets, happy to have both arms free now to turn my attentions to his sister.

Becca proves to be more of a challenge. I get back to the sofa just as she's attempting a kamikaze roll towards the edge. I lift her into position in my arms and try to get comfortable before round two begins. Her eyes follow my every move and there's a strange puzzled expression on her face as if she's trying to figure out who I am. Every time I try to slip the teat into her mouth, she turns her head away and flatly refuses to suck. Maybe she's testing me, maybe she's showing me who's the boss around here, or maybe she's just not hungry.

Reading my book is a definite no-go so I reach for the remote control and switch the TV on. I think perhaps a bit of background noise might just help to settle her, but she's having none of it. She's a born wriggler, this one. It takes one episode of *Emmerdale* and an hour of Corrie before she finally gives in and drinks her milk, falling asleep mid-suck.

It makes sense to bypass the basket and take her straight up, so I walk very carefully up the stairs with her in the crook of one arm, holding on tight to the banisters in case I trip and drop her. Once she's in her cot, tummy upwards as instructed, I dim the light and go back for Jamie.

It seems strangely quiet when I'm back in the living room by myself. It scares me to have the TV on too loud and maybe not hear the babies if they cry. There is a monitor but I've never been one to fully trust in technology. So, I switch the TV off, pick my pizza from the menu Syd has left me (along with a twenty-pound note that he refused to take back), phone in my order, pour myself a large glass of cider and open my book.

Is it odd that a thirty-one-year-old woman has never spent any time alone with a baby? I suppose having just a younger brother, and no cousins within a hundred-mile radius, and my small group of close friends still being mostly single, I just haven't come across a lot of mother-baby situations. Rosie has kind of opened up the way, been a pioneer, when it comes to kids. And, with two at once, she's certainly done it in style. I know I've done a lot of mocking in the last four months, joking about her being up to her eyes in sick, feeling sorry for her and all she's had to give up, dreading the day it happens to me, but I'm beginning to think I was wrong. What Rosie has is good. A loving husband, a proper home, and two little people who are totally dependent on her. There's a lot of love in this house.

Syd insists on driving me home. 'Can't have you waiting for buses at this time of night,' he says. It's only just after half past ten, but I can't pretend I would relish hanging about in the dark, so I say yes. 'And I haven't had a drink,' he adds, as if I might be worrying, which I wasn't. 'More than my job's worth.'

'So, how was it, really?' he asks, when we are driving and Rosie's no longer around to hear. 'I know Rosie won't admit it but she does worry a bit, whenever she has to leave them. Even with someone like you, that she trusts.'

'Does she? That's good to hear. I know I'm new to all this, but it was okay. Becca was a bit of a handful, fighting to stay awake, but absolutely no problems with Jamie. If you don't count trying to steal my jewellery!'

'Ah, there you are, see? You females are always the difficult ones. Obstinate, demanding, hard to please... We men are much more easy-going. And always looking for ways to pocket a few quid, of course.'

'Just a cheap chain, I'm afraid.'

'Never mind. He was just attracted by the sparkle, I expect. No idea of value yet. He'll learn!'

I laugh. 'You old cynic, you.'

'So, how's life, Carly? No bloke on the scene? No possibility of tiny feet pattering your way anytime soon?'

'I'm afraid not.'

'You're not still pining over old Jacky Boy, are you?'

'I don't know what you mean.' I watch his face, in profile, as the street lights throw a half-light into the darkened car, expecting him to turn towards me, but he keeps looking straight ahead at the road. 'And I have never pined in all my life!'

'You know perfectly well what I'm talking about. He's not for you, Carly, you do know that, don't you?'

'Yes.' I can't help remembering how close we had come to kissing and I'm glad of the darkness that hides what I know only too well will be showing in my face. 'But...'

'But what? Come on, you can tell me. I've said this before, but if you need anyone to talk to, you can trust me. It goes no further. I'm a safe pair of hands. Or ears, or whatever.'

'Look, I know it's stupid, and probably totally one-sided, but we get on so well, and it's great having him working in the same building, like it's fate or something. We had lunch one day, in the park. And a drink after work. He even carried my shopping! I like being near him, being with him...'

'I don't like the sound of this.'

'I love him, Syd, okay? You wanted to know, so there it is. I think I really do love him.'

'You can't love him, Carly. You only think you do. Because it's not real, is it? You hardly know him. And for the last five years you haven't set eyes on him, let alone had any idea what he might be doing with his life. So, he's back, and you still feel something. A spark. But that's not love, it's infatuation. Jack's like any other man. He makes mistakes. He might have been happy to meet up again, sent you mixed signals, flirted a bit more than he should, but you don't have to be drawn in. He's not worth it, and you're worth more, if that makes any sense.

Remember what I said earlier, when we had that idiot driver behind us? You can't do anything about other people or how they behave. Just concentrate on what *you're* doing. Be the better person.'

'I can't help it, Syd. Ever since we first met, all those years ago, it's only really ever been Jack. If only I'd done more at the time, thrown myself at him, begged him to stay. If only he hadn't had to go back home, he might not have married this other girl.'

'Molly. She does have a name, you know.'

'I know she does, but I don't want to think about that. Or about her.'

'Well, maybe you should. Because she's his wife, Carly. She's the one in the right here, the one on the moral high ground. She's the one who would be mortified if she knew about you, not the other way round.'

'There's nothing to know. Jack and I... we had a bit of a moment a week or two back, but nothing happened. Honest. I stopped it. Well, *we* stopped it. And I don't expect it to happen again.'

'But you'd like it to?'

'You know I would. He's the one, Syd. You know how sometimes you just know? He's the one, the only one, and I have no idea what to do about it. Except hope for a miracle, like his wife walking under a bus or something.'

Syd stops the car outside my flat and turns to look at me at last.

'I can't believe you just said that. Or that you could possibly mean it.'

'I don't mean it. Not really. It all just makes me feel so...'

'What? Jealous? Angry? You have to let this thing go, Carly. Let Jack go.'

'I'm trying.'

'Not very hard, from what I can see. How about I introduce

you to someone. I must have an available mate or two. Just for fun? It doesn't have to be anything serious, but you never know...'

'No, thanks, Syd. I think I'm okay without, for now.'

'Just a thought, that's all. But as for Jack, he's off-limits. I mean it. Stay away, all right? A bit of mild flirting in the office is one thing, but having a *moment* as you call it sounds like a whole other level. Think about Rosie. How do you think she'd feel if some random woman she's never met, or even heard of, was chucking herself at me? Oh, I know you probably think that's never going to happen, I know I'm no Brad Pitt, but I'm *her* Brad Pitt, if you know what I mean.'

I don't know what to say. I have never been lectured by Syd before, or by any man except my dad, and it feels wrong somehow, weird, him thinking he has the right to delve into my life, my heart, and tell me what to do. The trouble is, I know he's right. I've known it from the day I found out Jack was back. He's not mine. He never will be.

'And you probably don't know this, and it's not really my place to say, but I'm going to tell you anyway.'

I have my hand on the door handle, ready to get out of the car, but my curiosity gets the better of me. 'Haven't you said enough already?' I snap, grabbing my bag from the floor and staring at him.

'She's pregnant, Carly. I'm sorry, but it's true. He told me himself. Molly and Jack are having a baby.'

Chapter 20

Molly

They have not registered with a local GP since they came to London. It has been a case of waiting until one of them falls sick and then do it, which luckily hasn't happened yet, but with a third of her pregnancy already behind her, she knows it's time. The paperwork is quick and easy enough, the female doctor pleasant and welcoming, and now Molly is back at the flat, armed with a pile of leaflets and forms, and has already been booked in for her first meeting with a midwife. This is all suddenly starting to feel exciting, like an adventure she's only just setting out on.

She can't settle. Jack is at work, there is nowhere she needs to be, and she just wants to do something. There is only so much tidying and cleaning she can potter about at, and she doesn't fancy a walk, not while it's raining outside. So, she does what she always does. She pulls out her mixing bowl and a big bag of flour and raids the fridge for butter and eggs. When in doubt, bake!

She has been thinking a lot this last couple of weeks, about how she is ever going to find a job or some way of making money now there's a baby on the way. And they are going to need that second income more than ever now, what with a cot to buy, and clothes that get outgrown in weeks, a constant supply of nappies and all the other hundred and one things a baby is going to need. Of course, she knows that cakes are the answer, probably the only answer, but there are so many other women making birthday cakes, cupcakes, even gingerbread, and trying to sell from home or some weekend market stall. She needs to offer something a bit different, something there will always be a demand for. She can't believe many people buy gingerbread houses other than in the run-up to Christmas and, as she's already worked out, her tiny kitchen is never going to give her the space she needs to work on big elaborate wedding cakes, much as she'd love the challenge.

They rang Jack's family last night after he came home from work. It didn't really seem worth the trip all the way up to Norfolk on the train just to tell them the news, especially with money about to become a lot tighter and Molly's wrist still in plaster, so a phone call made sense. Of course, she had let Jack do the talking. She had told her mum and dad and it was only right he tell his.

She had been curious to know how he would play it. All excited, even if he was putting it on a bit, or just plain matter-of-fact? Build up the suspense to revealing a surprise, or just come right out with it? In the end, he had only had to hint at having something to tell them for Brenda to leap right in and guess within seconds. Molly had heard the squealing down the line from the other side of the room.

She smiles to herself. Brenda and Steve will make wonderful grandparents, just as her own parents will. The only problem is going to be the two couples battling over who is going to be first to meet the newcomer and who gets first push of the pram.

'Boy or girl?' Brenda had asked, once the phone had been

passed over to Molly and all the congratulations were out of the way.

'We don't know yet. We'll get the chance to find out at the twenty-week scan.'

'But which would you like?'

'I really don't mind.'

'I must admit I always wished I'd had a little girl. Oh, not that I don't love my boys, as you well know, but my life's been all about standing around at football matches and tripping over toy cars. And then the obsession with real cars, once they hit seventeen, and worrying myself sick about them out driving at night. Not to mention all the scraped knees and torn trousers and muddy boots...'

'I'm sure girls can be just as bad. I remember I was always falling over, and loads of girls play football these days.'

'I know. It just would have been nice to have a doll's house around the place, and to be able to have a go at plaiting hair or knitting something pink for a change... Oh, don't listen to me. The world's changed and I don't suppose anyone does all that pink or blue stuff anymore.'

As Molly stirs the cake mixture, last night's conversation keeps popping back into her head. Brenda was wrong. People do still do all that pink or blue stuff. It's everywhere she looks. Pink teddies, blue teddies, pink bedding, blue bedding, 'Welcome to the new baby' cards, almost all in either pink or blue. It's traditional. In fact, just a couple of months ago, before they'd left Norfolk, she had been to an old friend's baby shower and had been met by a whole room decorated with pink balloons and pink bunting, and they had all eaten off pink paper plates and drunk pink champagne. There had been absolutely no doubt that the baby was going to be a girl.

That was it! Babies mean celebrations, and celebrations mean cake! Lots of lovely cake. There has to be a demand, a big demand, for cakes made of pink or blue sponge, or covered in pink or blue icing. And biscuits too, shaped like teddies or bootees, and iced in the appropriate colour. Celebrating a birth or a christening. She wondered just how many babies were born in England, in London, even just in their own small area, every year, every month, every day? There would always be a demand, always parents and families somewhere wanting to celebrate with cake.

But, how about before the birth? Baby showers and gender reveals were a big thing these days, weren't they? The party she had been to was already awash with pink because the news was already out, but how about those occasions when a couple want to reveal the baby's sex for the first time? Inviting their friends and family round or making a video to share on social media, where they pull a cracker with a flurry of pink confetti cascading out from inside, or let loose a host of blue balloons to escape up into the sky? This is it. She's onto something. Gender-reveal cakes. That's what she can specialise in. Beautiful cakes with something pink or blue hidden in the middle, something you only discover once they are cut open or bitten into. Everyone picking one up and taking that first bite at the same time, the squeals when they all find out together...

Molly can feel the excitement mounting. There's something about cakes that has always excited her. The mixing, the adding of a new ingredient, the waiting to see how it comes out of the oven, the warm spongey top springing beneath her fingertip, the gorgeous smell that wafts through the kitchen, the thrill of planning and decorating. But this is different. It's a new kind of excitement, the start of something.

She wanted a business idea and now she has one. And there will be a market for it, she's sure there will. All the midwife appointments she will be going to, the clinics, the classes, the mums-to-be who she will meet. All she has to do is make up some samples, take photos, perhaps give a few cakes away to get reviews and opinions, print out some flyers or cards. She hasn't felt so positive, so enthusiastic about anything for a long time. It's time to let the ideas flow, to try things out, to mix and experiment and taste...

'Thanks, Brenda,' she mutters, as she reaches for a bottle of red food colouring and watches her mixture turning pink as she stirs.

Jack comes home expecting dinner but all she has made is cake.

'Bloody hell, Mol. What's all this lot for? Are we having a party?'

Molly looks at her watch. She has lost all track of time. 'Sorry, no, just trying out some recipe ideas. I didn't realise it's so late. Do you mind waiting to eat?'

'No hurry. I'll just go and get changed, then we can sort some food out, even if it's just scrambled eggs or something. One of these will keep me going for now.' He picks up a cupcake from the nearest plate and takes a big bite. It's too late to stop him.

'No! Jack...'

Molly hears him coughing before he's even made it to the bedroom. He comes back, a bit red in the face, a sticky coughed-up mess all over his fingers.

'What the hell is this?' he says, holding out his hand. 'I could have broken a tooth. Or choked to death.'

Molly knows she shouldn't laugh but she does. 'That'll teach you not to help yourself without asking first,' she says, reaching out and picking the glass marble out from among the crumbs. 'It was just a test run. How to hide things inside a cake. I didn't have any little teddy sweets or packets of edible glitter lying around, so I just used any old things I could find. You weren't actually meant to eat it.'

He looks at her as if she's totally mad. 'Teddies?' he says. 'Glitter? And why on earth are you baking cakes nobody's meant to eat?'

'Experimenting, that's all. With shapes and sizes and what fits in without any bits left sticking out and giving the game away.'

He looks at her as if she's gone completely mad.

'Just count yourself lucky I'd popped the marble in after it was baked and not before,' she says. 'A red-hot lump of glass could have been *really* dangerous!' She picks up another cupcake and cuts through the teetering dome of white buttercream that she has piled on top to conceal the hidey hole. The knife slides into the cake beneath, a cake that looks a very satisfying shade of bright baby-boy blue on the inside, and out from the centre pours a pile of pink Smarties. Would that work? For twins? One of each? Or should she try some sort of split-down-the-middle dual-colour cake? She's so fired up with ideas that she hardly notices Jack retreating to the bedroom, shaking his head.

Chapter 21

Jack

The IT project is coming on so well that the boss thinks it's time to test it out properly. That's why Jack has been hired, to lead on the testing, to get the new financial program set up on a few of the company computers alongside the existing one and choose a small group of staff from across all departments to start putting it through its paces. A trial run to iron out any problems before it goes 'live'. Jack didn't write the software, but he knows its success depends on him.

The whole idea of it makes him think about Molly and her cakes, testing out some new recipe on an unsuspecting guinea pig, otherwise known as her own husband, to see what works and what doesn't, what adaptations might be needed before it's let loose on anyone else. She's right, of course. New things do need to be properly tried and tested, although burying a lump of glass inside a cupcake might just have been a step too far. His own fault, according to her, for jumping in and biting into what was simply a prototype, without asking her first.

Molly has told him what she's planning and he has to admit it sounds like something that might just catch on, although with more sensible fillings, obviously.

There are ideas and suggestions flying around the room as the small IT team meet on Monday morning to talk through their options. Two men who work in the insurance quotes department have been sounded out already and are quickly chosen to help with the testing, and a woman who specialises in renewals and has been there forever. It's when someone says the name Carly Young that Jack is snapped out of his daydreams and back to instant reality.

'We'll need someone who's really hot on the current invoicing system to try out the new...'

Jack's brain has got stuck on the 'really hot' bit, as it so often does when he thinks about Carly. He's like a schoolboy with a crush. Or an itch he isn't able to scratch. Either way, there is unfinished business between them, and they both know it.

'Yes, she's our best bet from the payments team, I think.' His boss is nodding. 'Been here long enough to know the system inside out, and she's got the personality to put her thoughts across. Forthright. Honest. If anything's not quite right, she'll spot it and make sure we know about it. She'll need bringing up to speed though. A few one-to-one training sessions, to show what we need and how it all works. Jack, are you up for that?'

Jack grips his coffee mug and nods as vigorously as his boss. 'Yeah, sure. My pleasure.'

There's nothing Jack would like more than to show Carly what he needs, but there is a distinct line between work and pleasure and this is not the time or place to even think about crossing it. He has his career to think about, and a pregnant wife he really should be thinking about a lot more than he has lately.

He and Carly have already agreed that, whatever this unspoken feeling is that's been gently rumbling away between them, it's not going anywhere, that it can't and it won't. But he's not sure he believes that, even if she does.

His boss is right though. Carly does have personality,

honesty. Her opinions matter, even if her current opinion of Jack is probably that he's a randy married man who tried chancing his luck while his wife was away and who should know better. Still, this will give him the perfect reason to spend some time with her, to show her that the real Jack Doherty is an okay bloke if he's given the opportunity to prove it. Proper official time, at an office desk, that can't be misconstrued or misunderstood. He finds he's already looking forward to it, very much.

When the meeting ends, Jack grabs a coffee and goes back to his desk. The photo of Molly and her dog is still there, although it's been pushed aside by mounds of paperwork and a half-eaten sandwich he didn't get to finish yesterday and should have chucked away by now. He nudges it all even further towards the edge and rests his feet up in the middle of the desk. God, his shoes could do with a clean. He finishes the coffee, lifts his legs back down to the floor and leans forward, running his finger over the touch screen on his computer monitor and selecting the company phone directory. He doesn't want to email her. He wants to talk to her. And now he has a reason to do it. Ah, yes, there she is. Carly Young. Extension 357. He picks up the phone and dials.

'Hi, Carly. It's Jack.'

He's not sure quite what he expects. Not whoops of barely suppressed joy, exactly, but some sign that he's been forgiven for the near-miss kiss and that she is ready to carry on as if it never happened, maybe. A hint in her voice that she just might be pleased to hear from him. What he gets is professional Carly. Work-mode Carly. Calm, matter-of-fact, as if she could be talking to anyone.

'Jack. And what can I do for you this morning?'

He's tempted to make a joke out of it, to make some mildly smutty remark about what she might do for him, but if she can play things seriously, then so can he.

'I've got something I'd like to run by you. A proposition, you could call it.' There is a small silent pause and he races to fill it. 'Work-related, obviously. In case you thought I meant anything else...'

'Of course not. Even you wouldn't ring me on the work phone and suggest something so... inappropriate.' Is there a hint of a giggle in her voice? He can't be sure, but he hopes so.

'Not sure I like the *even you* bit, but no, of course not. Look, Carly, can I pop down and see you, or we could find a spare meeting room somewhere to have a chat? We're working on some big new software, as I'm sure you know, and I've just come from an IT team meeting. The thing is, we'd like your help. To see if you'd be interested in being a part of the testing process. We all agreed we need someone knowledgeable, honest, beautiful... Okay, I made that last bit up. Not that you aren't beautiful, of course... Oh, hell. I'm making a mess of this, aren't I? The truth is, your name came up and the whole team think you'd be great. Just the person we need. So, can I? See you, and talk about it? Sometime today?'

'Let me just check my diary.' He listens as she rustles some paper, puts the phone down, then rustles some more. Is she doing it on purpose? Making him wait? Who keeps an actual paper diary anymore anyway? She's probably just flicking the pages of a newspaper or something. At last, she comes back on the line. 'How about eleven fifteen? I can probably give you half an hour or so if that helps.'

'Fine, yes. I'll find us a room and send you the details.'

'Great. I'll look out for your message.'

And then she's gone. Jack is not quite sure what to make of

any of that. He's never known her to be so cool, so offhand. Not that he really knows her at all, when he comes to think of it, much as he might like to. And he's never worked with her, other than to pass the odd expenses claim through the system when he's had to buy something the stationery cupboard has failed to provide, and she's emailed him a standard reply.

He spends the next hour preparing some training notes to share with her, and printing off some screenshots to show her how things are going to look. Until now, this new software project has been really important to him, the chance to prove himself, to see something he has been such a big part of developing, moving towards fruition. This project is his baby. His career prospects, his reputation, his future rest on it.

But now he knows that his thoughts, his expectations, his energies, are all going to have to be shared with another baby, and the similarities are not lost on him. Being there right from the start, watching it grow, waiting nervously to see how it all turns out, so much of it out of his hands now, with all the responsibilities and worries that come with it. What if something goes wrong? There are two major projects running through his daily life now, side by side, each one just as important, just as life-changing, but only one of them that he chose to take part in, only one that he feels fully engaged with.

How do other men, men like Syd, cope? Diving into all this family stuff, sleepless nights, money worries, all the milk and mayhem and mess, and a wife who thinks and talks about nothing but babies anymore? It's not what he signed up for, but it's what he's going to get.

At five past eleven, he makes two coffees in polystyrene cups, shoving some sugar sachets in his pocket because he has no idea if she takes sugar or not, tucks all the other stuff he needs under his arm and heads off to the room he's booked. He wants to be there early, to show that he can be just as professional as she can. He has trouble with the handle on the door. It sticks and he almost drops the coffees as he tries to turn it using just his little finger. When the door finally springs open, he falls into the room, all hope of making a good impression lost.

Carly is already there. She's brought coffees too, in posh white mugs, and a proper china plate loaded with chocolate biscuits, and she's taken the better chair, the one by the window. He feels, for all the world, like the junior office boy walking into the boss's office, waiting to find out what he's done wrong.

'Hello, Jack. Come and sit down, quick, before you drop something!'

He just manages to balance the coffees on the table, only spilling a few drops, as the papers slip from under his arm and onto the floor. He scrabbles about, picking them up, feeling utterly flustered, his gaze resting on her long smooth legs under the table and the incredibly shiny high-heeled shoes she's wearing, reminding him again of how badly his own shoes need a good clean.

'Right.' He sits down opposite her, tucks his feet out of sight, takes a deep breath and gives her his best smile. 'Sorry about that. Shall we get started?'

'Oh, Jack, I thought you'd never ask.' She has a wicked glint in her eyes. 'Better close the door first though. We wouldn't want anyone to interrupt us, would we?' She reaches for the biscuits, picking one up and waving it at him, seductively. 'And I do so fancy a Hobnob!'

And then she bursts out laughing, and suddenly the old Carly is back in the room and all he wants to do is kiss the face off her.

Chapter 22

Carly

I think I'm going to like working with Jack. He makes terrible coffee and he has no taste at all when it comes to ties, but he knows his job, and he's clearly passionate about it. The new system sounds exciting, and a huge improvement on the old one we've had for years. It will make everything simpler, smoother, easier, and I'm really chuffed that someone somewhere suggested I was the person to help implement it. I wonder if that someone was Jack. If it was, I hope he picked me for the right reasons. All to do with my professional expertise and nothing to do with the fact that, even though I'm sure he would deny it, I know he still fancies me.

Our half-hour meeting actually overruns by a good hour, until my stomach gives an unexpected growl and we decide it must be time to stop for lunch.

'Fancy a walk down to the pub?' Jack says, bundling up the papers he has strewn all over the table. 'Get a pie and a pint? A girl can't live by biscuits alone, can she? And this is a business meeting after all. Perfectly legit. I might even be able to claim it on expenses.'

'Oh, no, you don't. I'm the one who has to approve them, remember, and filling me up with booze is not on the allowable list, I can assure you!'

'On me then. I think I can probably run to half a pint each and a plate of chips!'

'Money tight these days, is it?'

'Always is. Living in London's not like Norfolk, believe me. Everything costs more here. Beer, food, buses, rent... you name it.'

'Nappies?' I can't resist it. All this time we've been sitting here talking and he hasn't told me. Okay, I know this was a business meeting, but we're friends, aren't we? Or I thought we were. *Are.* He should have told me.

I've ruffled him, I can tell. He doesn't quite know what to say.

'Yes, Jack, I know. About the baby. Syd told me. I know he probably shouldn't have, but he did, so there we are.'

'Sorry. Yes, I could have said something, I guess. I'm still getting used to the idea myself, to be honest with you. Not actually told anyone at work yet.'

'Well, congratulations.' I push away all thoughts of his wife and her bulging belly, and what exactly she and Jack had been up to in order to put it there. 'You'll make a great dad.'

'Will I?'

'I have no idea! But it's what people say, isn't it? And what is there to it anyway? It's mums who do all the real work, we all know that. You just have to bring in the readies, and get home in time for a quick tuck-up in bed and a story. Even you should be able to manage that.'

'There you go again with the *even you* stuff. You don't have a very high opinion of me, do you?'

'I'm sorry.' And I am. I really am. When I look at Jack, I still see what I have always seen. The man of my dreams. The man I still do dream about, far too often for comfort, to be honest. It's not his fault I can't stop thinking about him, and there's no need for me to keep sniping away at him. 'Come on. Yes, we will go to the pub, and I'll buy the drinks, okay? A sort of wet-the-baby's-head thing.'

'It's not born yet, Carly.'

'Well, no excuse needed then. If I'm going to be on board for this project of yours, we'll be seeing a lot more of each other, so we might as well get to know each other a bit better over a drink or two. Friends, like we agreed, when we...'

'Let's draw a line under that, shall we? Start again?' He reaches for my hand across the table, and I think for a minute that he's going to shake it, but he doesn't. He lifts it slowly and carefully to his lips and kisses it, so gently it sends a delicious tingle right up my arm. It's probably the most old-fashioned, gallant and truly touching thing a man has ever done to me. Oh, Jack!

'Deal,' I say, my voice coming out in a funny little squeak, and we both stand up and walk into the corridor and towards the lift, leaving the empty cups and a plate of biscuit crumbs behind us. I can come back and deal with those later. I am going out to lunch with Jack, and nothing else matters right now. Gorgeous, handsome, totally out of bounds, Jack. I peer around, making sure Suze isn't lurking anywhere, ready to catch me out, shake her head and give me a good telling-off. But she's nowhere to be seen.

Jack behaves himself over lunch, and so do I. Now there's a baby on the way, there's a sense that the rules have changed somehow. I know that the flirting has to stop, even if the feelings haven't. We arrange another meeting, to sort through the IT project and my part in it, and then we go back to work, two floors apart.

I'm surprised, later, when I walk out of the building at half past five and find my brother waiting for me on the pavement. He's leaning up against the wall, head down, fiddling with his phone, when he looks up and realises I'm standing right in front of him.

'Sam. What are you doing here?' I have a sudden thought that it might be bad news, too bad for him to tell me over the phone. 'Nothing's happened to Mum, has it?'

'No. Don't worry, Carls. She's fine. Just passing, you know? And thought we might have a bit of a chat.'

'Passing? Sam, there's no way you ever have any reason to be just passing. Not around here. So, what's it really all about?'

'Come on, let's walk, shall we? Fancy a quick drink or a burger or something?'

It's too early to eat, so we head for the nearest pub, the same one I was in with Jack only a few hours ago. Sitting in the same seats would just feel too weird, so I aim for a different corner, closer to the TV. There's usually some sport or other that Sam's bound to want to watch. I fish my purse out of my bag. Although it was Sam's idea to come, he's still my little brother as far as I'm concerned – Mum and Dad's late-life miracle as they always used to refer to him although they weren't even forty at the time – and I don't suppose his plumbing apprenticeship leaves him with a lot of spare cash.

'Pint?' I say, leaning on the edge of the bar, and he nods.

'And a bag of crisps, if that's okay? I'm starving.'

'I'm not hungry yet, but you have some proper food if you want. Won't Mum have cooked you something by the time you get home though?'

'I wasn't actually planning on going home. Well, not for a while anyway.'

Now I am intrigued. 'Why?'

'It's that Anthony...'

'Ah, yes, Anthony. I've been meaning to ask you about him.'

'Oh, he's a nice enough bloke, don't get me wrong, but he's just...' He stops talking and shakes his head as if he can't put whatever it is into words.

We grab our drinks and Sam's bag of salt and vinegar crisps and sit down.

'You were saying? He's just what?'

'Just... there, I suppose. You know, there at home. All the bloody time. I can hardly move without tripping over him! If he's not having a cup of tea in the kitchen, he's helping her with the weeding and then they're having a takeaway or going out to some shop or garden centre together.'

'I thought you liked him? That you had a lot in common, bonding over the parsnips and all that?'

'I did. Well, I still do, I guess, but... that was when he was just some bloke I'd talk to at the allotments. And it was actually quite funny when I thought Mum was lining him up for you. He is so not your type!'

'You don't have to tell me that. And I'm quite capable of finding my own boyfriends without any help from Mum of all people.'

'Well, that's debatable, but we'll leave that subject for another day, shall we?'

'Bloody cheek!'

'But what I want to know is what we should do about it? About Mum and Anthony. With an H. Mustn't forget that bit.'

'Do about it?'

'Look, Carls, I don't mind Mum moving on. Dad's been gone a long time now and she's not old, is she? Well, not *that* old. We should expect that she might want to meet someone one day and have another go at love, marriage, whatever…'

'Marriage? You surely don't think things are that serious between them?' I take a huge gulp of my drink and have to swallow hard to stop myself from choking on it.

'Who knows? They haven't said anything to me, but he's becoming a sort of fixture, you know? And it feels a bit odd, uncomfortable, him being there, doing all the things Dad used to do. Using Dad's garden tools and his old wellies, sitting in his chair in the kitchen, helping himself to things from the shed. He even borrowed Dad's old umbrella when he went home one night last week and it had started to rain. At least he went home, which is better than him staying the night, which thankfully hasn't happened. Yet. I don't think Mum's quite ready for that, but it could only be a matter of time, couldn't it? Can't you just imagine him lying there, on Dad's side of the bed, slipping into Dad's dressing gown to come down for his breakfast?'

It's an image I really don't want popping into my head. It makes me wish Mum had been a bit more thorough and got rid of more of Dad's things. Still, the longer she holds on to them, the more likely it is that she's not ready to replace him. That's my theory anyway.

'He's too young for her. She wouldn't…'

'She might, Carls. Unless we stop her.'

'And how exactly are we meant to do that? I'm always telling her I'm a grown woman and I can make my own decisions, especially when it comes to who I go out with, so I can hardly deny her the same, can I?'

'Well, do you want a toy boy as a stepfather?'

I can't help laughing at that. 'He's a bit old to be a toy boy, Sam.'

'She's sixty, Carls, and he's in his forties. Think about it.'

I do think about it, and I don't like it.

'Do you think he makes her happy?'

'She laughs a lot more than she did. But watching Ant and Dec or Michael McIntyre can do that. And if it's affection she wants, she can get a cat. She doesn't have to make a fool of herself with somebody nearly young enough to be her son, does she?'

'Is that all there is to it, Sam? The age thing?'

'I dunno. Maybe.'

'Or would you feel the same whoever he was?'

Sam sips at his beer and gazes at the blank TV screen in front of us. 'He's not Dad, is he?'

'No. And nobody ever can be. But, if she's ready to find someone, I think maybe we just have to let her. If he's the one – the one who eventually takes Dad's place – then I don't think we can stand in the way. It's her life, her choice. It might not come to anything. Just friends, you know. But if... well, we can't help who we fall in love with, can we? In fact, maybe it's time you found a serious girlfriend yourself, then you can move out and not have to see them together all the time. Leave Mum to it. You must be cramping her style, turning up every evening and wanting to be fed, spoiling their alone time!'

He leans over and swipes at my arm. 'Pot, kettle, black! I see no serious relationship in your life, little Miss Independent! But, no, it's not gonna happen. Not for years yet. I'm way too young for all that getting tied down stuff. There's football, and pubbing, and having a laugh with my mates. Got to enjoy life while I'm still free and single, not have to ask permission from my wife every time I want to go for a pint. When I see it happening for you, I just might consider a change of heart.'

There's not a lot I can say in answer to that. What with the unexpected reappearance of Jack Doherty in my life, and finding I am far more fond of babies than I had ever imagined, I'm beginning to think that maybe, just maybe, I would rather like to change my life, fall in love and settle down after all. There's just one problem, of course. Who to do it with, now that Jack is not only married but soon to be a father, and even more out of the equation than he's ever been.

Chapter 23

Molly

Molly stands outside the gates and reads the words on the button pad. It's a school, but there are separate buttons for the children's centre and a sports hall too, all on the same site.

She rechecks her appointment letter and presses for the children's centre.

'Hello, can I help you?' a disembodied voice asks.

'Molly Doherty. I'm here for an antenatal class.'

'Come in.' There's a buzz, and the gate makes a small clicking sound as the catch releases.

As she swings it open and walks through, she hears footsteps charging up behind her and an arm reaches out to catch the gate before it closes.

'Ooh, just in time. Saves having to buzz again.' The woman is wearing a bright-red coat and pushing a double buggy that only just fits through the gap. She's puffing a bit from her speed spurt and Molly holds the gate back against the wall until she and the buggy are safely through. 'Sorry about that. I don't want to hold you up.'

'It's fine. I'm a bit early anyway.'

'I've not seen you here before. First time?'

'Yes. Can you tell?'

'That you're pregnant, no. Nervous, yes! You're not expecting twins, are you?'

'Oh, God, no. One's enough.' Molly immediately realises her mistake and feels herself redden. 'Oh, sorry. Not that having two isn't wonderful, but...'

'But not what you'd choose, right?' The woman laughs. 'I didn't have a lot of say in the matter. We get what we're given, don't we? But I wouldn't give them back now I've got them, believe me! No, I just wondered if you might be coming to TTC, that's all. The twins and triplets club. We haven't had any new members for a while.'

'Sorry, no. Antenatal class. In the children's centre.'

'Ah, yes, I remember those. Lots of exercises and breathing. A few gory videos. They'll have you practising bathing and nappies later too, with a doll, which I can promise you is nothing at all like the real thing, weeing and wriggling all over the place. You'll be in the room next door to us. Might see you after. A few of us tend to gather for a coffee and cake at the café over the road, if you fancy it?'

They reached the building at the end of the path and went in, each of them signing the register at the reception desk.

The woman turned as she was about to disappear into a room to the side. 'I'm late, as usual, so can't stop. But, what do you think? Want to join us for coffee and a chat when we're done?'

'Yes. Sounds good. I don't know any other mums yet.'

'Brilliant. You soon will. Bring some of them with you if you like, although from what I remember from my time in the class most are still working and have to get back there after. Oh, and I'm Rosie, by the way.'

'Molly.'

'See you later then, Molly. The Sunshine Café. You can't miss it. Nab a couple of tables in the window if you get there first.'

❧

As it turns out, they are there before her. A group of five women, so surrounded by bags and buggies, and all holding babies from newborn to toddler and at various stages of feeding, sleeping and crying, that they are spread over three tables and still don't seem to have room.

'Hello, Molly.' Rosie spots her as she opens the door, the delicious smell of good coffee and freshly baked cake instantly drawing her in. 'Come on over and find a seat.'

Rosie makes the introductions and Molly answers questions about her plastered wrist and how her accident happened. 'It should be healed pretty soon. Then this can come off. To be honest, I've sort of got used to it. I forget it's there sometimes, and it's surprising how you adapt and start doing things with the other hand, or gripping things differently.'

There is laughter and she realises that probably came across as a bit smutty. It all helps to break the ice though and, although she can feel her face reddening, she laughs too.

Molly has a look at the menu, and a waitress bustles over with a notepad and pen. The others have ordered and some are eating already.

'Just a latte, please. And a lemon cupcake.'

'Coming right up.'

'They do fantastic cakes here,' Rosie whispers. 'A bit pricey, but worth every penny.'

The others, Molly notices, already have coffees and various cakes and pastries in front of them, and are tucking in as they chat. If she is looking for her first customers, this is probably a pretty good place to start – with young mums so clearly fond of cake, and not afraid to pay well for it if the occasion warrants.

'First baby?' a blonde woman she thinks is called Jo asks, leaning across the table and blowing on the surface of her coffee.

Molly nods.

'Husband not with you today then?' She glances at Molly's left hand as if checking she hasn't slipped up. 'Only, I know they usually want couples at those antenatal classes. Not that mine ever came with me, the lazy so-and-so.' She laughs and rolls her eyes as she undoes a couple of buttons on her dress and eases a baby onto her breast in full view of the window.

'He's at work. And they said he wasn't really needed until later on, when we practise the breathing and talk about how he can support me at the birth.'

'Ha! The birth!' Jo laughs. 'That's the bit most men want to avoid like the plague! But, seriously though, Molly, classes are all well and good but anything else you need to know, just ask one of us. We've all been there, done that, got the T-shirt. Not much we can't tell you about or help you with. We've had all the scans, gallons of gas and air, epidurals, forceps, episiotomies, two Caesareans, and...' she looks around, as if counting in her head, 'thirteen babies between us. Ten of them twins. Not much we don't know!'

'Thanks. I haven't lived here long so I don't really have anyone else to talk to about any of this stuff.'

'No mum?'

'Oh, yes, but she's miles away, so it will have to be just phone calls for now.'

'Not quite the same, is it? I don't know how I'd cope without my mum.' Jo shakes her head and switches her attention to trying to eat her cake over the baby snuffling at her chest, carefully flicking away a few crumbs as they land on top of his head.

'So, Molly, what do you do?' Rosie asks. 'I bet you can't wait for maternity leave and a chance to put your feet up, eh?'

Here's her chance. She swallows. She may be a brilliant baker but she's no saleswoman and she's not quite sure how to broach the subject. 'Like I said, we haven't lived here long, and I don't work at the moment. Well, I don't go out to work, I should say. I'm working from home, trying to build my own business.'

'Oh, that sounds interesting. What is it you do?'

'I bake cakes.'

Suddenly, it feels as if the room has gone strangely quiet. They are all listening, as they probably have been all along.

'Wonderful. We like cakes, don't we, girls?' They all laugh as Miranda, a small brunette who hasn't said a lot up until now, licks her lips seductively and makes what can only be described as a *Harry Met Sally* orgasm sound.

'Lemon cupcake,' the waitress announces as she plonks a plate down in front of Molly and backs away, clearly unsure of what everyone is finding so funny.

'Tart,' Jo says, and everybody laughs again, looking at a shocked Miranda, before Jo quickly adds, 'I meant the lemon. I've had it before. It can be a bit tart.'

Once the noise has subsided and everyone is either dealing with a troublesome child or enjoying a few moments of peace and quiet before their own wakes up again, Molly pulls out a small pile of the business cards she has made on the computer at home and printed off onto sheets of white card. They look a bit on the amateur side, especially as she hasn't cut them all as evenly as she should, but they will do for now.

'If anyone's interested…' she says, hesitantly. 'I can do most things. Kids' birthday cakes, wedding cakes, christenings, although I don't have a very big kitchen so I'm keeping it small for now. And the new project I'm just starting up is gender reveals. Little cupcakes with coloured sponge or hidden middles. Blue or pink, or maybe both if it's one-of-each twins. A bit late for all of you, but maybe some of the pregnant women in the antenatal class might...'

'They'd love it!' Jo says, reaching for a card. 'Honestly, Molly, mums are always in need of cake. You should have asked them. Do it at the next session. You'll be surprised. I bet you get lots of takers. Actually, you couldn't manage something shaped like a rocket, could you? My eldest is five in a couple of weeks and mad about space. I couldn't find anything in Sainsbury's, and there's no way I have time to make one myself. If I even knew how!'

'And my sister's eighteen weeks preggers,' says Miranda, all signs of fake ecstasy now completely gone, a grizzly toddler draped on her shoulder and kicking at her arm. 'She'll find out the sex in a fortnight, and she's bound to want to do something a bit different to let us all know. And film it for Facebook. She loves all the attention, does Hannah. Can I give her one of your cards?'

'In fact...' Rosie says, slipping a small diary out of one of the pockets in her highly organised changing bag. 'We're thinking of having a party soon, at mine. We're not exactly what you'd call religious types so we haven't had a proper christening, but we've just found out that my husband's parents and brother are coming over from Australia soon and they've not seen these two yet. How would you feel about making us a sort of non-christening, welcome-to-England, meet-the-babies cake? We've pencilled in...' She flicks through the pages of the diary and settles on the page she wants. 'Yes, here, the middle of October. Probably the Sunday, starting in the afternoon and into the evening. Does that give you enough time? We'll be inviting the world and his wife, I expect, so it would have to be a pretty big cake! And, now you've put the idea in my head, let's have it half pink and half blue, shall we? Or a rainbow of colours. I don't fancy the traditional plain white churchy-type thing at all.'

Molly nods. She is overwhelmed at the response, from all of them. 'I'd love that. Give me your number and we can talk about it. The design, the size, the price, and when and where to deliver it...'

Rosie taps her number into the phone Molly passes to her and hands it back, taking one of the business cards with Molly's number on it. 'I'll stick it in my phone contacts later, but I've always preferred having things on paper. It's the teacher in me! I'm on maternity leave, from this school actually.' She waves her hand towards the school site across the road that they've all just come from. 'Glutton for punishment, coming all the way back over here every fortnight, but there are no twins clubs nearer to home. Luckily, none of the kids have spotted me so far, although it being the summer holidays the last few times has helped. Be warned though, I'll probably be marking your cakes out of ten when I get to taste them!' She smiles. 'Oh, I'm not serious, Molly. Don't look so worried. I'm sure your baking is delicious.'

'I'll bring a few samples next time, shall I? I'd feel a bit of a fraud without letting you taste them before you order anything.' Molly stops, embarrassed. She hardly knows these women but she is already assuming there will be a next time.

'That would be lovely.' Miranda's eyes have glazed over again at the thought of treats to come. 'We'd better not eat them in here though. It wouldn't go down too well, I don't think. Maybe we could meet in the park round the corner after the next TTC meeting, if the weather's good? I think your antenatal class should be on the same day, Molly. It usually is. Bring a rug and a few sandwiches. And we can always get our coffees to take away.'

'Sounds like a plan!' Rosie says. 'And I was hoping you might all come to the party as well. Kids too, of course. If we've got my husband's friends and family there, it's only right I should invite some of mine. Bring partners, if you want, although I'm sure some of them might not fancy a room full of strangers and screaming babies! The more the merrier though. I'll bring proper invitations next time we meet. And, Molly, maybe you can come a bit early and bring the cake with you on the party day. What do you think?'

Molly thinks that all sounds just perfect. Cakes to make, new friends who have included her so instantly in their group, a picnic in the park to look forward to, and a baby helpline on tap. She really has had quite a wonderful morning.

Chapter 24

Jack

There is something different about Molly. She has a sort of glow about her. Jack wonders if it's a pregnancy thing, a change in the hormones or whatever it is that kicks in once a woman's body realises it's got a baby on board. Whatever it is, she's definitely happier, softly singing to herself as she stirs at the gloopy mixture in her bowl and watches it turn blue. There is an earlier batch, the same but pink, lined up on the kitchen counter, and a big unopened box of icing sugar that makes his tummy rumble at the thought of what delights are to come. If he only gets to lick out the bowls, he'll be happy.

'I hope I've made enough,' she says, probably to herself, but he answers anyway.

'Enough for what?'

'I promised some samples, for a few possible customers. Cupcakes, mainly, but I thought I might try a few biscuits too.'

'You're giving them away? For free?'

'That's what sample generally means, Jack.'

'You'll never make any money that way.'

'Speculate to accumulate.'

He has to admit she's probably right, but he's quite surprised to hear her talking like that. Like a real businesswoman, who might just know what she's doing.

'And can you spare a sample or two for me, do you think?'

'If you're good, I might.' She gives him one of her sparkling smiles, with just a hint of naughty about it.

'I'll hold you to that,' he says, waving his hips in exaggerated circles. 'And you know I'm good. It's why you married me.'

She laughs out loud. 'Big-head! Now get out of my kitchen and don't come back until at least five minutes after the timer beeps.'

'I know to keep my distance when you've got a bun in the oven!'

She picks up a tea towel and swipes it at him. 'Not a bun. Cakes! There's a difference, not that I'd expect you to know that, as all you do is eat them. Just give it time for them to cool down, that's all.'

Molly's bun in the oven is sixteen weeks old already and according to her list of fruit sizes has now reached the avocado stage. Jack has never eaten an avocado and isn't sure he would recognise one if he saw one. The little fluttering movements she says she can feel in her belly are becoming more frequent. Sometimes she grabs at his hand and puts it there, hoping he can feel them too, but he's never really sure if he can. Until he can see it and feel it, this baby is a lot more real to Molly than it is to him.

'I'll pop out for a pint then, if that's okay with you?' He puts his jacket on and checks the pocket for his wallet and keys. A long cool beer in a pub garden somewhere is just what he needs. And a bit of thinking time too. He always said he wouldn't let work take over his life, that weekends were the time to get away from all that, but right now he finds he is thinking about it a lot of the time. The project, the deadline for getting it up and running, the dread of something going wrong.

'Fine. But no getting drunk. You know the effect too much beer has on you.' She looks down, pointedly, at his crotch area and shakes her head.

He kisses her on the cheek, dodging out of the way of her messy hands. How does she do that? Get the mixture all over herself, instead of keeping it in the bowl? Too much dipping and licking, probably. There is something faintly erotic about that thought, and he promises himself he really will have just the one pint and be back in time to sample whatever dipping and licking might be on offer tonight. It's been a while.

He isn't expecting to see anyone he knows. It's not exactly the poshest of pubs but the only one in walking distance to have any decent outdoor space. Yet, as he takes his pint from the bar and goes through into the garden, there she is. The girl who works downstairs, the one who sits next to Carly. He thinks her name is Susan, but he can't be sure. He remembers a meeting by the lift, when he had only been at Mandrake's a couple of days and she had come up to him and introduced herself, although come *on* to him would probably be a more accurate description. There had been something a bit too obvious about her that day, as if she was sizing him up. Making sure she grabbed his attention. The new boy. Fresh meat. He hopes she isn't going to do it again today, but there is someone with her, a bloke, so with luck he will be spared.

He tries to avoid her gaze, and heads for a table as far away as he can, but it's too late. She has clearly spotted him. He can feel the spark of recognition light up in her eyes from here. He tries not to look her way but he can't miss seeing her unhook the arm of the man she is with from around her shoulders as she sits up straight and uncrosses her bare legs. Fake tanned, if he's not mistaken. Her heels sink into the grass as she slides along to the end of the bench, grips the pole of the parasol above her head to steady herself and stands up.

'Hello, Jack,' she purrs, as she wobbles towards him. She probably thinks her voice is sexy but it is so not. 'What are you doing here? And on your own too.'

'Erm. Hi. Just out for a quick drink, making the most of the sunshine.' He tries not to make eye contact, hoping she might take the hint and go away. Behind her, he can see her date scowling at him. But she doesn't go away. She sits down, on the opposite side of the bench, lifting a leg up and over until it is under the table and she is sitting sideways on.

'No wife today?'

He would have thought that was obvious, but he shakes his head. 'She's busy.'

'Shame. I would have loved to meet her. You could come over and join us, if you're lonely. Sean won't mind.' She flicks her head towards the man at the other table, whose expression is still on the frostier side of friendly. It looks to Jack as if Sean will mind, very much indeed.

'No, no, I'm fine, thanks, Susan. Not stopping long.'

'Suze!' she says, correcting him. 'Nobody but my gran ever calls me Susan, silly.' Her laugh comes out like a screech, long and high-pitched. It really wasn't that funny, and he's not sure he likes being called silly.

'Sorry. Suze, of course.'

'I hear you've known our Carly for a while,' she says, not moving a muscle towards leaving. 'She seems to think very highly of you.' She pulls a face that he can't quite read.

'Does she?' He's starting to feel uncomfortable now. What has Carly said to this woman? How much does she know? He's suddenly very pleased that Molly isn't with him, or there could be some embarrassing explaining to do.

'Ten out of ten, she reckons!' She leans towards him and laughs like a drain. 'I can't deny you're bloody good-looking, but even so... You let a good one go there, you know. That girl would have followed you to the ends of the earth but what did you do? You went off and married someone else.' She teeters a bit as she unhooks her leg and tries to get up, and he realises that she's actually quite drunk. 'But you keep your hands off her, you hear? She needs you to stay away, for her own good. And for yours, if I find out you're messing her about again.' She waggles a pointed scarlet-tipped finger at him, like a teacher telling off a naughty child. The threat of untold consequences hangs in the air between them. 'Carly might think she loves you, but I hope she's sensible enough to know it would be a mistake. A great big stupid mistake...'

He watches her return to her own table and plonk down into the other man's lap, her fingers instantly latching back around the glass of wine she had left behind.

He shouldn't let the wild ramblings of a drunk women get to him. What exactly was all that about anyway? Was she warning him off? He hasn't thought about Carly at all today, but he does now. And those few words keep ringing in his head. *Carly might think she loves you.*

The kitchen is awash with cakes when he gets back.

'I think I've finally got it right,' Molly says, with a satisfied but exhausted smile. 'The recipe, the fillings, the icing... even the colours are perfect now. Oh, I'll still make the space-rocket cakes and the flowery stuff if someone orders them, but these are going to be my main focus from now on. Gender-reveal cakes are go!' She says that last bit in the voice he remembers from re-runs of that old TV show. *Thunderbirds are go!* 'Now all I need is a name for them, then I can get some professional business cards made up. Any ideas?'

The only idea that's running through Jack's head has nothing to do with cakes. Carly loves him. Carly thinks he's a ten out of ten. Carly needs to be kept away from him, for her own good.

'Jack! Are you listening to me?' Molly has boiled the kettle and is waiting for him to tell her whether he wants tea or coffee.

'Sorry, Mol. I was out of it for a moment there. Must be the effects of the sunshine.'

'Or the beer.' She laughs, pouring him a coffee anyway. 'Here, this should help. And you can have a cake now they've cooled down. Pink or blue?'

He looks at the half a dozen she's put on a plate beside their mugs. They all look exactly the same. 'How can I tell which is which?'

'Ah, that's the magic of them, see? You can't! And that's the whole point. What's inside is a mystery. Secret centres... A bit like us women, especially the pregnant ones!' She takes his hand and pushes it up under her sweaty T-shirt, and for the first time he feels it. That little kick, like a butterfly fluttering under her skin. And in that moment, it's real. This life, this baby, it's really happening. Whatever choices he once had are being stripped away from him.

'That's it! I can call them *Secret Centres*. What do you think?'

But Jack isn't listening again. Carly wants him, loves him even. And he knows he still wants her too. He had put her out of his mind for years. Just a silly fling, a moment that no one else need ever know about, a final before-the-wedding thing. He hadn't expected to ever see her again, thought she would have forgotten him long ago, moved on with someone else. But now he's back and she's still here, still single, and if her drunken mate is to be believed still into him, big time.

Jack thinks about her, about what might have been, far more than he should. He'd be kidding himself to deny it. But it's too late, isn't it? Molly needs him now, more than ever. His baby needs him. But he didn't ask for this baby, did he? He still doesn't really know if he even wants it.

What if Carly needs him too? Shouldn't he at least find out? Talk to her, make a proper decision, a proper choice, before it really is too late. Someone will get hurt whatever he does. He knows that. And he knows only too well that it could very easily be himself.

He takes a cake and bites into it. He tells himself it's like throwing a dice. Or flipping a coin. That fate will decide. Or luck. If it's blue, he'll choose Carly. If it's pink, Molly. If only it were that easy...

What's inside? Is it blue or is it pink? He dares not look. He closes his eyes and doesn't open them again until every crumb has been eaten.

Chapter 25

Carly

Anthony's here again. She hears them laughing even before she opens the door. This has been her family home for her whole life, yet suddenly she feels like an outsider, an intruder, someone who should be knocking before she walks in.

'Ah, Carly, love.' Her mum looks up as she comes into the kitchen, and waves her hand towards the draining board. 'Look at the lovely dahlias Anthony's brought. Grown them all himself too. Maybe you'd like some to take home with you? I'm not sure I've got enough vases to accommodate them all.'

What happened to *Hello* or *How are you*? It's all about Anthony these days. She hasn't even sat down yet and her mum's talking about her going home. Sam was right. This man is rapidly getting his feet under the table, and something needs to be done about it.

'Hi, Mum. And hello to you too!'

'Sorry. Enough of my babbling. Come in and have a cuppa. There's fresh tea in the pot. Sit down and tell us all your news.'

Us? Since when was she expected to tell Anthony all her comings and goings? 'Nothing to tell. Same old, same old...'

She pours herself a tea and pulls out a chair. She hates feeling awkward in her own home, but the strained atmosphere doesn't seem to register with either of them. A newspaper is spread open on the table between them, and the pen laid down beside it makes it obvious they have been tackling the crossword together.

'You don't happen to know the capital of Senegal, do you?' Anthony says, picking up the pen and chewing the end of it. 'Five letters. Got a K in it. Assuming we've got three across right, of course.'

'Sorry, no. I don't even know where Senegal is.'

My mother tuts. 'And you with an A-level in geography!'

I don't rise to the bait. A-levels were a long time ago and I don't remember much about lists of capital cities ever being on the syllabus.

'Oh, well, I'd best be off,' Anthony says, giving up on the crossword and hauling himself to his feet. 'Maybe you can finish it later, Joyce. Things to do, places to go. You know how it is...'

They don't kiss goodbye, which is a small mercy at least.

The kitchen falls silent in his wake. I drink my tea and watch her, but I can't read the expression on her face. She doesn't speak until she's moved over to the sink and her back's to me as she starts clipping the ends off the dahlia stems.

'You do like Anthony, don't you?' she says.

'I don't really know him, Mum.'

'He's become a good friend. He knew your dad, and they had a lot in common. The allotment, the crossword...'

'A good friend? Is that all?' I know I have no right to ask, but she's spent long enough delving into my love life, my choices, so it doesn't feel too out of line to do the same to her.

She turns to face me. 'Carly! What are you suggesting?'

'Just that he's here a lot, and that the two of you seem to be getting... what's the word? Close, I suppose. Is there something going on here, Mum? Are you two a couple now?'

She comes back to the table, a single stem clutched in her hand, and sits back down.

'Would it bother you if we were? Your dad's been gone a while now, love, and I am entitled to a life.'

'Of course you are. You're still young.'

She laughs. 'I wouldn't say that, exactly. But I still have a few years left ahead of me, God willing, and it would be good to enjoy them. You know, to have someone around to have a laugh with, to go out with sometimes. It doesn't have to mean he's trying to replace your father. Nobody ever could. I hope you know that.'

She's making me feel guilty now, for trying to trample on her chance of a bit of happiness.

'It's just that Anthony is so much younger than you, Mum. It unsettles me a bit. And Sam. Like I said, we know so little about him. Does he have his own house, for instance? Or a proper job?'

'What you are asking is whether he's some sort of gold digger, trying to take a gullible widow for everything she's got! You'll be asking about his prospects next, like some worried father protecting a daughter from a cad.' She sighs. 'Oh, Carly, you've got this so wrong. Anthony's not interested in me in that way. He's not about to move in or whisk me down the aisle, for my money or for my body! And I don't see him that way either.' She closes her eyes for a moment as if debating what to say next. 'You do know your dad was the only man I ever went to bed with? And that wasn't until we were married. Good job we turned out to be compatible and willing to learn as we went along, that's all I can say about that. There was no try before you buy for us! If we'd hated it, we'd have been stuck with it, for life.'

Do I really want to hear about my own parents' sex life? I

shudder and try to put the thoughts of Dad without his pants on aside. At least they were happy.

'No, I had a very strict upbringing, a very moral one,' she goes on. 'My parents had me late in life, and I think they found it hard coping with a child at all, let alone when I became a teenager. I was watched like a hawk as soon as puberty hit, believe me! No going off the rails or falling for some wrong 'un. They were sure every lad who came anywhere near me had evil intentions!' A vision of the Bennets and the wayward and very determined Lydia comes into my head, although nothing they did was able to stop that particular teenager from running off with a cad, was it? Pride. Prejudice. Both have a lot to answer for.

'Which is why I've always tried to be a bit more free and easy with you and Sam,' she goes on. 'Let you have your freedom, make your own mistakes, even if I might come across as a bit old-fashioned sometimes. Your granddad didn't hold with all that free love stuff in the seventies, or unmarried girls going on the pill. He saw it as his job to protect me, and my honour, come what may. He'd have been after *me* with a shotgun, let alone any boy who dared to try it on. I'd have probably worn a chastity belt if they'd known where to buy one! So, I'm not about to start dropping my drawers for just anybody now, am I?'

'Mum!'

'Look, love, I'm going to tell you this in the strictest confidence, okay? It's Anthony's business, and his secret to tell, but if it puts your mind at rest...'

I'm curious now, but I wait as she gathers her thoughts.

'Anthony is already in a relationship. He has a partner, someone he lives with, but... well, they can't go out together, enjoy trips to the cinema or the garden centre. I fill that gap in his life, just as he fills the same gap in mine. What we have together is not love or romance or sex. It's called friendship, Carly. As simple as that.'

'And this partner? Why can't they go out together?' It suddenly dawns on me. Why didn't I suspect it before? 'Is Anthony gay? Is that it? You're telling me that he's still lurking in the closet, or his partner is, and they can't be seen out holding hands? In this day and age? That you're his... cover, if that's the word for it?'

'No, Carly.' She puts the flower down at last. Its petals are a mangled mess now, she's been squashing them between her fingers for so long. 'Anthony is not gay. Absolutely not. He lives with a woman. Her name is Pauline, they've been together for twenty years, and he loves her very much, but she's not able to go out and do all the things other women her age can do.'

'Why not?'

She pauses for a moment, then takes my hand over the table. 'She has Huntingdon's disease, Carly.'

'Oh.' I wasn't expecting that.

'I don't ask him for all the day-to-day details but I know it's getting worse. Well, it will, I suppose. It's not curable, I know that much. It affects her brain, her movements, her coordination. Her memory and her speech too. From what I can gather, she gets very depressed, and a bit out of control at times, violent, not that she can help it, of course. I've seen bruises on his arms. And yet he stands by her, cares for her, stays faithful to her. He even gave up his job to be there for her. She has carers who come in, obviously, but he works for himself, from home, these days, so he can be there as much as possible. And that means he doesn't even have colleagues to chat to anymore. It can be very lonely, as I know only too well. So, sometimes he needs to get out and have a more normal life for a few hours. The allotment. Here... You surely can't begrudge him that?'

I don't really know what to say. I have misjudged Anthony so badly. And Mum too.

'I'm so sorry, Mum. I shouldn't have jumped to conclusions. Poor Anthony.'

'Well, that's exactly what he doesn't want. People to pity him, or to feel sorry for him. He wants to be treated just like anybody else, and have a bit of fun when he can, a chance to escape from the reality of their everyday life every now and then. And when he's here with me, we don't talk about all that stuff he has to deal with at home. We play music, we plant flowers, we wander down to the allotments and take a flask, we sit here and do the crossword. And, yes, you're right. Of course, he's much younger than me, but our friendship gives us both something we need, Carly. It has nothing to do with age. Or sex!'

'They aren't married though? No kids?'

'She knew she was carrying the gene. It's genetic, apparently, passed on by her father. She never knew him. He did a runner when she was a baby, but he left her with that. A ticking time bomb. And, as soon as she knew she had it, she was determined not to tie Anthony down, much as he was willing, keen even, to marry her. And she refused to risk passing it on to any children. Got sterilised to make sure it never happened.'

'That's so sad.'

'It is. He would have made a good dad.'

I flinch a bit, remembering saying the very same thing about Jack. 'So, what happens now? When I see him? Do I pretend I don't know, make out you haven't told me?'

'No, that would be silly. And dishonest. He's not ashamed of his situation, he just prefers not to broadcast it, but I will tell him that I've confided in you. Besides, I get the impression things will be changing sooner rather than later.'

'What do you mean?'

'Do you need me to spell it out for you, love? I don't think that Pauline has long left, that's what I'm saying. She's had a few falls, infections, a couple of bouts of pneumonia, and she's just getting weaker, less able to fight. Her body's giving up, and Anthony believes that maybe she is too.'

I go for a long walk when I leave Mum's. Life really is a sod sometimes, isn't it? Who knows what deadly disease any of us might catch, or what bus might come whizzing round the corner and knock us down at any minute? Yet, here I am, wasting my life as if I have all the time in the world. Maybe my mother's been right all along. I should have found someone by now, settled down, got married, had a couple of beautiful children. Be less Carly and more Rosie!

Why didn't I meet someone like Syd? Caring, understanding, a real family man? Instead, I was stupid enough to pin my hopes and all my romantic fantasies on a man I can't have. Just because he is drop-dead gorgeous and has beautiful deep-brown eyes, and makes my knees go weak! I must be the shallowest woman I know.

Chapter 26

Molly

It is October already, the day of her own gender-reveal scan fast approaching, and, after six weeks, Molly has just had the plaster removed from her wrist. She wriggles her hand about, happy to have it back in full working order again, and thinks how lucky they are to still have nice enough weather for a picnic in the park, even if it means keeping coats on and bringing umbrellas just in case.

She has invested in a special two-tier carrying case, so she can safely transport the sample cupcakes and the tin containing Jo's son's rocket birthday cake on the bus, but it's heavier than she had anticipated and her wrist, unused to doing the work lately, is aching, even though she has tried to take most of the weight in her other hand. She has had to stop for a few minutes to put everything down and catch her breath. Maybe she should have looked for something with wheels.

She spots Rosie ahead of her, pressing the button at the school gate, and rushes to catch up with her.

'Hello,' Rosie calls, waving a hand before returning it to the handle of the double buggy she is struggling to manoeuvre through the gate. She seems to manage it with a sideways shunt of her hip before Molly can help her, and holds the gate open for Molly to follow her through. 'They should warn people that you need a special driving test before getting let loose with one of these buggers,' she says with a laugh. 'Oh, sorry. I meant buggies, obviously! Anyway, far more importantly, I can see that you've brought cake. Lovely!'

Molly nods towards the bag over her shoulder. 'And a rug and sandwiches, fizzy water, some fresh fruit salad...'

'You could do with a buggy yourself, just to carry stuff in. And you put me to shame. I've only grabbed a packet of biscuits and an apple. Oh, I've got plenty of milk with me, for these two. Didn't have time to sort out a lot for myself. Somehow their needs always come first these days, but you'll find that out soon enough.'

'I'm happy to share. I've brought far too much.'

'You can never have too much when it comes to food. Especially cake. See you after our sessions, okay? If yours finishes after ours, the park's literally just round that corner. We'll be under the biggest tree.'

Molly signs the register at the reception desk and goes into the room where the antenatal class is held. It's a bit less daunting the second time around. There is a screen set up at the front, and the chairs have been laid out in a small horseshoe shape, so they are probably going to watch a video. Nothing too gory, she hopes. She recognises a few faces from last time and nods hello, then settles herself in a chair in the second row. This doesn't quite seem the time to start touting for business, but she grips a small bundle of her new *Secret Centres* business cards in her pocket and decides to try broaching the subject when they stop for tea and biscuits and a chat at the end.

The film is about some of the changes they can all expect in their bodies over the coming months. About stretch marks and feeling tired and food cravings. She smiles to herself as some of the women mutter about fancying dried apricots or tinned pears or lumps of coal. One has started licking at ice cubes while she watches TV and another admits to sending her husband out at midnight in the rain to try and track down a Mars bar, because nothing else would do.

When the refreshments come out and Molly opens up her case and offers them some of her cakes, they all turn their noses up at the plate of custard creams provided and pounce on her as if they haven't eaten for a week.

'Mmm, pink and blue. What a brilliant idea.'

'Ooh, they're great. Sign me up for a dozen of those.'

'I'll be phoning you just as soon as I've had the scan.'

'Yummy. I do hope I'm having a girl, cos the pink sponge is just so pretty.'

The compliments and the orders are flying in fast. Everyone is taking a card, or several so they can share with their friends. One girl works for the local newspaper and promises to be in touch about a feature and some free advertising. Molly gives them a sneak peek at Jo's commissioned rocket cake too, and there's another round of excited chatter and requests for a cake made to look like a garden shed and another like a pair of ballet shoes.

She notices the class leader, in her blue nurse's uniform, listening in at the back of the crowd, and worries that she shouldn't really be hijacking the class like this, until the woman steps forward and asks about a retirement cake for one of her midwife colleagues, and if it would be indelicate to ask for a cake with a model of a newborn baby on top, with umbilical cord still attached. She knows it will appeal to the woman's sense of humour. Molly laughs along with her and assures her that with icing just about anything is possible, and that she will enjoy making something a bit different for a change. Another card changes hands.

Molly closes the case before everything gets devoured. She wants to make sure there are enough cupcakes left for the girls at the picnic. By the time they all start to collect coats and bags, she feels she has gained not only new clients but more new friends too.

&

'So, how is everything? Bump growing? Skin glowing?' Her mum is on the phone later that afternoon, trying so hard to be a part of a pregnancy she is missing out on seeing develop in the flesh.

'All fine, Mum.'

'And London? Are you settling in yet? I hate to think of you all alone when the baby comes.'

'I won't be alone. I have Jack.'

'Of course you do, but he'll be at work, won't he? And it can be lonely, being at home all day with just a baby for company. I remember it well. Still, at least I had my mother close by, and my sisters.'

'I wish we were nearer, Mum, and that you could pop in whenever you want to, but that's not going to be easy, is it? I have made some friends though. Other mums, and mums-to-be. We had a picnic at lunchtime today. Lots of babies for me to practise on! It was a bit chilly, but I really enjoyed it.'

'Oh, that's nice.'

'And the wrist is better, the plaster came off yesterday, so that makes everything a bit easier. Maybe I could come up there for a few days soon, before I get too huge to travel! I've been busy building up the cake business and it's early days, I know, but I think I can make it work. I've got quite a few birthday cakes to make, and lots of people want to order the gender-reveal ones once they've been scanned, but I'm sure I can find a few days to slot you in!'

'That would be lovely, Molly. We do miss you, you know. Me and your dad, all your friends. And the dog.'

'And I miss all of you. Let me check with Jack when he gets home. And if he can't get a few days off, I can always come by myself. The beauty of not having a boss to have to please! And I promise not to break any bones this time.'

'You'd better not. You keep that little grandson of mine safe now, you hear?'

'I will, Mum. But it could be a girl, you know. I keep telling you that.'

'Nonsense. I'm never wrong, you'll see. So, I won't be needing any of your special gender thingies. Not to tell me something I already know.'

Molly puts the phone down and sits for a while with a cup of tea. Is it a boy? Her mum will be having her believing it too, if she's not careful, but with a fifty–fifty chance either way, it won't be that big a miracle if she's right. Before long, Molly's eyes are starting to close. Despite being in London, their street is surprisingly quiet. Unless she opens a window, she can't hear the traffic. It should make it easier when she's trying to get a baby to sleep, or catching up with her own sleep between feeds. She has watched the twin mums and seen how manic everything can get. At least she's only having one.

Her dreams, in which she is being chased by a giant rabbit wearing ballet shoes and a nappy, are interrupted, thankfully, by the door slamming shut as Jack comes in from work.

'Busy day?' she asks, yawning.

He nods, and comes over to peck her on the cheek. She notices that he smells faintly of beer but chooses not to mention it. So, he's had a quick drink on his way home. Alcohol is the last thing she fancies nowadays, not that it would be allowed if she did.

'You too, by the look of it. What's tired you out? I don't smell any baking.'

'No, I had my antenatal class today, and then a picnic with some of the women I've met. I did tell you this morning.'

'Did you? Sorry. Let me get changed and then you can tell me all about it. The class, especially, and anything you think I should know.'

'There's so much to know you wouldn't believe! This whole pregnancy thing is a revelation, Jack. Stretch marks and constipation and chomping on lumps of coal in the middle of the night, and we haven't even started talking about the actual birth yet. Pain relief and pushing and piles! I'm just glad it's us women having to cope with the pregnancy and not you men, or it would never happen.'

'You're right there.' She sees Jack shudder as he disappears into the bedroom.

She glances at the clock and is surprised to see it's already nearly seven. Jack's home later than usual and she's been asleep for ages. She's done nothing about dinner. She can't keep using being pregnant as an excuse to put her feet up and live on takeaways. There's a chicken pie in the freezer, and some frozen chips, and the fridge is bursting with far more carrots than feels anywhere near normal. When she comes to think about it, she has been nibbling on them quite a bit lately, just washed under the tap and eaten raw. It occurs to her that she may have found her own pregnancy craving. Still, at least it's a healthy one, and, if the tales her mother used to spin her can be believed, it could just help her to see better in the dark, which will come in handy for night-time nappy changes. No wonder she was dreaming about rabbits!

Chapter 27

Jack

Jack is pleased with the way the project is going. More importantly, his bosses are pleased too. Another two or three weeks of testing and tweaking and it can all go 'live'. Soon after that, when everything is running smoothly, he will be moved on. There are other projects lining up, plenty for him to tackle once this particular one has been completed, so he knows his future is secure, even though his time at Mandrake's is coming to an end. That's how being a consultant works. A bit like temping, going where he is needed, making new friends, building his CV and his reputation. His new company is not about to go bust as the last one had. He will be with them long-term, or for as long as he wants to be.

But for the next few weeks, he will be working in the same building as Carly, seeing her often, and having to find a way for them both to deal with that. Being colleagues, friends, and nothing more. If only the might-have-beens and the what-ifs didn't keep popping into his head. Is it really too late? It's madness to think that way, but there's something about her that has grabbed hold of him and is not quite willing to let go.

Since that encounter in the pub garden, he has tried hard to avoid her mate Suze, yet somehow she keeps appearing. Coming up to his floor with messages or invoices in need of querying. Hovering near the lifts. Giving him that evil stare of hers that seems to have replaced the sensual come-and-get-me look she had directed at him when he had first arrived. She seems to have appointed herself as Carly's protector, some kind of gatekeeper, making it her mission to keep watching him, and to keep them apart. Far from warning him off though, her determination to save Carly from the clutches of a married man has become like a red rag to a bull. It is not her place, nor her business, to come between them or decide whether they should see each other or how they should behave. It's how he feels, and just as importantly, how Carly feels, that matters, and as they have no choice but to be thrown together, this is a relationship, whatever form that might choose to take, that they have to figure out for themselves.

He has another meeting with Carly later this afternoon. He has told himself, and her, that his diary is full, that four thirty is the only time he could manage, but he knows that's not true. He has chosen a late-afternoon slot knowing that, by the time they are finished, everyone will be going home, that he can quite legitimately suggest a quick drink somewhere, so they might finally be able to talk things through, away from the office, and work out where they go from here.

'Oh, I can't, Jack. Not tonight. Sorry. I've got a driving lesson at five thirty. Syd's meeting me outside the front door. You should pop out with me and say hello.' It's only four twenty-five but they have both got here early and Carly is spreading out her notes on the desk in front of them, her pen poised, the tip just brushing her lips as she concentrates. She is wearing a bright-pink shiny lipstick, and he just wants to reach over and kiss it. Kiss *her*. He mustn't. He doesn't.

'It's just that... well, there was something I wanted to talk to you about.'

She looks up, her hand and the pen it is holding slipping back down onto her lap.

'About the project?'

'No. There'd be no need to go out for a drink to do that. We can cover that here. It was... you and me, I suppose.'

He's sure he can see the hint of a pink tinge creep up over her face. She looks a bit uncomfortable, yet her eyes continue to hold his gaze. She braves it out and doesn't look away.

'Is there a you and me?'

'I sometimes think there will always be a you and me, Carly. Whatever else happens...' He stops, an image of Molly and some faceless future baby crashing into his thoughts, just as it probably is into Carly's too. 'I get the feeling we still have unfinished business. Oh, that's not a very good way to describe it, I know.'

'It's not, no. This, here, is business.' She taps the pile of papers on the desk. 'And that's no problem, is it? It's all going well. We're going well, working together like this.'

'We are. But you know that's not what I'm talking about. It was something your friend said to me. Suze...'

'Suze? When did she talk to you? And what did she say? God, I wish she would just butt out. She's hardly a world expert on relationships herself. One minute she's all loved up with that Sean, they're getting on great, then he's been spotted with another woman and she dumps him, then she's all over him again. I can't keep up. I just wish she'd make up her mind. Go on, what's she said? Something horribly embarrassing, I expect.'

'It doesn't really matter what her exact words were. She was more or less telling me to leave you alone, to stay away or else...'

Carly laughs then. 'And I bet you were really scared, right? What's she going to do? Whack you with one of her high heels? Throw a drink in your face?'

'I wouldn't put it past her to do either of those, actually. But the point is that I don't want to have to find out how you feel from your friend. I want – no, I need – to hear it from you. Do *you* want me to stay away?'

'Not easy, when we work together.'

'Aside from work, I mean.'

'This is all a bit heavy, Jack. And we *are* at work, aren't we? With a project to worry about and to talk about, and less than an hour to do it in before Syd gets here.'

'Later then? After your lesson? You could meet me somewhere. We can't just keep ignoring it, can we? I know we agreed to let it go, but it's not that easy, is it? That kiss, all those years ago. What so nearly happened, and why we let it. Did we do the right thing, Carly? Walking away from all that... I don't even know what to call it... attraction, lust, something more than that? I couldn't get you out of my head for weeks afterwards, and being back here has just made it all so real again, what I felt back then, what I'm pretty sure you felt too. It's like the bloody great elephant in the room every time we get close to each other.'

'But you married someone else. We can't ignore that, can we? Or the fact that she's pregnant? I told you before, I can't be the third person in all of this, the bit on the side, the dirty little secret. Your wife doesn't even know I exist, and I hope to God it stays that way. But I know about her, and that means I have a choice, whereas she really doesn't.'

'What if I told her?' He has no idea where that has just come from, but suddenly he means it. Come clean. Do the right thing. Get it all out in the open and sod the consequences.

Carly gapes at him, her pink lipstick mouth poised as if to say something that fails to come out.

'I mean it, Carly. What if I told the truth? Told her everything?'

'There is no everything. Nothing to tell. We don't really know each other, Jack. We fancy each other rotten, I admit that much. But we've never even slept together. What we have is no basis for big confessions, for wrecking a marriage. I don't want to be responsible for that.'

'How do we know, if we don't give it a try?'

'I can't do this. I can't have this conversation. Not here. We're at work. Someone could walk in. And we haven't even started to talk about this project that means so much to you.'

'It's not the only thing that means so much to me, and you know it.'

'The baby...'

'That's below the belt, Carly. I never wanted a baby. I still don't know if I want a baby.'

'A bit late for that. You're having one, like it or not. It's not going away.'

'I know. It's just... look, Carly, I haven't really talked about this before. Well, only to my mum and dad. But I've been in this position before.'

'Position?'

'A pregnancy I hadn't planned, hadn't expected. I was just a kid really. We both were.'

'You and Molly?'

'No, no. Before Molly. A girl from school. The typical stupid snog behind the bike shed kind of thing. Except it was actually a barn full of pigs. And I was all bravado and raging hormones, and thinking nothing could touch me, you know. The big *I Am*. Not stopping to think. When she told me she was having a baby, I totally lost it. Shouted, swore, blamed her, denied it, tried to wriggle out of it, the lot. I'm not proud of myself, but I was seventeen. I knew nothing about abortions or how to get one, and I didn't have the cash anyway. There was nothing I could do but own up to it, tell Mum, who told Dad, and before I knew it I was marched down to this girl's house and there was this big pow-wow that seemed to go on for hours. Angry voices and tears and shame... Well, it all got sorted, quickly and quietly, Dad paying, the girl going away for a while, taking time out of school.'

'*The girl?* Listen to yourself. Didn't she have a name?'

'Yes, of course. Sorry. I'm making her sound unimportant, aren't I? And like it was all her fault, and I'm the only one affected by it all. Katie, that was her name. But at the time I admit I didn't really give a thought to her, how she was feeling, even though it was her body, her baby, her choice to make. I was a selfish pig, I really was.'

'And you're still doing it, Jack. *Her* baby? It was yours too.'

'Oh, God, I know. But it ended... well. Oh, I know that well isn't the right word, but things could have been worse. Nobody found out. They moved house quite soon after, took her away from the village, and I never saw her again, but those few months, from the moment she told me until the day she left, were the most traumatic of my entire life.'

It's not until she takes hold of his hand that he realises it's trembling. 'Does Molly know?'

'No. Nobody does. I didn't see the point. It's history.'

'Is it though? It's obviously had an effect on you, a huge one. No wonder you're a bit rattled, but it's very different this time, isn't it? This pregnancy was unplanned, yes, but you're older, and you're married. You're not some Willoughby-type character, seducing young girls and getting away with it.'

'Who?'

'Never mind. He's in a book. *Sense and Sensibility.*'

'Oh, right. I can't remember when I last read a book.'

'Really?' She looks shocked. 'I can't remember a time when I wasn't reading a book. But, look, what I mean is that times have changed. And so have you, I hope. No need to go running to Daddy for a handout. No shame in what you've done. Your wife is pregnant. Your *wife*, Jack.'

'I know. But it's brought back a lot of that old feeling. Of it all happening again, things being out of my control, things I might not even want. I feel trapped, Carly. I'm not even sure why I married Molly, to be honest with you. I think maybe I was trying to just do the right thing, be respectable, honourable, you know, because I hadn't been the first time. Once we had slept together, with condom very securely in place, I felt I owed her. Loyalty, a future... I couldn't be that Jack-the-Lad bloke I'd been before.'

'But did you love her, Jack? Do you love her now?'

He pauses, not sure what to say. Did he? Does he?

'I thought so. Life was comfortable, easy, ticking along... until I met you.'

'I'm sorry, Jack, but you need to grow up. Grow a pair. Being a couple and making a baby together isn't meant to make you feel scared or trapped. Take responsibility, like you said you wanted to. Make a proper choice and stick to it. Not just what's right for you, but for her, and the baby.'

'But it's not just them, is it? It's you too.'

'Oh, come on, Jack. I didn't get you into this mess. You did that all by yourself. You have to decide what you really want.'

'I'm trying. I really am.'

'Well, try harder. Because I'm not going to be messed about. Do you really want to own up? Just walk away from a perfectly good marriage? Start some new life with me? Because, let's just say, in this ridiculous fantasy of yours, that you confess all, tell your wife about me, leave her and your unborn, unplanned child, and come to me. What happens if I want a baby? *When* I want a baby? Have you thought about that? You'll be on the same old treadmill all over again, won't you? Another do-you-don't-you-want-this situation. It seems to me like you're running away from something with no idea what you're running into. You haven't thought about it properly. Any of it.'

'Then talk to me. Help me to think about it properly, because what I do know is that I can't stop thinking about you, and that's no way for me to live, and it's not fair on Molly. Better she knows.'

'Is it? Really? I'm not sure I'd want to, if I was her.'

'But I have to do something, Carly. I feel I'm in limbo here, stuck in the middle, and I don't know what to do. Tell me, what did this Willy bloke do? In the book?'

'Willoughby! He put his philandering behind him, fell in love with a girl called Marianne, but went off and married someone else. For money. Broke poor Marianne's heart, and quite possibly his own as well. But she survived, and she married someone else after a while. Someone safe and steady, who really loved her.'

'Right. Not sure what lesson I'm meant to learn here.'

'Well, let's just say I'm keeping my options open. Holding out for a hero! But there's really only one way to learn, Jack, and that's from your own mistakes, although it would be much better if you stopped making them. But, okay, I agree we can't leave things between us like this. We'll talk later. After my driving lesson, although God knows how I'm going to concentrate on bloody three-point turns with all this going on in my head.'

'Where?'

'Not in some pub, with people listening. God, what if I cry? Or you do?' She laughs then, but he can see she's not finding it funny. She's scared, just as he is. 'I may live to regret this, but come to my place. We can be sure of some privacy there. Fran will probably be home. My flatmate. My chaperone! But we can go into my room if she is. And I can make us something to eat, if you like. Just stay away until after Syd drops me back. I wouldn't want him to see you coming in and get the wrong idea. He's another one who's been trying to warn me off, although a lot more subtly than Suze wading in with her size nines.'

'Deal. I'll tell Molly I'm working late. She won't mind. Saves her having to cook, and she'll probably have nodded off before I get back anyway. Or I'll say that I'm meeting up with Syd. It'll kind of be true if I come out and say hello to him before your lesson.'

'Are you a natural liar or have you had lessons?'

'It's just easier to tell a half-truth sometimes, and why rock the boat before we know if we want to get off?'

She looks at him strangely, but picks up her notebook and pen again, tearing out a page, scribbling her address down and passing it across to him.

'Quarter to seven, okay? Now, let's do what we came here for, shall we?' She lifts her wrist and looks at her watch. 'Keep it professional, at least while we're here. I've got a list of things I need to ask you, and we don't have long left before I have to go.'

He has been so determined not to be late that he's totally misjudged the journey and turned up twenty minutes early. The car will be back at any minute with Carly and Syd in it, and he's promised to stay out of sight. He's pretty sure he knows which direction they are going to be coming from, so he strides off the other way, hits the nearest corner, and turns down the street to his left. There are a few small shops up ahead and he goes into one that looks like a cross between a grocer, a newsagent and an off-licence. Should he buy her something? Chocolates? A bottle of wine? A lottery ticket, in the hope they'll win a fortune and he can walk away into a new life without leaving his pregnant wife without a roof over her head?

He spends ten minutes browsing the overstuffed shelves, aware of the man behind the counter watching him suspiciously as if he's some kind of robber about to demand he open the cash register and hand over the takings. Not wanting to hang about any longer, he selects a bottle of white wine from the fridge and the best of a selection of semi-wilted flowers from a plastic vase near the door, and pays the extra ten pence for a carrier bag he only really needs because the flower stems are dripping water down his trousers. And then he's back out on the street and cautiously approaching Carly's flat, ready to backtrack round the same corner at the slightest sighting of a learner car. There isn't one, so he assumes she's back now and that Syd has already gone.

He examines the plaque on the door and rings the bell for Flat 3. There is no fancy electronic entry system, just the faint sound of the bell ringing somewhere inside and feet pounding down the stairs, before the door opens and Carly ushers him in. She is still wearing the clothes she had on at work, as is he, of course, and that all just makes the whole meeting feel a bit too formal.

'I brought wine,' he says, holding the bag out in front of him. 'Just corner-shop stuff, I'm afraid, but you did say you might cook...'

'Oh, okay, thanks. These for me too?' She has taken the bag from his hands and is admiring the flowers, lifting their petals to her nose. 'They never seem to have any scent these days, do they? Pretty though.'

She closes the front door and he notices the scuffed skirting boards, dodgy lighting and threadbare carpet in the hall and on the stairs behind her. There's a vaguely musty smell too, from a lack of windows and fresh air. It reminds him of the entrance to his own block. Standard stuff, presumably. Functional, just about clean, shared by several people, none of whom are keen to do anything about it.

'Come up then. Fran's here, but she's busy ironing, so she won't bother us.'

They stop in Carly's small kitchen and pop the wine into the fridge.

'Talk first, or eat?' she says, turning her back towards him and reaching for plates from a cupboard above her head. 'It'll only be something simple. Pasta okay?'

'Fine. Not that I'm all that hungry, but it will be nice to sit down together. Will Fran be joining us?' He nods vaguely in the direction of the rest of the flat and the woman he has yet to set eyes on.

'Do you want her to?'

Jack laughs. 'Not particularly. Three's a crowd and all that.'

'No, we usually do our own thing when it comes to food. She's more of a chips and chocolate girl anyway, to be honest.'

'Okay, we'll eat first then, shall we? Or talk while we eat, if you like.'

He slides into a wooden chair on one side of the table and watches as Carly measures out pasta and sets a pan of water to boil. She starts frantically chopping at tomatoes and slicing mushrooms, and from the straightness of her back he can tell she's tense.

'This should feel nice,' she says, still facing away from him. 'Cosy...'

'But it doesn't?' he asks.

'It's a sort of homely couples thing, isn't it? Making a meal after work, sitting down together to talk about our day. We never had that, Jack. We never even had a first date, did we? We're not a couple. And now it's too late.'

He stands and takes her hand, easing her away from her chopping and into the chair opposite him. He studies her fingers as he grasps them over the table.

'I'm sorry, Carly.'

'What for? For never taking me on a date? For marrying someone else? For the babies you didn't want? For coming back to London and turning everything upside down again?'

'All of the above.'

'This has to stop, Jack. I want us to get along, to be friends, to be able to work together without this constant feeling of... oh, I don't even know what it is. Uncertainty, I suppose. So, we have to just put the past aside and get on with it, don't we? Being colleagues. Keeping our distance for as long as you're working at Mandrake's. Forgetting everything else. Living life as it really is. You telling your wife anything about us, past or present, would be crazy. It wouldn't achieve anything except a lot of upset, and for what?'

'A chance. One worth taking?'

He can see the tears forming, and tightens his grip on her hand.

'No.' She tries to pull away from him, but he won't let her.

'I want to kiss you, Carly. Please. One last time, if that's how it has to be, but just come here, will you? You're unhappy, I can see that. Let me...'

And she does. She stands up just as he does, and moves towards him, the tears trailing down her cheeks now and making her eye make-up run. He pulls her in against his chest and feels her breathing. He has never wanted her more.

He lowers his head at the same moment she raises hers and their lips meet. She is warm and soft. Her mouth opens, pressing hard against his own until her lips part and his tongue touches hers. Her hand comes up to the back of his neck and her fingers find their way into his hair.

'Oops! Sorry.'

They pull apart. There is a short, very round woman standing in the open doorway, her face red, maybe from embarrassment, or maybe she always looks that way. This must be the elusive Fran. She backs away. 'I was just going to make a cup of tea. I'll come back...'

'It's fine. Come in. It's your kitchen just as much as mine.' Carly returns to her chopping board. 'This is Jack, by the way. Jack, Fran.'

They manage an awkward hello as Fran flips the kettle on.

'Can I get one for either of you? Or a coffee?'

'No, thanks,' they both say together, and silence returns while Fran busies herself with teabags and a mug and Carly pours pasta shapes into the pan.

'I'll let you get on then. Enjoy your meal.' She scurries away, closing the kitchen door after her.

'Well, that was a bit...'

'Our fault, Jack, not hers.' She is concentrating on the tomatoes which have been chopped so finely now they are turning to mush. 'Maybe we should continue our... conversation... in my room once we've eaten.'

'Or now. The food could wait.'

'I suppose it could.' She puts her knife down and turns off the heat under the pan.

She reaches for his hand again and leads him out into the narrow hallway. He catches a glimpse of Fran through the open door of what must be the lounge. She is holding an iron in one hand and a half-eaten chocolate bar in the other. She doesn't look up as they pass.

Carly's room is just as he would have expected it to be. Very tidy, with bookshelves lining one wall and a double bed, neatly made, with pink covers, against the other. He can see the top of a tree through the window, and hear the faint hum of traffic. They stand for a few seconds, just looking at each other, as if neither of them can be quite sure what is supposed to happen next, or if they really want it to.

'I really care about you, Jack.' She says it so quietly he wonders if he might have imagined it, but the look in her eyes tells him he hasn't. 'I think I'm probably half in love with you already, and it would be so easy to let myself fall the whole way, head first, no holding back... but I can't, can I? And I have no idea what to do about it.'

There is only one thing they can do. At this moment, anyway. Later doesn't matter. What happens after this doesn't matter. Not anymore. They have waited so long.

He wraps his arms around her and slips a hand underneath her top, letting his fingers roam up her bare back, pulling her closer. She lets out a small groan and does the same to him, each of them exploring the other's hidden skin, tentatively, gently, for the first time.

The bed is inches away and he's not sure who makes the first move, but they are on it now, his body alongside hers, his hands moving around to the front of her top and easing it up and off over her head as a book slips off the pillow and hits the floor with a thud.

Chapter 28

Carly

What the hell am I doing? I'm lying, half-naked, with the man of my dreams snogging my face off, and I just know it's not right. You know how that happens sometimes? When you've waited forever for something, and built it up in your head, and then when you suddenly get it, you realise it's not really what you expected, not what you wanted at all?

I roll away, as best I can when he's half on top of me, and plonk a hand over each nipple. Not that he hasn't already seen me in all my glory, or had a good feel of them, but this isn't a conversation I can have with my bare chest on full display.

'No, Jack.'

'No?' He sits up. 'But I thought you wanted...'

'So did I.'

'If it's being careful you're worrying about... Condoms...'

'No, it's nothing to do with condoms. I just can't do it. *We* can't do it.'

'Speak for yourself. I most certainly can.' He lowers his gaze to his open trousers and the prominent bulge that just seconds ago was pushing urgently against my thigh. I get a glimpse of his underwear, bright red with some kind of superhero design that, in any other circumstances, would have had me in fits of giggles or recoiling in mock horror. Mr Darcy emerging from the lake he most certainly is not.

'We were meant to be talking, remember? And eating. And sorting things out once and for all.' I'm desperately trying to cover everything up and willing Jack to do the same. 'Not having sex.'

'Right. Okay.' He says it but I'm not sure he means it.

'Please, Jack. I don't sleep with married men. I told you that before. Not even when that married man is you. I have wanted you, so badly, but I've been blind to a lot of things, things we really can't change, so it has to stop here, right now. I'll get over it, I have to, and this... this is not happening. I can't let it.'

'But Mol...' He's said it automatically, without thinking, started to call me by her name. And that's when I know I've done exactly the right thing in stopping this right now. 'Oh, God, Carly, I'm so sorry. It's just habit. A slip of the tongue. Forgive me.'

I sit on the edge of the bed, my back turned towards him so he can't see my face, or my boobs. I lean down and rescue my book, smoothing its cover and checking it's not damaged in any way. It's a new edition of *Persuasion* that I've only just started to read, leather-bound in red and gold, and suddenly making sure it has survived seems to be all I can focus on, the only thing that matters.

'Nothing to forgive,' I force myself to say. 'She's your wife, and I'm not. Simple as that. I'm sure it's her name that always comes out of your mouth when you're in a... situation like this. Now, we can go back into the kitchen and eat that pasta, like civilised people, old friends sharing a meal and a glass of wine, or you can go home now. Either way, none of this ever happens again, and we don't talk about it again either, okay? And Molly never has to know. We're done. Finished. It's best for all three of us, I know it is, believe me.' I manage to find my top, lying in a heap on the carpet, and pull it back on, keeping my back towards him, not bothering to locate my bra and have to fiddle about with the hooks while he's watching me.

'If you say so. If a woman says no, she means no. I am aware of that, and I respect that, but are you sure? We could be really good together. We fit, don't we?' He looks up at me with his big brown puppy eyes and I so want to back down, to whip off all of my clothes again and lie back down on the bed and let myself melt into him, but it's too late for that now. I'm letting him go. I have to.

It's dark outside but the street lights are on. I lift the curtain and watch Jack walk away down the street.

'You okay, Carls?' Fran stands behind me and rests a hand on my shoulder.

'I will be. Nothing a bottle of wine won't put right.' I'm not sure that's quite true but I'm not about to spill all to Fran, and wine always helps, doesn't it?

'Fancy a chocolate as well? I've got a whole box of truffles unopened. The good Belgian ones. I'm happy to share.'

'Do you know, I think I do. I've gone off the idea of that pasta now. Let's pig out on whatever we fancy tonight, all the stuff that's bad for us, and hang the consequences.'

'I tend to live my whole life that way.' Fran sighs and pulls me into a big blubbery cuddle.

I lower the curtain and turn away from the window.

'So that was the famous Jack?' she says, shoving the ironing board back into a cupboard and ripping the cellophane off the chocolates. 'Not quite as handsome as you and Suze have had me believe.'

'Really? Are you blind?'

'No.' She laughs. 'Just gay!' It's the first time she has openly admitted it, to me anyway, and I feel kind of flattered that she's able to say it. Maybe it's a night for confessions all round. 'So, he's not my type, obviously. I take it things didn't go well. In the bedroom, I mean. A bit of a flop, was he?'

'Fran!' I giggle. 'No, everything seemed in good working order. Just a change of heart, on my part. A last-minute one, but let's just say I came to my senses, just in time.'

'Good. Affairs with married men rarely work out. Especially ones with kids. And you're better than that, Carls. In fact, if you weren't quite so straight, I'd make a play for you myself.'

I am about to laugh again, but something in her face tells me she just might mean it.

'Now, where's that wine you mentioned?'

'In the fridge. Jack bought it. Maybe I should take it and give it back to him, at work?'

'And the flowers?' She must have spotted them in the kitchen, propped up in an old milk bottle because I was too busy cooking and kissing and making a fool of myself to have bothered finding a vase. 'Don't be daft. Gifts are like engagement rings. Men give them, with expectations, or from guilt or whatever but, whatever the outcome, women are not obliged to give them back. That wine is officially yours. Well, ours now. I'll get the corkscrew.'

'No need. It's a screw-top bottle.'

'Either way, it looks like the only kind of screw either of us is going to get this evening.' Fran gives me a cheeky wink, and goes off to get the wine.

The rest of the evening rolls by on a glut of sugar and booze and some old cheesy rom-com film we discover on a TV channel we don't usually watch.

'Syd's invited me to a party,' I say, suddenly remembering the chat we'd had outside as the driving lesson came to an end.

'From one married man to another,' Fran mutters, shaking her head.

'Absolutely not! Syd is great, just the sort of man I wish I could bag for myself, but he belongs fairly and squarely to Rosie. No, they're having a bit of a do. Partly to take the place of a christening for the twins, as neither of them has set foot in a church for years and they just want a family gathering without all the religious side of it, and partly to welcome Syd's parents and brother who are coming over from Australia for the first time since the wedding. Rosie did mention it the last time I saw her but they've picked a firm date for it now. He said I could bring a mate if I want to, as I don't have a *proper* plus-one. The cheek of it! I don't suppose you fancy coming, do you? I'm pretty sure Suze will be there. And he's bound to have asked Jack, so I could do with all the moral support I can get.'

'Will he bring his wife, do you think? Jack, I mean.'

'If he's got any sense, he'll be trying to keep the two of us apart, and it's not as if they know her. Jack worked with Syd years ago and they've had the odd beer together since Jack's been back, but that's all.'

'Plus-ones are invited though, remember?'

'True. But I'm sure he can get away without bringing her. He doesn't even have to tell her, does he? Having us both in the same room would be asking for trouble. He's not that stupid. In fact, he may not even go himself.'

'I could come with you, I suppose. I'll have to check my busy diary, of course.' Fran laughs. 'But you never know, I could get lucky. There might be some tasty unattached women there. Apart from you, I mean.'

I reach over and flick at her with a cushion.

'Yes, of course I'll come,' she says. 'Beats sitting in, drooling over Julia Roberts and stuffing myself with yet more chocolates, doesn't it? It's time I got out more. And it's a sort of christening, so if there are no women, at least there'll probably be cake.'

Suze drags it out of me, just as she always does. There is something about being together in the confines of the small staff kitchen that always brings out the latest gossip. It's not unusual to go in there and find someone in tears or whispering their secrets to a friend and clamming up the moment they realise they've been rumbled.

'And you definitely mean it? No more Jack Doherty?' Suze has stopped with the kettle held in mid-air and is peering into my face, looking for clues.

'Apart from at work, yes. I do mean it. One hundred per cent.'

'Thank God for that. It's been wearing me out, trying to keep the two of you apart. But I was only doing it for your own good, you do know that?'

'Yes, Suze. And because you love a bit of scandal and can't bear not knowing every last detail of everyone else's so-called love lives!' She hands me a mug of coffee and we wander back to our desks. 'What's the latest with Sean, by the way? It's time I turned the tables and interrogated you for a change.'

'Well, actually, I do have some news on that front.'

I don't know how I missed it as soon as she held that kettle up in front of my face. There's only a great big sparkling diamond on her finger!

'Oh my God!'

'Yep. He asked me last night. Bended knee, ring in a red velvet box, the works...'

'And you said yes? Are you sure about this?'

'Of course I said yes. He's single, he loves me and, unlike some I could mention, he doesn't have a pregnant wife lurking at home. He's a catch, Carly. And I'm the one who's caught him.'

'And the other-woman incident?'

'All a misunderstanding. It was just some old school friend he happened to have bumped into. A hug hello and a chat about old times. It was nothing. Water under the bridge, and long forgotten.'

'Well, congratulations. Wow! What a surprise.'

'Drinks at lunchtime? Celebrate properly?'

'Of course. Have you set a date yet?'

'Early days, Carly. Give me time to get used to the whole thing first, but I thought maybe next spring? I like the idea of blossom on the trees and a bouquet of white tulips. Bridesmaids in something all pale pink and lacy.'

'So, you have thought about it then?'

'Well, what girl hasn't planned her own wedding by the time we get to our age? I knew exactly the kind of dress I wanted and where I'd like the venue to be long before Sean came along. And now he has, he's the last piece to slot into the puzzle. My fantasy groom finally has a face. Don't tell me you haven't done the same?'

I sort of half nod, because I don't want to admit that I really, really haven't.

Chapter 29

Molly

Rosie's cake is finished. Or maybe that should be cakes? Over several phone conversations, they have decided on two separate tiers, one having a fairly traditional white christening look, but without the religious crosses or church bells that neither Rosie nor Syd feel any need for. There are baby shoes and bottles in alternate pink and blue icing arranged all around the edge and models of the babies themselves sitting together in the middle, with tiny dummies in their mouths. The other cake, in honour of the visitors from Oz, is a riot of brightly coloured sugar-paste balloons against a background of bright blue sky, with streamers laced around little dancing kangaroos and koalas. She has worried that it will look a mess, the two halves, representing the two reasons for the party, having no obvious connection, but they will be separated onto two levels of a chrome stand, a good six inches apart and offset at an angle, so they won't actually touch. The wording piped around the lower board simply says *Welcome*, and that seems to cover both bases. It's unusual and unconventional and fun, and actually pretty cool, even though she says so herself.

Molly has spent the whole of Friday on the finishing

touches, keen to put it all together as near to the party date as possible to make sure the sponge tier is as fresh as it can be, even though the fruit tier for the christening half has been sitting in its tin, soaking up the sherry, for more than a week now.

She stands back and admires her handiwork, the cakes carefully placed separately in two large white boxes, ready to be delivered to the party. She has ordered a taxi for Sunday, knowing how impossible it will be to carry the boxes safely on a bus, and plans to get there early enough to get the cakes set up in pride of place before Rosie's other guests arrive. She wonders if it would be okay to leave a few of her new business cards alongside it, in the hope of getting more orders, or is that a tad too mercenary at a friend's party? She'll take some anyway, and play it by ear.

Jack has been working late again. Once or twice this week he's not been home until she's already in bed. By the time he comes in this evening, the kitchen is tidy again, the work surfaces wiped clean and, apart from the boxes pushed back into a corner, there is nothing to show for all her hard work.

She makes them both a cup of tea and puts her feet up in front of the TV. She feels tired and Jack looks it too but, true to form, the baby isn't. She can feel it moving, a little flicker below her ribs, and lays her hand over it. They say you should talk to it, sing to it, and that it will hear you, but she feels silly doing that in front of Jack, so she just massages gently over the bump.

'I finished that big order today,' she tells Jack as he slumps into the chair opposite. 'For the girl I met at the clinic. And I've got some more gender-reveal cupcakes to make in the morning. I think the business is slowly starting to take off. There's someone from the local paper coming to take photos and talk to me next week, for a feature on the small businesses page.'

'That's great. I'll be able to retire soon then? And buy myself a Lamborghini!'

'Not sure about that. A second-hand hatchback one day, if we're lucky, maybe. With room for a buggy in the boot. But the cakes might bring in enough money to help pay for some of the baby stuff at least.'

'And how is our little avocado today?'

'Keep up, Jack. We went past the avocado stage a while back. She's at least a full-sized mango by now, and on the way to being a sweet potato!'

'She?'

'Well, you know what I mean. He or she. We'll find out in another week, but until then it doesn't feel right to keep calling this little one *it*.'

'She, he, it... I feel like I want to combine them all and start calling it the little shit. But I don't suppose you'd be over keen on that, would you?'

She gives him a stern look but laughs anyway. 'Maybe not.'

'Fancy doing anything tomorrow? While we still can.'

'Not really, if you don't mind. I get so tired, and you've been working your socks off. I think me and this little one could do with a bit of a rest. Can we just spend the day lazing about here? Together? And, by the way, I'm not sure about the *while we still can* comment. Having a baby won't stop us doing things, Jack. Or I hope not anyway. In fact, it would be nice if we can start doing more. London has loads of great places to take a baby to. Parks, that museum with the huge dinosaur, the zoo, the river...'

'It might be a bit soon for museums, Mol. Not really something a baby can appreciate.'

'Okay, you could be right, those can wait a while, but I'm beginning to see the advantages of being in London now. I wasn't sure I could settle here, but the baby will make a difference. I'm quite looking forward to going out and introducing him, her, it, shit or whatever, to some squirrels or monkeys. Or an elephant. Do they still have elephants at the zoo? I must find out. And having made some friends really helps too. We can walk our prams together. Which reminds me, I'll be out for a few hours on Sunday, delivering the cakes, and I've been asked to stay on for the party. Quite a few of the other mums and babies will be there. You're welcome to come.'

'Probably not really my thing, so I'll give it a miss if that's okay. I might pop out myself and grab a drink or two if you're not going to be around. I won't be late though. I'll probably be back before you are, once you and these other mums get chatting.'

'And don't forget I want us to go up and see Mum and Dad soon. I thought maybe straight after the scan next Friday? We'll be able to tell both families at the same time whether we're having a boy or a girl. Although Mum's convinced she already knows.'

'Yeah, okay. Book us onto the train. And I assume we'll be taking some of those new cakes of yours with us? The coloured-middle ones?'

'Of course. I'll have to make them quickly that afternoon, once we get back from the hospital though. Or do it early and make some of each, as I have no idea which colour I'm actually going to need!'

'No inkling? No preference?'

'You know I haven't. Nothing we could do to change things now, even if I did. It's your little swimmers that made that decision months ago.'

'Clever little buggers. If their swimming's anything like mine, we're lucky they made it at all. Probably struggled up your tubes doing doggy paddle!'

'Lucky?' She picks up on that one word, looking for the positivity that has been so clearly lacking lately.

'What?'

'You said we're lucky. Is that how you feel now, Jack? Because I know it was all a shock to you, that you hadn't really planned on being a daddy just yet.' She looks at him, studies his face, still not quite able to figure out how he feels. There is something distant about him, and it worries her. 'But you are happy about it now, aren't you?'

He comes and kneels down next to her chair and pulls her towards him, her face resting into his shoulder, so she can't see his expression. All she has are his words.

'Of course,' he says. 'And, like you said, Mol, nothing we can do to change anything now anyway, is there?'

Chapter 30

Jack

He's been a bloody idiot. He's known it all along, deep down, but now he has to face it, and deal with it. Fancying another woman is not a crime. Half the men he knows are at it. But trying to get that woman into bed, telling her he wants to leave his wife for her... what was he thinking?

Since that evening in Carly's room, he has kept his distance from her, and from Suze, as much as he can at work, and tried his best to show more interest in the baby, because he does love Molly. He really does. Things may have settled into being more homely than wildly passionate lately, but he supposes that happens to all couples in time, and he can't really imagine a life without her.

Carly was right. This is not the same as the first time. Molly is no silly teenager, giggling as she lay on her back in a field with too many alcopops in her belly and her knickers round her ankles, desperate to prove how grown up she is and panicking like mad as soon as it all goes wrong. This baby, the baby of now and not of then, may not have been planned but this is not the same stupid careless mistake. Not this time. Molly wants this baby, so much, and is already in love with it. And with him too, hopefully.

Molly has changed though. She's not such a quiet country mouse anymore. Coming here to London was a huge step for her, but she has done it, for him. And now she is building a life of her own, making new friends, going into business, making plans. She's even going to be interviewed for the local newspaper. He feels proud of her and, somehow, worrying though it is, he knows that she would survive without him if she had to. If he left her now, she would be desperately upset, and angry, and she would never understand, but she would survive. She would go home, to the village and her parents and everyone who loves her, and she would have the baby, a child he would rarely see and would probably never form a proper connection with, because of what he had chosen to do. This baby has given her a new determination, a purpose, something beyond her life with him, something he knows she will cling to above all else.

Maybe that's it. That's why he has been feeling so unsettled, so unsure of what he wants, where his future might lead. It hasn't just been about seeing Carly again, the thrill of starting some illicit secret affair. It's about Molly growing into an independent woman, blooming into impending motherhood. It's about not being needed, being the spare part, the outsider now that Molly has someone else to love. He shakes his head. He hates to admit it, even to himself, but he's jealous. He's jealous of a little unseen mango-sized blob of a person who hasn't even been born yet, who has no name, yet is already pushing him out. He wants unconditional love, to be wanted, needed, to be the centre of someone else's world. Carly's world? Molly's world? Does it even matter which, especially now he realises, suddenly, that he is not?

He has been on some crazy seesaw these last few weeks,

rocking backwards and forwards between two women, wanting them both. A classic wanting-his-cake-and-eating-it situation, which is pretty ironic considering the dominance of cakes in Molly's life and in their own kitchen lately. Forget special boy or girl centres. He has thought it before, but she might as well fill her little cupcake thingies with some kind of Carly versus Molly stuff. Bite into one at random and have the decision made, like flipping a coin. It's never that easy though, is it? And now the decision has been made for him. Carly has stepped away, told him to forget about her, to go back to Molly. Not that he actually ever left her. In his head, in his fantasies, in some future la-la land that was never going to be maybe, but Molly need never know about that. Sweet, dependable, trusting Molly need never know.

Jack sits in a noisy pub, half watching the TV screen, which is semi-obscured by a group of teenagers, standing in a circle, most of them looking barely old enough to be in here, let alone downing pints. Having promised Molly a lazy Saturday at home together, he has only popped out for a magazine she wants and a loaf of fresh bread, but it has started to rain, and he doesn't have a coat with him. Any excuse! He has come across Syd by chance, taking a quick breather and an opportunity to use the Gents between driving lessons. Saturdays are his busiest day and there's no time to nip home for lunch.

Jack laughs at Syd as he finishes his pint of lemonade, taking the slice of lemon out and sucking at it until the sourness makes his eyes water.

'More than my life and job's worth to get caught drinking and driving,' Syd says, totally unembarrassed, dropping the nibbled rind onto his empty sandwich plate. 'Not that I'd ever do it. It's a dangerous game, and I have a wife and kids to think of now. They need me in one piece. So, you can stop the sniping about my choice of liquid refreshment. There's nothing wrong with lemonade, I can tell you. Perhaps you asking the barman to stick a paper umbrella in it was a step too far, but laying off the booze and being responsible for a change is no laughing matter. You should try it sometime.'

Jack makes a mock salute. 'Yes, boss. But yeah, you're right. I can't go breathing beer fumes all over the baby when it comes, can I?'

'No news about what you're having?'

'Scan's next week. Friday.'

'And you'll be there?'

'Hope so. I'm pretty busy at work, but I'm sure I can get away early. It's not until mid-afternoon.'

'Well, make sure you get a picture. Everyone'll be drooling over it, trying to work out who it looks like, whether it's smiling or waving its fists about, and which way up it is!'

'I just want to see if it's got a willy or not. This "what is it?" thing has gone on long enough now. If it has to be some kind of fruit or veg, I'm hoping for a cucumber!'

'No idea what that even means, but it sounds vaguely phallic, so I'm guessing you want a boy. Well, what man doesn't?'

'I haven't actually said that out loud yet, but yeah. A boy would be good. Only one thing wrong with it though. It would mean having to admit the mother-in-law has been right all along.'

'The women are always right, Jack. Haven't you figured that out yet? If you want an easy life, the women are always right! And my mum's over here now, so I've got yet another woman telling me what to do. I'm just glad we don't have the room and they're all shored up in a hotel! Don't forget the welcome party tomorrow, by the way, if you can make it. I'd like you to meet the folks, especially my brother, Daz. I get the impression he's thinking of staying on for a while if he can. There's only just over a year between us but he always did follow me around, copying whatever I did. My little shadow, although not so little these days. He's a good six inches taller than me and he's got muscles like Popeye! Living in the UK and getting a job over here is the logical next step for him, while he's still single and fancy free, and now I've been the advance guard and shown it's possible! I can't see Mum being very happy about losing both of us, but he needs to spread his wings a bit, and she'll always have Victoria.'

'Your sister?'

'Yeah. Married with a six-year-old. Which is why she's not come with them. A kid in school. A husband not able to get away from work for long enough. And the cost. The air fares aren't cheap. No, our Vic's not likely to be emigrating anytime soon. Mum can be confident of hanging on to one of the brood!'

After Syd dashes away for his next lesson, which Jack is pleased to discover is not with Carly, he sits alone for a while, savouring his beer. It hasn't really occurred to him before but he misses his own brother. They might be like chalk and cheese but he's always been there, from occupying the bed on the other side of their childhood room to standing beside him as his best man on the day he got married. He's quite looking forward to seeing him, and all the family, when they go home next weekend. It's been too long.

He peers out of the frosted glass behind him and is fairly sure the rain is easing off. He picks up Syd's discarded pink paper umbrella, shakes the liquid off its cocktail-stick handle, folds it down carefully and slips it into his pocket. It will give Molly a laugh when he brandishes it later and tells her it was the only one he had with him and it didn't quite manage to keep the rain off.

He hesitates at the door, looking both ways, before heading for the little row of shops with the baker's right slap in the middle. It's a small family-run place, somewhere he had once thought Molly might find herself a job, or a few hours' casual work at least. But she has bigger ideas these days, and a bigger belly, and he can no longer imagine her there behind the counter, in a fitted green overall, on her feet all day, pushing someone else's cakes into paper bags.

He can smell the bread already. It entices him in, and makes him buy far more than they need, but he can never resist a good thing. He almost forgets the magazine Molly has asked him to find, but doubles back to the newsagents before he's got as far as the corner. They have flowers outside too. He pushes the thought of Carly and the bouquet, if you could call it that, that he'd bought her that night when he'd gone to her flat, from his mind. It's ages since he's bought Molly flowers. He knows what she will say, making a joke about what he has to feel guilty or sorry about. But she will love them anyway, and appreciate the gesture, even if the choice is somewhat limited and they come without all the fancy cellophane and ribbons.

He picks out the biggest and best-looking bunch. He has no idea what they are, except that they are pink and white and pretty. Will she read something into that? That he's decided they're having a girl? That that's what he's hoping for? They have nothing in blue, so he can't even buy a bunch of each. But colour-coded flowers could be the way to go when they tell his parents next week. Molly will want to do it with cake, but he has to have some say, doesn't he? And his mum's always on some kind of diet. She will prefer flowers to cake, although a pile of cupcakes, whatever colour their middles might be, will no doubt keep his dad happy.

He realises that he's starting to look forward to telling them, to sharing the excitement. Because, fired up with Syd's enthusiasm for the joys and responsibilities of fatherhood, he knows deep down that it is exciting, and a special privilege, bringing a new life into the world.

Chapter 31

Carly

I go in through Mum's back door, like I always do on a Saturday, but there's no one sitting in the kitchen. I'm into the hall before I hear muffled voices coming from behind the half-open dining-room door. I guess that Anthony is here again. It will be the first time I've seen him since Mum told me about Pauline, and I'm not quite sure how to play it. Saying something straight away, offering sympathy, could feel very awkward and out of place, but not saying anything looks like I don't care. As it turns out, the choice is taken out of my hands.

'Carly,' Mum says, standing up as I enter the room. Anthony is sitting with his back to the door, leaning forwards, elbows on the old wooden dining table, his head in his hands. 'There's been a bit of bad news.'

'Oh. Do you want me to leave?'

'No, no, come in, love, please. Anthony's going in a minute anyway. Pauline's taken a turn for the worse. She's in the hospital, and he has to get back there.'

He turns to face me now. 'Hello, Carly. Sorry to spoil your Saturday. The last thing you want to see is me sitting here blubbing.'

'No, really, don't be silly. I'm so sorry. Is there anything I can do?' Stupid question, I know, but it's what we're conditioned to say, isn't it?

'Thank you. Nothing any of us can do, I'm afraid. Even me. Except just be there for her. I had to pop home for a few bits. Change of clothes, for me as well as her. A few toiletries, her favourite perfume. If this is it... well, I'd like her to be looking her best. It's how she'd like to go. Clean nightie, her hair nicely brushed...' He lowers his face again, eyes closed, then takes a deep breath and stands up. Mum reaches out a hand to steady him.

'I could come with you. For moral support?' she says.

'Thank you, Joyce, but no. We went into this thing together, Pauline and I, the two of us against the world, and we'll end it the same way. But I really do need to get back to her now. I just felt I should tell you what's happening, in case I disappear for a while. You've been my rock these last few weeks, and I want you to know how much I appreciate that.'

Mum throws her arms around him and gives him a squeeze. 'My pleasure, love. And do let me know, won't you? If anything happens, if you need anything, anytime, day or night. I can't bear to think of you all on your own. At least when I lost my George, I had Carly and Sam to help me. But I do know what it's like, so call me, please. I mean it.'

She lets him go and he nods. I move aside to let them through into the hall, listen to the opening and closing of the front door, and wait until Mum comes back in. She looks very tired and pale.

'Memories of Dad?' I ask her, thinking back to his last night when we all waited for the inevitable.

'They never leave me, but yes, especially now. It's never easy, is it? Saying goodbye?' She slumps into a chair and I go and put the kettle on. A cup of strong tea has always been her go-to comfort blanket.

'Sam at football?' I place the tea in front of her and tip some Rich Teas – the only biscuits I could find – onto a plate.

'Where else?'

'I'll stay a while today then. Until he's back. Never mind Anthony, I don't like to think of you being on your own either.'

'I'll be okay, Carly. I'm made of stern stuff, you know. And it's not as if I ever met the girl.'

'Sad though. What's happened to her? If you don't mind me asking.'

'Pneumonia, again. There's only so much a body can take. It's awful to say it, but I do wonder if it will end up being a happy release, for both of them. An end to all the years of pain and stress, and her slowly deteriorating like that. Her going... well, it will give him a chance of getting some sort of real life back, while he's young enough to enjoy it.'

'And there's really nothing going on between you two? No hint of a future romance brewing away?'

She leans across the table and gives me a pat on the wrist. 'No. I've already told you that. It was a friendship that served us both well, but to be honest I don't think he's going to need me long-term. Once he's back at work, able to mix with people his own age, no longer in need of a shoulder to cry on...'

'I'm sure you mean more to him than that.'

'Maybe, but once she's gone, which sounds imminent I'm sorry to say, he's going to have a lot to deal with for a while, and after that I hope he can rebuild his life and move on. He won't want an old biddy like me clinging to his shirt-tails then, will he?'

'I guess we all have to let go sometimes and move on, don't we?'

She gazes at my face. 'Something you're not telling me, Carly?'

'Nothing specific. Just coming to the conclusion that you may have been right all along.'

She laughs, almost spitting a mouthful of tea all over her lap. 'Did I just hear you say I was right? That has to be a first!'

'Well, with all the pearls of wisdom you've dished out over the last thirty-odd years, you had to strike lucky eventually.'

'And which particular pearl has struck home?'

'The settling down one. The one that says I don't want to end up on my own like poor old Miss Haversham, wallowing in a wedding that never was, and it's time I found myself a nice bloke who isn't a total dick.'

'I'm not sure I ever used those exact words, but yes, I do recall once or twice saying something along those general lines.'

'Once or twice?' It's my turn to splutter. 'You've been drumming it into me ever since puberty!'

'Glad to know it's finally sunk in then. But I have to wonder, why now? I thought the string of no-hopers was never going to end.'

'One no-hoper too many, that's why. The last in a very long line fell at the final hurdle and he's not going to get back up again.'

'You're talking in riddles. You do know that, don't you?'

'Sorry, Mum. Just that this one was different from all the others, and I really thought I could love him and live happily ever after, but I can't, and I won't. So that's that. End of.'

'Ah, I see.'

'Do you?'

'Married man, by any chance?'

'How did you know?'

'All those pearls of wisdom have to come from somewhere, you know. Call it experience. Or a mother's intuition.'

'Anyway, I didn't... you know. I didn't allow it to go too far. Only in my stupid head. So now, I'm going to do what you told me to do all along. Find a nice, steady, faithful, and most of all available man and try to find what you and Dad had.'

'You don't just find that, Carly. It's not an instant thing, no matter what you might hear about all that love at first sight nonsense. You have to build it, work on it, make it what you want it to be. Yes, it helps to have the right man to do it with, but love really doesn't grow on trees. Once you have it, though, there's nothing else quite like it. I'd rather have comfortable and trusting over all the angst and fireworks exploding passion any day.'

I remember something Jack said a while back, about his life with Molly being comfortable and easy until I came along. He made it sound dull, lacking in some way, but suddenly it sounds very much like love, even if neither he nor I had realised it.

'A man you can share all your hopes and dreams with,' Mum goes on, oblivious to my brief lapse in concentration. 'To live with side by side every day, faults and problems and all. That's real love, Carly. What your father and I had. What Anthony has with his Pauline. And then, one day, all too soon, it's gone, snatched away, and your life is never the same again.'

'Poor Anthony.' I reach for her hand and feel it shaking. 'And poor you.'

I stay for the afternoon, watching some TV and reading *Emma* for what must be at least the fourth or fifth time, while Mum potters about with a duster and plumps cushions that absolutely don't need to be plumped. I guess she's just keeping busy, finding things to do to keep her mind off whatever's going on at the hospital. We realise neither of us has eaten since breakfast and make up a quick late lunch, just sandwiches and a piece of cake, and I finally persuade her to sit down and watch a film with me until Sam comes back. I don't like the idea of leaving her on her own and, to be honest, I don't have anywhere else to be.

'What shall we plump for?' she says, rummaging through her shelf of old charity shop DVDs, and I laugh to myself at her use of the 'plump' word as visions of her perfectly placed chubby cushions jump into my head. '*Pretty Woman?*'

It's the film she always picks, mainly because she has a not-so-secret crush on Richard Gere. And I'm a sucker for a romance, especially an unconventional one. Obviously.

'Good choice. Got any popcorn?'

'Not the sort of snack I tend to have stashed away in the cupboard, but I can probably run to a cheapo supermarket choc ice in the interval.'

We laugh, and the spectre of a dying Pauline temporarily leaves the room.

Chapter 32

Molly

Molly hasn't been to a party for ages. She takes the time to do her hair nicely, pulling it up and back and securing it in place with a glittery clip shaped like a butterfly, chooses earrings that are not too big and flashy but still catch the light as she moves. It's October and sunshine is far from guaranteed so she settles on a warm longer-length dress with a daisy pattern that she can still – just – get into without having to resort to buying something new from the maternity range. It's an afternoon party, and there will be a lot of kids there, so there doesn't seem a need to go for high heels or tons of make-up. She slips on some flat shoes and a cardigan and bundles the bare necessities into a huge shoulder bag, along with the chrome cake stand which only just fits if she pushes it in sideways, then carefully picks up the cake boxes.

'Sure you don't fancy coming with me? To meet a few new people? Carry me home if I get legless?' She laughs as he shakes his head. 'See you later then. Be good!'

'Always,' he says, opening the door, taking the boxes from her hands and carrying them down to the taxi for her. She watches him from the car window, waving her off from the pavement, as the taxi takes her around the corner and she can no longer see him. It would have been nice to go together but she can understand why he's reluctant. Her new-found independence and her expanding circle of friends are liberating, and it's exciting to see her business start to grow, but pregnancy is making her feel tired and inexplicably weepy lately, and she looks forward to getting back home. There's nothing quite like the comfort of familiar arms to fall back into before bed.

Rosie's house is small, but warm and welcoming. She has hung streamers and balloons around the living room, and the table, covered in a crisp white cloth, is already laden with plates of food. The smells of warm sausage rolls and something cheesy mingle and fill the air.

'I've left space for you,' Rosie says, pointing to an area in the centre of the spread. 'For the *pièce de résistance!*' She is lifting the lid from the first box and peering in, anxious to get a glimpse of the cakes. 'Ooh, this is great,' she says, her voice as excited as a child's. 'Come on, let's get it all out and set up before anyone else gets here. And before those little horrors of mine wake up and start yelling for milk. I dare not get changed until they've had their feed or I'll be greeting the guests with stains all down my front!'

'When are people due to arrive?'

'Well, my husband's just gone to pick up his parents and his brother from their hotel. It's only right they get here first, as guests of honour. Everybody else... well, anytime from three o'clock. I don't expect anyone to stay particularly late. It'll be getting dark by six, and having a small house means open doors and an overspill into the garden, so it will be getting chilly too. And I want it to be a party for the babies, not some boozy late-night knees-up! Although there will be wine, of course. And beer. Go on, have a seat and I'll make you a coffee or something. I'm assuming you're not into wine at the moment?'

'Better not.' Molly touches her tummy. 'Tempting though it is!'

'Won't be long until you can have a sneaky glass again. I'm breastfeeding but the odd one doesn't seem to hurt.' She raises her voice as she disappears out of the door. 'And I need it sometimes, believe me!'

Molly sits back on a squashy sofa and slips her shoes off. Her feet and ankles are feeling a bit swollen and she's pretty sure Rosie isn't going to mind. That's the beauty of other mums. They understand.

She can hear the kettle starting to boil in the kitchen just as one of the twins wakes up and starts grizzling upstairs, the sound amplified through the baby monitor beside her.

'Can I help?' she says, padding barefoot to the doorway and finding Rosie in the small kitchen, spooning coffee grains into cups. 'I could make the coffee, or get the baby for you.'

'Thanks, Molly. Instant okay for you?'

Molly nods. 'Of course.'

'It's not easy, this trying to be in two places at once lark! That's Jamie you can hear, and Becca won't be far behind. Honestly, I need the arms of an octopus sometimes. Be grateful you're only expecting one. But the coffee's done now, so if you don't mind taking them through, I'll pop up for his lordship.'

Like a well-oiled machine, Rosie soon has both babies fed, changed and ready to party, and leaves them lying quietly in their baskets while she goes up to get herself ready.

The front door opens and Molly hears voices in the hall. The family are here already, and she feels a sudden nervousness as they pile into the room, carrying wrapped gifts and champagne and an enormous bouquet of flowers.

'Ah, hello. You must be our cake lady. Rosie said you'd be here early. I'm Syd, the other half!'

'Molly.'

There follows a round of introductions and handshakes and a lot of cooing over the cakes, in pride of place on the table. Syd's mother makes a beeline for the babies, hovering for a moment as she tries to decide which one to pick up and cuddle first. His dad flops into an armchair, the flowers resting on his belly while he waits for Rosie to appear so he can hand them over, and the brother, whose name Molly has already temporarily forgotten, follows Syd to the kitchen in search of a beer.

Molly is glad when Rosie comes running down the stairs, wearing a lovely blue-and-silver top and a pair of loose trousers, with not a hint of a milk stain in sight. 'Ah, Molly, you've met everyone. That's good.' She looks at her watch. 'We'll be deluged soon, just you see. A houseful, and a garden full too, probably, but at least the weather's good. I bet the girls from the group get here first. Eager for a bit of grown-up company and some free food!' She kisses her parents-in-law, takes the bouquet to the kitchen to find a vase and comes back with Syd and his brother in tow, cans of beer in their hands. 'Music please, Sydney,' she says, grabbing her husband by his free hand and twirling herself around. 'Nothing too loud or wall-shaking though. The last thing I need today is crying babies.'

All the girls from the twins and triplets club have come, along with their hordes of lookalike children, but not a single partner. 'Oh, my Dave would hate it,' Jo says, rocking her twin girls in their double buggy as her five-year-old son, Toby, runs around the garden chasing bubbles. 'This is his chance to get a couple of hours' peace, or a snooze in front of the telly with a beer in his hand. Believe me, where there are this many kids all together in one place, you won't find many dads hanging about. Not willingly anyway.' She laughs and takes a long swig from her can of alcohol-free lager. 'Mmm, if I close my eyes, I can almost convince myself this is the real thing!' she says, grabbing Toby just as he is about to whizz past and straight into someone carrying a tray of glasses.

'At least you've got a partner,' Miranda moans. 'I'm having to manage these two terrors on my own.' Her boys are just at the starting to walk stage now, and are tumbling about on the grass, giggling over a ball.

'Your choice, sweetie. What did you expect when you did your thing with the turkey baster? Kitchen utensils aren't known for their parenting skills, are they?'

'It was not a turkey baster,' Miranda replies, indignantly. 'I went to a proper clinic, Jo, as you well know. Donors are checked and regulated and everything. I just hadn't expected to end up with the two for the price of one deal.'

'You and me both! Who'd have twins by choice, eh? Still, count yourself lucky it wasn't three.' Jo looks across at Berni, the only TTC member with triplets, and sighs with relief. 'That woman's a bloody marvel. I mean, we were born with two boobs for a reason, weren't we? Where the hell are you meant to put baby number three? Must be a continual queueing system. One off, one on, one waiting in the wings. Like juggling three bean bags with only two hands.'

Molly leans back in a folding garden chair and closes her eyes for a moment, her hand across her tummy. One baby is just fine. Quite enough. She has no idea how any of these women cope with more.

'Hey, Molly. Wakey-wakey!' Rosie is at her side now, with a couple of newcomers in tow.

'I wasn't asleep!'

'Of course not. Just resting your eyes, I know. My Syd says that all the time. Anyway, I've brought some friends over to meet you all.' Molly looks up at the rather round red-faced woman with big frizzy red hair who is standing beside Rosie, blocking out what there is of the sun. 'This is Fran, a possible future client for you, Molly, as she's a great lover of cake!'

'Cheek!' Fran nudges her, but seems to take it in good part.

'And this is Carly, best friend of many years standing. Carly and Fran share a flat. The other member of the gang is Fran's big sister, Suze.' She snorts. 'Well, not bigger than our Frannie in the size sense, obviously, just age-wise. I have no idea where she's just disappeared to. I seem to have lost her on the way through, but I'm sure she'll catch us up later. She's just got engaged so she's probably dragged the poor bloke into the understairs cupboard or something! Now, girls, meet Molly, who made the cakes for me. And these are some of the mums I've met at the twins club. Or should I say other gluttons for punishment!' Everybody laughs, although Fran is not looking quite so happy now. One dig too many about her weight maybe?

'Excuse me a minute, all of you. Feel free to introduce yourselves,' Rosie says, seemingly unaware of any discomfort coming from Fran's direction. 'That sounds like the doorbell again. More guests. I don't know where I'm going to put them all. At least the clocks haven't gone back yet or it would be getting dark before we know it. And we'd better hope it doesn't rain, cos it'll be a hell of a squeeze if everyone ends up indoors!'

The two newcomers pull up chairs and settle down beside Molly, each already carrying a glass of wine. The smaller one, Carly, puts her hands around her drink protectively as Toby hurtles past again, clutching a mangled sausage roll, and almost knocks it out of her grasp. 'Kids, eh? Who'd have them?' she huffs, seemingly oblivious to the fact that Molly is actually having one, but Molly doesn't put her straight.

'So, you made those fab-looking cakes in there?' Fran says, positively drooling at the very thought.

'I did, yeah.'

'A great idea, the two halves being so different. Something for everyone, and not your traditional christening cake either. Our Rosie's never been the religious type. I just wish they'd hurry up and cut the damn things, so we can all have a piece. It's bloody torture, all this look-but-don't-touch stuff!'

Molly laughs. 'I hope they live up to expectations.'

'I find cake usually does, even if men may not.' Jo has wedged a squirming Toby between her knees now and is bribing him to sit still with yet more food, most of it sugar-coated, piled high on a paper plate. 'Excuse my cynicism, but they're only really good for one thing, aren't they? Men, I mean.'

'What? Putting up shelves?' Miranda has finally settled her two in a sleepy heap on a blanket, and collapses on the grass beside the others. She pulls what looks like a hand-knitted cardigan together at the front and starts doing up the buttons. 'I'd just as soon have a go myself.'

'Yeah, we all know you don't need a man. For anything!' Jo makes a rude gesture that even Miranda can't help but laugh at. 'Sisters are doing it for themselves! With a bit of help from the turkey baster.'

'All right, Jo. Joke over now, okay? Anyone would think you were on the booze. Oh, look.' Miranda takes the can from Jo's hand. 'This one's the real thing. A strong one too. Not an alco-free at all. You've mixed the lagers up. Accidentally on purpose, I wouldn't be surprised. And we all know, the more you drink, the looser your lips get.'

Jo bursts out laughing. 'I reckon we've all got pretty loose lips after giving birth to this lot!' She waves her arms around to indicate the gaggle of assorted children surrounding them. 'No wonder Rosie's put us down here at the bottom of the garden, away from all the normal well-behaved people. Like we're a different species. Still, you'll be next to join us, Molly. Believe me, your life, and your nether regions, will never be the same again. Better start those tightening exercises now, before it's too late!'

Some of the other mums laugh, but Miranda has been quiet ever since the quip about doing it for herself. They all know Jo wasn't talking about shelves. Molly wonders if Jo has gone too far, discussing what must be a pretty private thing for Miranda with anyone who'll listen. She can't imagine what would lead a woman to go to those lengths. Having babies without a partner. Using donor sperm. It's not as if Miranda is that old, grabbing at a last chance before her fertility levels plummet. But it's none of her business. Or theirs. Somebody really needs to change the subject.

She turns towards the women sitting beside her. Time to start a new conversation. 'So...' she begins, intending to ask them about their jobs or their shoes or anything unrelated to baby-making, but Carly is staring at her in a very strange way, as if she's suddenly seen a ghost or something, and Fran is staring at Miranda, as if... well, as if she fancies the pants off her. And it looks pretty much like the attraction could be mutual. Ah, maybe that explains the lack of a partner in Miranda's life. A male one, anyway...

'Oh no, Toby!' Jo's strident voice rings out as her son suddenly slumps forward, lets out a strangled gulp and, without anywhere near enough warning, is promptly sick all over her lap. There is a frantic scrabble among all the mums as they delve into changing bags looking for cloths and wipes.

As Molly turns her head away, the sweet sickly smell making her stomach churn in sympathy, Carly stands up, abruptly, making her chair totter. 'Are you okay?' Fran says, her gaze pulled abruptly away from Miranda. She reaches out a hand, but Carly shakes her off and walks back into the house, without saying a word, her face as white as a sheet.

'Sorry,' Fran says. 'Not sure what that was about. She's usually the life and soul of the party. And a bit of vomit's never bothered her before. Probably needs the loo, or starting a period or something. Now, when are they going to let us at those wonderful cakes? Tell me, Molly, are they fruit or sponge?'

Chapter 33

Carly

I can't believe it. It's her. It has to be. A Molly who makes cakes. I didn't put two and two together at first. Well, why would I? She's the last person I expected to find lolling in my best friend's garden. But as soon as someone said she was pregnant, it all fell into place. There just can't be that many cake-making Mollys who also happen to be pregnant, can there? That would be taking coincidence a step too far. But why her? And why here? I had no idea that she and Rosie had ever met.

I do the only thing I can do right now, and that's escape. If I stay there looking at her any longer, young Toby might not be the only one being sick on the grass. I rush back into the house, hurtle up the stairs and into the bathroom, shoving the door shut and slipping the bolt across. Thank God nobody else was in need of a pee or I'd have been left hanging about on the landing, scared stiff that someone I know might see me and I'd have to make up some sort of explanation. Because I know I must look like shit. I certainly feel it. Blame it on a dodgy sausage roll? Not very kind to the chef, who happens to be Rosie and is right now downstairs totally unaware of having brought the viper into the nest. That's not very fair either, actually. I could just as well cast

myself as the viper. She is Jack's wife, after all, while I'm just…
well, what exactly am I? I take a deep breath and try to stay
calm. I'm sure Molly is a very nice girl. It's just that she's the last
person I ever wanted to meet face to face.

And, as for social media, I haven't dared go there. If I were
to find her Facebook page, I might stumble across their wedding
photos or something equally horrifying. While I've avoided her,
both virtually and in real life, I've been able to tell myself she
doesn't really exist. But she does, and she's here, and I have no
idea what to do, except wait for my breathing to calm down and
my shocked face to return to something like normal, and get the
hell out of here. Fast. Except my bag's still out there, next to my
abandoned chair, in the garden. Suze. I need Suze. She's the
only one who will understand, the only one I can rely on to help
me, rescue my bag and think up some excuse for my sudden
departure. Where the hell is she?

I have a pee while I'm here, even though I don't really need
one. Then I slosh a few handfuls of warm water over my face
and look in the mirror. I could just about pass as okay, if nobody
looks too closely.

I slide the bolt and open the door just a crack. I'm lucky.
There's no one hovering. Suze. Where can she be? The last I
saw of her was when she arrived, just after Fran and me, with
her new fiancé in tow, and they came up here to find a place to
put their coats. They can't still be in Rosie's bedroom, surely?

The giggle gives her away. She is in there, the dirty mare!

Forget Suze's modesty, if she even has any these days. It's
not even four in the afternoon yet, for heaven's sake, and a
christening party as well. There's appropriate and there's
downright flooze, if that's even a word. I fling open the bedroom
door, half expecting to see a pair of naked buttocks bobbing
about on the bed, but she's over by the window, messing about
with a safety pin and squinting at a tiny button that seems to

have come off her dress, unfortunately right at boob level, so there's a fair amount of lacy balconette bra on show. Sean is sitting on the edge of the pile of coats, looking bored and moaning about needing a drink, although he is definitely having a good look at her cleavage while he waits.

'Carls. Thank the lord! Come and give us a hand. You're so much better at this stuff than I am. Every time I try to stick the pin into this fabric, I stab myself. I know I shouldn't laugh, but there are times when I wish I wasn't quite so well-endowed. I'm starting to look like an overstuffed pin cushion!'

'Never mind that. You'll never guess who's here. Out in the garden.'

'No, I probably won't, as it could be anybody from Jeremy Clarkson to Genghis Khan. You're gonna have to give me a clue.' She hands me the pin and I do my best to slot it through both halves of her dress front and close it together. 'There. Done. Now can I have your attention, please? This is a matter of life and death.'

'Is it? Ooh, now I'm interested. And we've only been here ten minutes!' She casts a glance in Sean's direction. 'Go on,' she says, as if she's giving permission for a child to leave the table. 'You can go and get that drink now. And I'll have a white wine while you're at it.'

As soon as he's gone, I grab her by the shoulders to make sure she's looking at me properly. 'It's her.'

'Who's *her*? Carly, what are you going on about?'

'Her. Molly. Jack's wife. She's here. Sitting outside, all happy and pregnant, surrounded by all these mothers and babies, like butter wouldn't melt. Like she belongs here. At Rosie's party, for God's sake. *Our* Rosie.' I grab Suze's hand and pull her to the window, making sure I don't disturb the net curtain, our faces close together as I point. 'Look, that's her, over by the rose bush. The one sitting next to Fran. In the flowery dress. It only turns out she made the damn christening cake. What are the chances of that?'

'Right. I see.'

'And there's my bag, see? I've only gone and left it out there. How am I meant to get that back now?'

Suze pulls me back from the window. 'You walk out there and pick it up. Easy as that. But, Carly, why exactly does any of this matter? It's not like she knows who you are. Or like anything has actually happened between you and Jack, who is *her* husband by the way, so I'm not sure why you're being all high and mighty. Blimey, Carls, if she had any inkling, it should be her mad at seeing you here, not the other way round. She doesn't, does she? Know about you, I mean?'

'God, I hope not.'

'Then calm down. Take a breath. There must be enough people here to lose yourself in, to keep your distance. Nobody says you have to be best buddies, or even talk to her if you don't want to. You don't even have to eat any of the cake if you're worried it might choke you!'

'Oh, ha, ha. Make a joke, why don't you? Look, I think I should go home. I just don't feel right about us both being here. I don't feel... comfortable. You can go outside and get my bag, tell Rosie I'm not feeling well or something, and I'll just slip quietly away, okay?'

'Or you can be a grown-up about it and stay. Rosie's been your closest friend for years. Although I like to think I come a close second! It's not very nice to lie to her, is it? Or to not be here to celebrate the babies, or to meet the long-lost Aussie family? I hear Syd's brother, Daz, is a bit of all right. And why should I do your dirty work and tell a pack of fibs anyway, just because you're being a total coward? I'm sure this Molly is a perfectly normal person. Nice. Friendly. Well, she must be for Jack to have married her. Let it go, Carls. Let it go...' She twirls around, bursting into song, the words of the *Frozen* hit ringing out across the room, and then she laughs out loud, and takes a little bow. I wonder if she's had a drink or two already before she even got here. 'There is no you and Jack, remember? Whatever you might have hoped for never happened, did it? Nothing to feel guilty about.'

'Guilty? Who said anything about me feeling guilty?'

'Well, if you ask me, guilt is the only possible explanation. I mean, you can't actually hate her, can you? You don't know her. You've never met. And she's certainly not someone to be scared of. She knows nothing, so she's not coming after you with a meat cleaver, or a divorce petition. So, guilt's all it can be. You can't face the poor woman because of something you only ever did, or thought about doing, in your own head.'

I sit down on the bed, somebody's coat zip pushing into the back of my leg, and close my eyes. I think back to that moment, in my room, when we so almost did a hell of a lot more than something that was only happening in my head. There were clothes coming off, bare flesh, nipples, tongues... But we stopped, didn't we? So maybe Suze is right. I'm blowing this up out of all proportion.

'It all sounds mad to me,' she goes on, oblivious to what I'm thinking, remembering. 'A drunken kiss years ago, that's all it was. We've all been there, got a bit swept up in the moment. And he wasn't even married then, was he? No matter how bloody good it was, it's done. Get over it. Like he did, when he married Molly and not you. And you had your chance to go for it properly and you bottled it. Both of you did. Couldn't go through with it. Or so you say?' She looks at me enquiringly, checking I've told her the truth. I nod. 'That surely tells you all you need to know then, doesn't it? It's never going to happen. Not now, not ever. Time to find yourself a bloke of your own. An available, unmarried bloke, not some fantasy lover you've never even screwed. And no time like the present. There's one downstairs, right this minute, all the way from down under. No baggage, except his rucksack or swag bag or whatever Australians call it. So, let's go track him down, say hello, and you can have a dance or something, prove you've still got it... and then you can go out there and rescue your own handbag. With your head held high.'

'Okay.' I don't know if I really mean it or if it's simply the only option. There's nothing to lose. I stand up and pull my dress straight. 'Do I look all right? Make-up not smudged or anything?'

'You look gorgeous, as always. And this Molly probably won't stay long anyway. It's not as if she's a real friend, or known Rosie for years, like us. She's only here because she made the cake. It's like inviting the vicar along to the party after a church do. They come to be polite, have one sherry and leave.'

'Let's hope you're right.'

'I'm always right. Well, about most things, most of the time. Ready?'

'As I'll ever be.' Am I? Really? God knows.

We're halfway down the stairs when the bell rings. The glass is frosted so he's a bit blurry, but I still know it's him. I would recognise him anywhere. His height, his hair, the way he stands, everything...

'Jack!' I squeal, grabbing Suze by the hand and dragging her back up the stairs again, my heart pounding, and just making it to the safety of the landing as Rosie opens the front door.

Chapter 34

Jack

Jack rings the bell and waits for someone to answer. He can hear the sounds of the party from out in the street. Not a rocking the rafters sort of sound, but a happy sort of hubbub, a mixture of laughter and chat coming from an open window, with Abba singing away in the background, and the squealing of kids from somewhere out at the back. He won't stay long, just long enough to show willing. Syd was a good mate once, and it will be nice to see Rosie again and to meet the elusive brother from Oz he's heard so much about. But he wants to be home before Molly gets back, especially as he hasn't even told her where he's going. Why hasn't he? It's not as though there's any need for secrecy. Even if Carly does just happen to be here, they will have met by chance, won't they? Neither of them has planned it. They just happen to know the same people.

The door opens and Rosie is standing there, looking just the same as when he last set eyes on her, more than five years ago. A bit chubbier in the face maybe, but just as young and pretty as ever, and nothing to mark her out as the mother of two he now knows her to be. Syd's a lucky man.

'Jack! Wow, it's so good to see you. Come on in.' She beckons him over the step, but then changes her mind and throws her arms around him instead, enveloping him in a big hug before finally closing the door and taking him by the hand, leading him along the hall and into a room packed with people. 'Syd said you were back, but it's lovely to actually see you. And married now!'

'Yep. And you two are parents already. Makes us all sound old, doesn't it?'

'Speak for yourself. Getting married and having babies is the best thing I ever did. Best thing anyone can ever do! Keeps you young. Or on your toes anyway. Your turn next?'

'It is. Didn't Syd tell you? First one due in March.'

'No, he didn't!' She hugs him again. 'You men are useless when it comes to gossip. I had no idea. Congratulations!'

Syd is standing half in and half out of the kitchen, as if hedging his bets as to which group of guests he should be paying attention to. The older family members and neighbours, sitting on armchairs with cups of tea and trying to have a conversation above the din, one of the women, who must surely be Syd's mum, cooing over the two babies she is holding in the crooks of both suntanned arms, or the men propping up the draining board with cans in their hands, talking rubbish about football and the state of the world?

'Jack, my man!' He lurches forward to shake Jack's hand, not letting go of it as he steers him into the kitchen. 'Beer?'

Rosie smiles indulgently and steps away, clearly knowing when she's been beaten. 'See you later then, Jack. I'll leave you with Syd. Food's in here, when you're ready. I'm going out into the garden for a while.'

Jack opens a can, nods a hello to his fellow drinkers and finds a space by the washing machine. Why do the men always hover in the kitchen at parties? It feels like some unwritten rule, steering clear of female conversation, avoiding being expected to dance. There's a certain safety and solidarity in sticking to male company.

Syd's brother, Daz, is dominating the conversation, his Australian accent and suntanned skin making him stand out from the crowd as he answers questions about crocodiles and spiders and whether he's ever been to Ayers Rock. Jack smiles to himself, imagining what Molly might ask if she were here. The only things she would want to know were if he'd ever visited the Ramsay Street set from *Neighbours* or met Kylie Minogue. Perhaps he should ask, just so he had some anecdote to take home to her.

After a while he chucks his empty beer can into the bin, squeezes back through the kitchen, clapping Syd on the shoulder as he passes, and steps into the living room. His stomach is rumbling and Rosie had mentioned food.

The first thing he sees, in pride of place on the table, is the two-tier cake he'd last seen sitting on the worktop in his own kitchen this morning. What? How did that get here? He looks around in confusion. Surely this can't be the party Molly had been going to? Taking the cake to? The one she'd made for the woman she met at the clinic? But, of course, it must be. Her client, her new friend must be Rosie. Syd's Rosie. Did Molly ever say the party was for twins? She might have done. He can't remember. Or perhaps he hadn't listened properly in the first place. But it's definitely Molly's cake. And that must mean that, unless she's already left, she's here somewhere.

Should he stay? Slip away quietly? Or go looking for his wife, with a surprised '*What-are-you-doing-here?*' look on his face? Not that he'll have to try to look surprised. He really is. Thank God there's no sign of Carly. That could be a bit awkward. No, very awkward.

He grabs a sausage roll and stands chewing it while he takes a look around and plans his strategy. One of the babies is starting to get grizzly and the woman who must be Syd and Daz's mother is trying and failing to calm it down. Any minute now Rosie will hear and come back from the garden. He really can't just go. What if she says something, mentions him to Molly? The mysterious missing Jack who had only just arrived and has vanished without saying goodbye? The one who used to lodge with Syd and is still working in IT? No, he has to front this out. He swallows the final mouthful and aims for the open back door.

Molly is sitting on a folding chair at the bottom of the garden, surrounded by women and children. There is a lot of noise and several of the babies are in mid-feed, the number of exposed boobs making him feel decidedly uneasy, but it looks from here as if Molly's asleep. Her eyes are closed anyway. Maybe she prefers not to witness such a white wobbly mass of breastfeeding flesh at close hand either.

He picks his way down the path and arrives in front of her. 'Mol?' He says it quietly, in case she really is asleep, but her eyes fly open and she gives a little jump.

'Jack? What are you doing here?'

He kneels down beside her. 'I was going to say the same thing! My mate, Syd. You know, the one I used to work with when I was in London before, the one whose sofa I slept on... well, this is his party, his house... I said I might pop by for a bit, to see Rosie again and wet the babies' heads, as you were out anyway.' He's babbling, and he knows it. 'I had no idea this was where you were going too. We could have come together if we'd known.'

'Oh! Rosie's one of my new friends, from the baby clinic. She never told me her husband's name. It never came up. I never made the connection...'

'Me neither. But we're both here now, so shall I get you a

drink? Bring you out some food? Or do you want to go soon? You look done in.'

'I can't leave until they cut the cake, can I? So, yes, I'll have a Coke or a lemonade or something. No ice though. It's starting to get a bit chilly out here. Oh, and maybe a couple of tuna sandwiches. Thanks.'

'Oh, who's this then?' One of the women, with a voice like a foghorn, looks at him curiously. 'Is this the baby daddy?' She laughs, and the lager she's drinking bubbles back out of her nose in an ugly snort. Clearly drunk in charge of a child, or quite possibly more than one, although it's hard to tell which baby belongs to who and, thankfully, this woman is not one of those baring her breasts.

'Yes, this is my husband, Jack. Jack, this is Jo. And this is Miranda, and Fran...'

He nods and smiles, with no hope of remembering their names, although Fran looks kind of familiar. He mumbles a vague sort of communal greeting and disappears back towards the door and the food table.

Some of the men have emerged from the kitchen. Daz is at the centre of the conversation again, a samosa halfway to his mouth, but it doesn't quite make it to its destination. And there she is. Carly. She is standing with her friend Suze from the office, right next to the plate of sandwiches he needs to reach, both of them looking as if they're listening intently to Daz. Suze is definitely flirting with him in that obvious giggly way of hers, even though there's another man right next to her, scowling, a hand wrapped possessively about her shoulders. It's the one he saw her with in the pub garden that time when she'd warned him off. He hadn't looked too happy that day either. Clearly the jealous type. At least if he kicks off, Jack thinks, the focus of everyone's attention will stay away from him.

Carly's back is partly turned and she hasn't yet spotted him but he can't avoid her. Normally, he wouldn't want to, but today is different. He feels a bit like a sandwich himself, the sliver of limp cheese trapped between two slices of bread. The two women in his life are both here, just an open door keeping them apart. There is no way out. He just has to act naturally, and hope that Molly stays outside and Carly stays in. And then take Molly home, as soon as humanly possible.

'Carly!' He touches her on the arm.

She turns slowly. There is something in her expression that makes it obvious that seeing him here is no surprise.

'Hello, Jack. I wondered if you might turn up.' She forces a smile.

'Well, I probably won't stop long. I felt I should look in, you know. For Syd.'

'Don't leave early on my account.'

'No, no, I wouldn't.' He lowers his voice. 'Look, Carly, we're okay now, aren't we? Friends? We did say that we can't avoid each other, what with work...'

'Yes, but I didn't realise that would mean having to meet your wife. Your pregnant wife.' Her cheeks have gone red. He's not sure if it's the warmth of the room, or embarrassment. For a moment, he thinks she might be about to cry.

'Oh. I'm sorry. Have you...?'

'Outside. I didn't know who she was at first. Too stupid to put two and two together.'

'I'm sorry, Carly. Really.'

'Yes, you said that already. But there we are, it's done now, and she doesn't know who I am, or anything about me, so no harm done.'

'No, I suppose not. I will do my best to keep you apart though, assuming that's what you want?'

'Of course it's what I bloody want. But when has that ever mattered to you, Jack? Now, I suggest you get whatever it is you've come for and go back out to be with your wife. I'll see you at work as usual.'

'Right. Of course.' He reaches for a paper plate and piles it with whatever is nearest. Carly's tone worries him. Her voice seems to have gone up an octave and she's giving him that woman scorned look that could so easily lead to trouble. She wouldn't, would she? Say something to Molly, something to bring it all out into the open? Whatever she's said about them staying friends, he is not totally sure he can trust her. Not now she's been confronted with the enemy. Is that the right word? Hopefully not. Her rival, at least.

'Everything all right, Carly?' Daz has stopped talking long enough to notice that the atmosphere has changed. He's turned away from Suze and is looking at Carly now. Looking at her as if he fancies her, which he very likely does. Carly is a beautiful girl. She deserves to be fancied, loved... to be happy.

Jack turns away, balancing the plate of food in one hand as he pushes through the throng in search of Molly's Coke.

'Cutting the cake in five minutes!' Rosie calls, to anyone who might be near enough to hear her, and Jack sees a couple of people reaching for their phones, ready to get the best position for a photo.

When Jack comes back through from the kitchen, Daz has guided Carly to a couple of chairs next to the wall and is topping up her glass from a bottle of champagne. Where did he get that from, the smooth sod? They don't look his way at all as he steps outside and shivers in the chilly late-afternoon air. He'd better tell Molly about the cake cutting. It's what she really wants to see and the only reason they're still here. At least he knows where Carly is sitting now, so he can aim for the other side of the room. And then get them both out of here as quickly as possible, before there's any chance of trouble.

'This is egg. I asked for tuna!' Molly says, eyeing the mound of randomly selected food with suspicion, and Jack finds himself saying he's sorry again. It's starting to become a habit.

Chapter 35

Carly

Daz is all right. I'd thought he was a bit loud at first, a bit too full of himself, but he's funny, and he's kind, and he's definitely flirting with me. It's good to be with a man who isn't trying too hard, isn't riddled with guilt and indecision, isn't married to somebody else.

Suze and Sean have moved off in search of beer, or somewhere to sit, maybe even back upstairs for a private snog. I'm still not convinced they were only up there trying to fix a button, or exactly what it was that had made it ping off in the first place. Since the surprise engagement they've become embarrassingly touchy-feely. But being left alone with a good-looking Aussie isn't such a bad thing, and I quite fancy a bit of touchy-feely myself. The last attempt had not ended well.

I laugh when Daz whips out a bottle of chilled champagne from a cool bag he's hidden under the table. How long has that been there? And why? He discreetly pops the cork, smothering it in the trailing edge of Rosie's best tablecloth to muffle the sound.

I watch Jack go scuttling back to her outside, and I try my hardest to forget he was ever here. Easier said than done.

'Can't have a celebration without some bubbly,' Daz says, oblivious to my discomfort, producing two plastic glasses and pouring us a good-size measure each. I take a sip. It's still deliciously cold. Daz struggles to reinsert the cork and fails, so he slips the upright bottle back into its camouflage bag and props it against the wall to stop it from falling over.

'Won't there be some later, for the babies?'

'Babies don't drink alcohol, Carly,' he says, trying to keep a serious face. 'Second-hand maybe, via Rosie's boob if she's been at the booze, but generally they prefer milk.'

'I know that.' I giggle, swiping at his arm and almost spilling his drink. 'I meant that Syd might open a bottle later, for everyone to toast the babies.'

'You can't toast babies, Carly,' he says, a mischievous twinkle in his eye again. 'Too wide. They'd get stuck in the toaster.'

This time I laugh out loud, snorting bubbles down my nose, and he makes a big thing of slapping me on the back so I don't choke.

'There,' he says. 'I've saved your life now, and that makes you forever in my debt.'

I don't notice at first that Fran is standing next to me. I suppose it's inevitable that she'll find herself at the food table at least once every half an hour or so. Fran and food tend to go together like the horse and carriage in some old song, or bread and butter might be a better analogy. She's watching me and Daz with an obvious curiosity that I know is going to lead to the third degree when we get home. Lights in the eyes, thumbscrews, the lot. But it looks like food is not her main reason for being here, for a change. She holds out her hand with my handbag in it.

'Sorry to interrupt,' she says, pointedly, but she's smiling. I can't help wondering how things are going between her and that girl outside. 'Your phone was ringing in your bag, a couple of times actually, so I thought you might want to check it.'

'Thanks, Fran.' And thank you, thank you, to whoever has been ringing. That saves me the tricky how-to-rescue-my-bag-from-the-jaws-of-death dilemma.

'I thought I saw your Jack outside,' she says.

'Not *my* Jack, but yes, he's here. With his wife.'

'Oh, right, I see.' She gives me a strange look as if she wants to know more but I'm not about to give it to her. And certainly not in front of Daz.

'Well, I might as well stay here for now,' she says, clearly resigning herself to having to wait until later to interrogate me. 'Rosie says they're about to cut the cake. And you know me. First in the queue...'

That's more like the Fran I know and love. But she's right. Within seconds everyone seems to be swarming in from all directions, crowding round the table as Syd appears with the most enormous knife, its heavy handle decorated in big silvery swirls, the blade super-shiny. I suspect it's the one they used for their wedding cake and that it has been carefully wrapped and hidden away somewhere ever since. It's certainly not your usual everyday kitchen knife. A sudden image flashes across my mind, straight out of one of those old Agatha Christie TV murder mysteries. A fancy knife, dripping with blood, someone out for revenge, a body in the conservatory, a trail of clues...

'Silence, please,' Syd bellows, abruptly forcing my wayward thoughts back into the present, and I notice, just in those two words, how Australian he sounds. The acquired London edge to his voice fades away, and he is back to his roots, probably something to do with being surrounded by his own family for the first time in ages. He goes on to make a short speech about how proud he is, of his wife, his children, being here among all the people that matter to him, and I see Rosie wipe away a tear as she rests an arm across his shoulders. He thanks her for putting on such a wonderful spread, thanks us all for coming, thanks Molly for baking the cakes, and if he was even a tiny bit religious he would probably be thanking God by now too. I'm pretty sure he's close to tears himself, but a few beers always did bring out the sentimental in him.

'Now, where are the real guests of honour?' he says, beckoning his mum to bring the babies forward. He takes one and Rosie takes the other, each simultaneously planting little kisses on the tops of their small fluffy heads. 'To the little people who have changed our lives, who make our lives complete, who *are* our life...' He cradles a baby in the crook of one arm and lays the tip of the blade on top of the white cake, the christening half of Molly's double concoction, and slides it down into the centre. 'To Jamie and Rebecca.'

Everyone cheers and Syd's dad pops more champagne as Rosie gives the baby back to her mother-in-law, goes into the kitchen and fetches a stack of plastic flutes just like the ones Daz and I are already trying to hide behind our backs. I'm not sure jumping the gun and guzzling the celebratory champers ahead of the rest of the guests is quite the done thing.

Jack is on the other side of the room. It's a small room so he's actually only a few feet away, but it might as well be a mile. He accepts a small glass and downs it in one. His pregnant wife shakes her head. She has an unborn child to protect. Her eyes are on the cake, watching it being cut and handed round, waiting to see if people like it. She smiles to herself as the congratulations pour in. She steps forward and silently slips a few little cards onto the table, as if she's hoping to attract more business but is too shy to make a big deal about it.

Jack leans against the wall, his eyes lowered. He can't look at me. Or doesn't want to. Suddenly, he feels like a stranger to me, a dream I once had, one I have finally woken up from, and I can't believe I was so scared to come downstairs. If anyone's scared, it should be him. The one with everything to lose if the truth ever comes out. It gives me a momentary feeling of power. That, at last, I am the one who has the upper hand. A few words in Molly's ear and I could change both their lives forever.

But what has she ever done to deserve that? Nothing. So, I won't say a thing. Won't do anything to rock the boat. It would be vengeful and cruel, and I'm better than that.

Jack may be tall and good-looking and clever, but he's far from perfect. I know that now. He has his faults, just like everybody else. If I'm looking for my Mr Darcy, then Jack definitely isn't him. I think I may just have to stick to the fantasy screen version after all, go back to drooling over Colin Firth, dripping wet shirt and all. Real life has a nasty habit of letting people down. Of letting *me* down, when it comes to men anyway. If Darcy existed for real, I bet even he would have his faults. He'd snore or fart or something...

I watch Jack now, still sheepishly avoiding my gaze. And wait for that magnetic pull, the lurch of feeling that always comes, but this time it doesn't. I realise that I don't really know this man, or what his real life is like. And that Molly is just an ordinary, perfectly nice woman whose whole future I could so easily have wrecked, but didn't.

No. We're finished. Over. Done. He is standing there, waiting and, as his wife turns back towards him, I can see her shape, properly, for the first time. Her rounded waistline swells inside her dress, and she looks tired. She takes his hand, leans into him, then tilts her face up and kisses him gently on the very edge of his lips. There is an easy intimacy and a familiarity to it that has nothing to do with me. They are a couple, soon to be three. They fit. And in that moment, the what might have been disappears, just like that, quietly, with a little inevitable pop, like the cork coming out of a champagne bottle, never to be forced back in again. Jack looks across at me and gives me a tiny nod, then they say their goodbyes to Syd and Rosie and they leave. Together.

I pick up one of her cards. *Secret Centres*, it says, in small but fancy print. *Celebratory and party cakes. Gender-reveal cakes a speciality.* It gives her phone number, her website and email addresses, her Facebook handle, all those important details that, along with actually seeing her real-life-in-the-flesh face, I have tried to avoid for so long. I am tempted to slip it into my bag, to keep it, but I don't. I put it back on the table with the others.

My bag! I suddenly remember what Fran said, that my phone had been ringing out in the garden. I fish it out from the depths and look at the screen. Two missed calls. Two text messages. All from my mother.

'Let me give you my number while you have your phone out.' Daz takes it from me and taps his number into my contacts, before I have a chance to say anything. Not that I'm going to stop him. 'Maybe we could meet up while I'm still in England?' he says, pressing a few buttons on my phone and finding my number, which he quickly saves on his.

I nod. 'I'd like that.'

I take the phone back and open Mum's messages. Short and sweet, factual, although I can only imagine how she must be feeling. It's Pauline. She's gone.

I didn't know the woman but I feel a wave of sadness for her, and for Anthony. He loved her, and she was so young to die. It's all so unfair, but then, life so often is, isn't it? I make my excuses and go up for my jacket, which is buried halfway under Suze and Sean, but I grab it anyway. I have to go. Anthony will be needing Mum, and Mum will be needing me.

She's sitting by herself in the dark when I get there. There's a cold cup of tea in front of her on the kitchen table, and a mound of screwed-up tissues.

'Oh, Carly,' she says, reaching out and hugging me, so tightly I can hardly breathe.

'I'm sorry, Mum. Anthony must be devastated.'

'Yes. He knew it was coming, of course, but it's still a shock, isn't it? When it actually happens...'

She's thinking about Dad. I know she is.

I ease myself out of her grip, flip the light on and refill the kettle. While it's starting to boil, I walk into the dining room and find a half-empty bottle of cheap brandy in the sideboard. It usually only comes out at Christmas, to help set the pudding alight, but I think she needs it today.

I make her a mug of tea and pour a good-sized slug of brandy into it, then place it in her cold hands. 'Here. Drink this. Or just hold it for a while. It will warm you up.'

'I can't help thinking of him all alone. If he'd had children, at least there'd be someone to share the burden, help him with the grief...'

'But he didn't, Mum, and you know why.'

'Poor man. I don't know what I would have done without you and Sam, when we lost your father.'

'Let's not go there, eh? Bringing it all up again is only going to upset you. And me, probably. Where is Sam anyway?'

'Out with someone. A girl, I guess, but he's keeping it all very close to his chest. I know nothing about her at all. I never do, with any of his girlfriends. He never brings them home, you know.'

'Doesn't want you overdoing the matchmaking probably, or putting them off!'

'I don't. Do I?'

'Only joking, but you do tend to share your opinions quite... shall we say, generously?'

'Which means I interfere, I suppose?'

'You mean well, Mum. Now, come on, what are we going to do for Anthony? Give him a call, get him over here, offer him a bed for the night, or do you think he wants time on his own? We could make him a casserole so he doesn't have to cook.'

'I don't know. I thought I knew him so well, but now I have no idea what he might want. I doubt if he'll be thinking about food at all. Death changes things, doesn't it? He'll have so much going on in his head. All the practical stuff, the funeral arrangements, who to tell... and there'll be all the memories too. The good ones and the bad. They play over and over in your head, you know, like a film on a loop. It's a terrible time, those first few days. He'll be needing a damn good cry too, but sometimes that takes time to come. And the last thing I want is for him to think I'm some interfering old woman, like you obviously do.'

'No, Mum. You're caring, that's all. You want the best for everybody.'

She gives me a watery smile. 'I do, Carly. It's just that I don't always know what that is. But I think we'll give Anthony a bit of space, for tonight at least. I've spoken to him on the phone, but there's not a lot more I can do for now, and he has a sister who's driving down from the Midlands in the morning. He knows where I am when he needs me. *If* he needs me.'

We sit for a while in silence, until my phone beeps with a message. It's Fran. She's taking Miranda and her kids back to our place, and she's going to cook them all a meal, as if she isn't already stuffed full of cake! But I'm pleased for her, I really am.

'Shall we watch a film?' I say eventually. 'To take our minds off things.'

'But don't you want to get off home?' Mum looks up at me,

and there's an unspoken pleading there in her eyes. 'I don't want you to feel you have to stay.'

'Fran's got company, so I'm in no rush to get home, Mum. In fact, I may not live here anymore, but this house is my real home. Always will be.'

'Okay then.' She smiles properly, for the first time since I got here. '*Pretty Woman?*'

'Yeah, why not?' I say, leading her into the lounge. 'Have you got any of those choc ices left? Or a can of cider or beer or anything? I've had a bit of a bad day myself.'

'Want to tell me about it?' She touches my hand. 'No interfering, I promise.'

'Yeah, I think I do, actually.'

'Well, if it's the same man you've hinted at before, the married one, and I'd bet anything that it is, then all I can say is he's not worth it.'

'As simple as that?'

'Yes, sometimes it really is. If you love him and he loves you back, wonderful! Nothing you can't overcome. But any other combination is never going to work. Equals, Carly. Or move on. That's all I'm going to say. It has to be a two-way thing, like it was for your dad and me.'

'And Anthony and Pauline?'

'Maybe. I never met the girl, but from the way he spoke about her, it sounded like true love to me, despite all their problems. And that's what I want for you, and for Sam. All I've ever wanted.'

'I know, Mum. And it's all finished, I promise you. I met his wife and I felt so ridiculously upset and unsettled, and guilty, even though we never... well, you know. And none of it's her fault, is it? No, I'm done with married men, and pining for what I can't have. It probably wasn't worth having anyway!'

'Good for you, love.'

'But I met someone new today. Someone fun and uncomplicated. And single! He's Rosie's brother-in-law and he's called Darren or Darwin or something like that, although everyone just calls him Daz. And we really seemed to get on well. It's early days but if I do see him again, if I let myself get too close, then there could be a pretty big stumbling block up ahead, because he lives thousands of miles away... in Australia.'

'Distance is irrelevant, Carly, and you're making problems before they even exist. Take it a step at a time. See how you get on, and if it's meant to be... well, just listen to your heart, and go where it takes you. To the moon and back, if necessary. At least you can get to Australia on a plane. No space rocket required! Now, get that DVD on. I'm in need of a bit of Richard Gere.'

'Oh, yeah? Which particular bit?'

'Carly! I swear I have no idea what you mean. I'm a respectable widow woman, I'll have you know. I must say, though, I quite fancy a wedding on some hot sunny beach, with the sand between my toes, and a lovely new floppy hat.'

'Let's not get ahead of ourselves here, Mum. I've only just met the guy.'

'Oh, I'm not talking about *your* wedding, Carly. I'm talking about me and Richard Gere. Well, we can all dream, can't we?' And then she curls her legs up on the sofa beside me and we settle in for a bit of much-needed romance.

Chapter 36

Molly

It's Friday, the day of the scan, the one where they will finally find out the sex of the baby, and Molly is quietly excited. The plan is to head for Norfolk this evening, straight after the appointment, and share the news with both families before they tell anyone else, although her mum is still insistent that it won't be news to her. She already knows that the baby is a boy and it always has been.

Molly is busy baking. She's heard about a little market a short bus ride away that's held on alternate Sundays and she's thinking of taking a stall before Christmas, selling decorated cupcakes with snowy toppings and trying out a range of gingerbread biscuits in festive shapes, as gifts or for hanging on the tree as decorations. She has made a small trial batch of gingerbreads as a present for Sian and Ralph, who she hasn't seen since the accident in their hall, using a dog-shaped cutter and adding red icing collars, little eyes and a black tip to the tails. She just knows they'll love them.

She is making cakes to take home to Shelling too, of course. She could hardly set up a gender-reveal cake business and not make some to mark her own big moment. Her parents have booked a table at the Brown Cow for dinner, but there will always be room for cake. She smiles at the thought of them all round the table, her own family and Jack's, doing a countdown and then biting into the cakes at the exact same moment, everybody finding out together whether the secret centre is pink or blue.

She lays out all the ingredients, the two bottles of food colouring standing side by side. There won't be time after leaving the hospital to come back and bake, if they are to catch the early evening train. She knows it will be a waste but there is no option but to bake cakes with middles in both colours, and then throw the 'wrong' ones away, maybe feed them to the pigeons outside the station. They won't care what colour they are.

Molly sings along to a tune on the radio as she works. She hadn't expected to settle in London, much as she had been willing to give it a try, but being pregnant, making friends, and getting absorbed in her baking, have given her new purpose. Yes, a bigger flat with an extra bedroom, and definitely a bigger kitchen, would be nice, but that would all come in time. There is only so long a baby can sleep in a small cot beside their bed. It, he, she will need a room of its own soon enough. And Jack will want to move onwards, upwards too. There will be better jobs, more responsibility, more money. Maybe more children too. She thinks he has finally got his head around the idea of becoming a dad and, while still not exactly singing about it, there has been a sort of acceptance lately, maybe even a touch of excitement. He's still asking regularly about which fruit or vegetable he can compare it to, so that has to be a good thing. And he does know what the soon-to-be large banana or bunch of carrots look like, which is an improvement on the mysteries of the artichoke dimensions the baby has apparently reached this week. Jack wouldn't know how big an artichoke was supposed to be if his life depended on it. Not that she would either!

She stirs the cake mixture with a big wooden spoon. Something about the physical effort, the idea of her own gender-reveal offerings made lovingly by hand, keeps her away from the electric mixer this morning. They are going to be bigger than usual, simply because they are hers and Jack's. In her head, she counts out how many cakes she will need for the family, then adds a few more to allow for possible damage en route, and another one for Flossie, the dog.

Jack was in a rush this morning. It's only a few days before his pet project goes 'live'. She knows very little about it, just that it has to go well. It's a matter of reputation, satisfaction, pride. His first really important piece of work since they arrived, his first chance to prove himself to the consultancy firm he works for now, a step on the ladder towards the next challenge, whatever and wherever that might be.

She had made a grab for him as he left, laying his hand on her belly, planting a kiss on his cheek. 'You won't forget, will you? This is important, Jack, and I want you there with me. To meet our baby together. The appointment is at four o'clock, so I need you back here by half past two really to allow plenty of time, if we're going together on the Tube, and taking our weekend bag and the cake carrier with us. We are, aren't we?'

'Of course. Well, I hope so. But you know how it is. I might get held up, and you can't carry all that stuff by yourself, so if I'm not here by three, get a taxi to the hospital and I'll meet you there. Worst-case scenario though, because I will do my absolute best to get home in time so we can go together.'

'Looking forward to finally knowing?'

He nods. 'And to proving your mum wrong if it's a girl, obviously.'

She had nudged him, laughing. 'She won't like that!'

She wonders if Jack is secretly hoping for a girl. And, if he is, is it only to get one over on her poor mum? He'll be teasing her forever if she's wrong.

The phone rings just as she's putting the cakes into the oven.

'Mum. Talk of the devil! I was just thinking about you.'

'All good, I hope?' her mum says, not waiting for a response. 'Just calling to check on your train time. Your dad will come and meet you at the station. But don't you go telling him, will you? On the drive over. I want to be the first to know.'

'Of course I won't. Jack's mum will be bursting to find out too, and it's only fair we tell you all together. We're hoping to catch the five thirty train, so we should get in to Norwich about twenty past seven. We're pushing things a bit with Tubes and traffic and everything, and knowing what hospitals are like the scan could well be running late, so if we're unlucky we might have to catch a later one. Then it could be quite a late dinner, I'm afraid.'

'That's fine, love. The rest of us will meet in the pub for a drink anyway, then your dad'll bring you straight there to join us. Oh, I'm that excited I don't think I'll be able to eat a thing!'

'Well, leave room for cake.'

'Oh no. Nothing sweet for me, love. I'm watching my waistline. Just my usual pie and mash.'

Molly smiles to herself. Pie and mash is her mum's idea of a diet. With lashings of gravy too, probably! 'You'll want this cake, Mum, I promise you. See you later.'

Molly blows a loud kiss down the line and hangs up.

When the cakes are cool, she carefully slices the top off each one, scoops out a hollow in the middle and spoons a big dollop of pink-stained butter icing into half of them, then lays the spongey tops back on to make a mound and smothers the whole thing with a thick swirl of pure white icing to stick it tightly back together. She repeats the whole procedure with the blue, then lifts and checks each one, making sure no tell-tale colour is seeping out anywhere. She has kept the sponge itself a neutral cakey beige this time, not wanting to risk the tiniest glimpse of colour emerging through the outer casing of icing on the way. Trains can be bumpy, and there must be no accidental reveal before she is ready.

She gazes at the finished cakes with pride, then has a minor panic trying to remember which plate holds the pink centres and which the blue. But, of course, she knows. She's a professional now, and not about to make that sort of silly mistake. She writes a quick note to label them anyway, just in case she forgets. She gets the cake carrier ready to load later, picks up a gingerbread and bites its little doggy head off with a satisfying crunch, then goes to the bedroom to pack their bag for the weekend.

It's quarter to three and Jack isn't here. Molly sits, with her coat and shoes already on, the bags at her feet, the cakes carefully encased in their carrier and her handbag on her lap. She knows she is tapping her fingers on the arm of the chair and wills herself to stop. It's no good getting impatient or worked up about it. It's not good for her blood pressure.

She wonders if there's time to make a cup of tea, especially as she's heard that a full bladder can help to get a good scan picture, or is that only in the earlier stages? But then, bursting for a wee on a busy Tube train doesn't sound like a comfortable experience and it's not one she fancies risking, so maybe another drink is not such a great idea after all.

She looks at her watch again. Still only ten to. She knows, and so does Jack, that she was being extra cautious in her planning. The walk to the Tube station, and the walk to the hospital at the other end, are easy enough to work out. It's just the trains themselves that can be temperamental. She opens her phone and checks for the latest updates, but there are no reported delays. She's panicking over nothing. The whole thing won't take more than an hour at the most. They still have time if he hurries up and gets here.

It's three o'clock, and time to give up and call a taxi. But she calls Jack first, just in case he really is almost here, desperate to make it in time, as excited as she is. Apparently not. She listens to his phone ringing and ringing, then his answerphone messaging kicks in.

'Hi, this is Jack Doherty. Busy right now, but not too busy to call you back. Leave me your name and number.'

Maybe he's on his way, underground, out of signal. Or right outside the door already and about to put his key in the lock. She moves to the window and peers out. He's not there. Still, the light-hearted, casual tone to his voice makes her want to yell at him. 'Busy? Busy doing what?' Doesn't he know this appointment matters more? Has he even remembered?

'Where are you, Jack? We're going to be late. I'll have to meet you there now.' She tries not to sound too annoyed, but she is. This is so typical of him. There's no real enthusiasm, no excitement in him. Nothing to match the way she feels about this baby. There never has been. 'Call me back, please.'

He doesn't.

Chapter 37

Carly

Thank God it's Friday! It's been one of those weeks where I've been snowed under with work and hardly had any time to breathe. Jack's IT project has been gathering pace over the last few days, with everything on track to go 'live' next week, keeping everyone on their toes, and I can see, whenever I've bumped into him, that he's stressing over it. Soon his three months at Mandrake's will be over, and he will be gone. I'm still not sure how I feel about that.

I went out with Daz on Wednesday. It really is early days, and I don't want to do or say anything to jinx it, but let's just say it went well. He really is a lovely guy, and it's going to take a while for me to tire of hearing his tales of life in Oz, if I ever do. It all sounds so exciting and exotic, and hot. And so is he, by the way. Hot. No doubt about that. And quite some kisser!

Fran and her new 'friend', as she still insists on calling her, were up late last night, talking, drinking, laughing, until about two in the morning. Eating too, I expect, knowing Fran as I do! And the empty tin of Quality Street I spotted in the bin this morning speaks volumes. I don't know if Miranda stayed the night or got a cab, but there was no sign of her when I got up.

No kids with her, I'm pleased to say but, even so, all the happy noises made it hard for me to get to sleep, the walls are that thin. It makes me wonder just how much Fran heard that time – the only time – that Jack was in my bedroom, and I squirm with embarrassment at the memory. There are some things you just don't want your mates to hear. If things ever get that far with Daz, I'm only going to invite him over when Fran's out. He is staying in a hotel though, and I've always loved a nice hotel room, with crisp white sheets, and little complimentary shampoos, and room service if you fancy a snack and you're already in your PJs, so you never know...

Jack's asked me to meet him for a quick catch-up, purely work-related, before the weekend, and I'm heading for our usual meeting room, a pile of print-outs under my arm, and our usual coffee order balanced in my hands. I can't stop long though. I've worked through my lunch hour so I can leave early today and Syd is picking me up outside for a driving lesson after work. Though I say it myself, I think my driving's going pretty well. We're talking about booking a theory test soon and then the real thing soon after. Streets of West London, beware!

I'm here first, so I settle myself at the table and spread my paperwork out in front of me. Jack's good at his job. The old and new payment systems have existed side by side for a few weeks now, making extra work for all of us, but it's certainly proved that it's on track and that it works! Whenever I have found a problem, he's always managed to fix it. It's just the final push of the button left to do and our old system will vanish into the ether as the new one magically takes its place, or that's how I like to think of it anyway. If only there was a magic reset button to close down what's left of Jack and me, and set me off on a brand-new path to love and life, but I guess that's all down to me now. With a little help from Daz, if I'm lucky.

I wonder if there will be a leaving do for Jack when he goes.

Is that likely for a consultant only brought in for a few months' work? I hope so. I'd like a chance to say goodbye, and without all the angst that surrounded our previous one, five years ago. I want to wave him off without that burning desire to rip his clothes off (well, I tried that and it was a disaster, wasn't it?) and without the tears in my eyes this time. Not that I can guarantee that, because I did love him and I will miss him. In another time and place, we could have been good together, a proper couple, if only...

The door handle rattles up and down noisily and he finally lunges in, almost tripping over the door frame. I smother a giggle. His clumsy entrances are starting to become a habit. 'Bloody doorknob,' he mutters, righting himself. 'It's time they got that fixed.'

'Knobs can be troublesome, Jack.' I am laughing out loud now. 'Treat it more like a woman. Less of the firm grip and more of a gentle touch, that's all it needs.'

'Yes, I'll try to remember that,' he says, grinning as he sits down opposite me and reaches for his coffee. 'God, Carly, I've hardly stopped today. I even forgot to charge my phone last night, I've had so much running through my mind. It went flat as a pancake, and I've had to leave it plugged in at my desk. I've not even managed any lunch, let alone found time for a coffee. So, thanks for this.' He lifts his cup, takes a long sip and nods. 'Just the way I like it. Hot and strong.'

'Don't say it, Jack.'

'Say what? That it's the same way I like my women? Am I really that predictable?'

'Oh, yes. You really are.'

'I don't suppose you've brought biscuits as well?'

'Afraid not. I can run and get some though, if you're starving.'

'No, I'll be okay. Best get some work done. I have to be

somewhere else quite soon. With Molly.' He peers at his watch and shakes his head. 'I was hoping to get away sooner, but it's too late now. I won't make it home in time, but she knows to get a cab without me and I'll meet her there. So, let's get on with this, shall we?'

<h1 style="text-align:center">Chapter 38</h1>

<hr>

<h2 style="text-align:center">Jack</h2>

Jack sits back in his chair and stretches his shoulders. Things have gone well. There are no problems, no last-minute glitches. The final stage of the project is on track, and then he will be out of here. No more Mandrake's, no more sleepless nights, no more missing meals, no more Carly.

'Thanks, Carly,' he says, reaching out and laying his hand on her wrist. She stops shuffling her papers into a pile and looks at him, those big blue eyes of hers shining at him.

'What for?'

'Agreeing to be our guinea pig, testing out the system for us. For me. Doing it so efficiently, so well...'

'Too much flattery and you'll be giving me a big head.'

'You deserve it. The flattery, I mean. Not the big head!'

'Thanks. I've enjoyed it. You're very easy to work with, Jack.'

'And I'm sorry about the way things worked out between us. I acted like a total prat, didn't I? I know there's no reason to see each other after I leave, but you never know. We have mutual friends, so it could happen, if Syd has another party or Molly makes your wedding cake one day!' He sees her smile at that. 'I don't want there to ever be any awkwardness.'

'Me neither.'

She stands up and gathers her stuff.

'I hope you're happy, Carly.'

'I'm getting there.'

'That bloke at the party? Syd's brother?'

She looks down at the carpet but not before he sees her blush. 'Sorry. Not my business anymore, if it ever was.'

'No.' She hesitates. 'Good luck with the baby, Jack. It won't be like the last time, I promise you. Molly seems nice, and fatherhood just might be the making of you! Now, I really do have to go. I've got a driving lesson soon.' She picks up the empty cups and walks out, closing the door behind her, and he sits for a moment, relishing the silence. His stomach growls hungrily.

Maybe she's right. Being a dad will be okay after all. He hopes so, anyway. Something clicks inside his head. Dad? Baby? Oh, God, the scan! He looks at his watch. It's quarter to four already. How did that happen? He grabs for his laptop and papers, picks up the pen he's dropped on the floor, and almost knocks his chair over in his haste to get out of here. All he has to do is collect his coat, with his wallet in it, unplug his phone, ring to tell Molly he's on his way, find a cab and dash straight to the hospital. They're bound to be running late. They always are, aren't they? She'll never forgive him if he doesn't make it in time. And he realises, suddenly, that he won't forgive himself either. He wants to be there, to see their little artichoke baby moving on the screen, and he really, really needs to be there when they finally find out if it's a boy artichoke or a girl one.

He grabs the door handle and yanks it down hard. Too hard. With a strange clunking sound, it loses contact with the door and comes away in his hand. No! This can't be happening. He should have listened to Carly. Treat it gently, she'd said. Bloody door. It always has given him trouble, and now…

He tries to get a grip on the door itself, to find a way of easing it open, but without its handle it won't move. He needs a tool of some kind. The pen? He pokes it at the edge of the door but it's too fat, too round. He needs something flat, like a screwdriver or a knife, to get a bit of leverage. A paperclip, even. He looks around the bare room. It's set up for meetings, a so-called 'quiet' room. There is no phone, no cupboard, no drawer that might present him with what he needs. Frantically, he rummages in his pockets. Oh, why couldn't he be more like his brother? Working on a farm, Richard would never be without a Swiss Army knife somewhere about his person at the very least, and probably all sorts of other useful things too. Lengths of string, screws, nails, you name it… God, he hasn't even got a coin that he could try twisting against the mechanism, to release the catch. Everything's cards these days. Bugger!

There's nothing else for it. He'll have to make a total dick of himself and bang on the door, shout out for help, like some damsel in distress in need of rescue.

'Hello!' he says, loudly, but just short of a real out-loud cry for help. Nothing. He thumps on the wood and yells again, a bit louder this time. Outside in the corridor, all is quiet. This room is tucked away in a corner. It's not called a quiet room for nothing. Nobody hears him. Nobody comes.

Chapter 39

Molly

Molly clambers out of the taxi and the driver helps her remove her bags and cakes and places them on the pavement. She finds her purse and pays him in cash, then watches him drive away. She has made it with ten minutes to spare, enough time to try calling Jack again before going inside where the big red 'No mobile phones' signs will shame her into turning hers off. She's never been sure if the ban is because phones interfere with hospital equipment in some way or if they just want a bit of hush in there.

It goes to answerphone again. She's torn between worrying that something terrible has happened to Jack (an accident, ambulances, blood all over the road) and being bloody mad at him for letting her down. In her heart she has a pretty good idea which is likely to be closer to the truth. Jack never did want this baby. Sometimes she's felt that he's almost scared of it and all that comes with it. Maybe this is his way of letting her know it's over, that he doesn't care enough about their baby, if at all. She's going to have to do this whole parenting thing on her own.

She lays her hand over her bump. Today it will stop being some faceless veggie-related mass of cells and become a real boy or girl at last. Like Pinocchio! She has no idea why that thought pops into her head, but it makes her smile. Her mum will be able to start knitting clothes in the right colour now, and they can start looking through the baby-name books, because they will actually know what it is. Or *she* will. It doesn't look like Jack will be here to find out. She gulps back a threatening tear, switches her phone off and heads inside.

❧

'Mrs Doherty?' She has been staring at the same page of a magazine, not taking in a word, when she is called in, right on time.

'All alone today?' the woman says, as she washes her hands and points Molly towards the bed. The name badge on her uniform says that she is called Angela Harris.

'My husband's been held up.'

'Oh, that's a shame. I could call the next lady in before you, if that would help. See you after. It might give him a bit more time to catch up?'

'Thank you. That's very kind, but there was nobody else in the waiting room.'

'Oh, well. Best crack on then, eh?'

Molly lifts her top and winces as the cold gel squirts across her bare skin.

'Are we ready to take a look at this little one?' Angela says, and they both turn their heads towards the screen.

Chapter 40

Carly

'Hi, Syd, how's things?' I open the driver door and climb in.

'Not bad. Although, to tell you the truth, Carls, my back is killing me. Too long sitting here, wedged in and doing nothing. I really need a bigger car. Or longer legs! Do you mind if I have a fiddle with the seat? It won't take long.'

'Of course not. I'm not in any rush. I've finished work for the day.'

'Wish I could say the same!' He climbs out and kneels down on the pavement. It's a busy road and we're not in a proper parking space but I keep my eyes peeled for any passing traffic wardens as he fiddles with the controls.

'There!' he announces, as the passenger seat slides backwards and he adjusts the angle of the back. 'Lucky there's nobody sitting behind me or they'd get their legs crushed!'

'I don't suppose there's ever anyone sitting behind you, is there? Learners aren't likely to bring a friend along.'

'Oh, you'd be surprised! I've got one teenager whose mum insists on coming on every lesson. Thinks I'm about to run my hand up her kid's thigh or something. It wouldn't be so bad if my pupil was a girl!'

I laugh, do up my seat belt and check in the rear mirror.

'Hang on.' Syd has one leg in the car but he's stopped in mid-bend. 'Did you hear that?'

'Hear what?'

'Someone just called my name. Or I think they did.' He gets back out of the car and looks around. I lean forward and peer out too. Someone is banging on a window, way up above us. The window flies open and a man's head emerges.

'Syd! Carly! Help!'

It's Jack. Waving his arms about, up on the second floor. What the hell is he doing?

'Jack? What's up, man?' Syd is leaning backwards as he looks up, taking the opportunity to place his hands at each side of his back and give it a good stretch. 'Where's the fire?'

'No fire,' Jack shouts down. 'The door's stuck. To the room. Handle's broken. I can't get out.'

I get back out of the car and look up too, and there he is, like some modern-day male equivalent of Rapunzel, stuck in his tower.

'The door handle? I did tell you, Jack...'

'I know you did. And you were right, but that's no help to me now, is it? Please, Carly, can you come back inside and let me out? Like, now? I'm in a bit of a hurry. It's the scan today. You know, the big one that tells us the sex, and I'm already late. Molly will kill me...'

A couple of passers-by, pensioners in macs, have stopped and are looking up anxiously, as if someone's about to attempt a suicide and jump out of the window.

'Sex? Did he say something about sex?' The old woman tuts and drags the old man away. 'Disgusting!'

I can't help laughing. 'What's it worth, Jack? I am supposed to be having a driving lesson, not sorting out your knob problems.'

'Oh, stop messing about. This is serious. As many coffees as you can drink. Or ciders. Or a massive bunch of flowers. Anything... Just come and get me out. Please.'

'Better do as he asks, Carls,' Syd says, leaning his elbow on the car roof. 'Anything for a mate, eh?'

The lift is slow in coming but I make it to the second floor and head for the meeting room. The handle, or the half of it that should be sticking out of this side of the door, is lying on the carpet in the corridor. What am I supposed to do? Fit it back on somehow?

'Jack?' I tap on the door and he's there, on the other side, immediately giving instructions, the relief in his voice obvious even though I can't see him.

'It just needs something to slot in next to the catch, to release it. Anything. A knife from the kitchen maybe? Or go and find the caretaker, if we have one. Do we have one?'

'Old Archie, you mean? The handyman? He only comes in twice a week, and today's not his day.'

'The knife then? Quick, Carly. I can't miss this scan. I really can't.'

'I thought you didn't want this baby?'

'Well, I do, all right? I was there when it was made and I'll be there when it's born. I'm a dad, Carly, or I soon will be. And I need to be there. Pink or blue? It matters, Carly. It's taken me a while to come to my senses, but it matters, okay?'

I thought it would hurt to hear him say something like that, but it doesn't. Jack is finally facing up to his responsibilities. Good for him. And for Molly too.

It takes another five minutes, but together we do it. The door opens with a satisfying click and Jack bursts out, giving it a final frustrated kick before he runs off towards his desk. I'm not sure if I'm still needed, but I follow him anyway.

'Oh, shit. I didn't switch the socket on.' He tugs the charger away from the wall. 'My phone's been plugged in for hours and it hasn't charged at all. I need to ring Molly. See if it's too late.'

'Use the office phone.'

'I can't. I don't know her number. Who remembers mobile numbers these days? It's all saved in here.' He holds up his dead phone and for a moment I think he's going to chuck it in the bin or hurl it at the wall. 'I'll just have to get to the hospital as quickly as I can and hope she hasn't gone in yet.'

'Need a lift?' I don't know why I say that. It's not even my car.

'Yes!' And then we're running down the stairs because the lift is taking too long to come, and back out into the street, and he's trying to climb into the back of the car. 'There's no room,' he yells at Syd, who's trying to catch up with what exactly is going on here. 'Who has their seat that far back? Where am I supposed to put my legs?'

'Other side, mate. Try the other side,' Syd says. 'Where are we going, by the way? Cos it looks like you're coming with us, right?'

'The maternity hospital. Quick as you can!'

Syd gestures to me to swap sides and I slide into the passenger seat, amazed at just how far my feet can stretch out, not even reaching the front of the footwell, which is just as well as I remember this is a dual-control car and I don't want to touch a pedal I shouldn't.

I look in the mirror. Jack is looking at his watch again. 'It's ten past,' he announces. 'I'm already too late. I just know it. I've blown it. I'm in the doghouse, big time.'

'Better start practising your begging then, mate. Woof, woof!

Seriously though, I'll do my best to get you there.' Syd's in the driving seat now, ignition on, watching the flow of the traffic, waiting for a gap. 'I remember that moment, seeing Rosie's scan and finding out what our two little blobs were. One of each for us, but who knows what you've got brewing away in there? Can't have you missing out on that now, can we?' Suddenly Syd sees his chance and the car shoots off from the kerb with a loud squeal of tyres. It feels like one of those *'Follow that car'* moments you see in the movies. 'Lean back and hold on to your hats!'

Chapter 41

Jack

Why does it take something as stupid as a broken door to bring everything into focus? He has been feeling trapped for a while, not really knowing what he wants, where his future lies, but finding himself actually trapped, unable to get out of that room, unable to get to Molly as he'd promised he would, having no choice, that was something else entirely. He knows what he wants and it's Molly. He can't imagine not having her in his life, can't imagine that little baby being brought up without him.

Jack has been too involved in work, too involved in himself, to see what really matters. He's not some frightened teenager anymore. This is not some accidental pregnancy to run from. It's Molly. His wife. The woman he loves. And this is their baby. Something they have made together, and will love together, see moving on the screen together, willy or not, if only he can get to the scan in time. If only she can forgive him if he can't.

The car slips through the traffic like a knife through butter. Syd, it has to be said, is a bloody good driver. If there's a gap, he gets through it with inches to spare. If there's a light about to change, he manages to time getting through it perfectly. What would have taken him God knows how long on foot and by train takes Syd less than twenty minutes.

It's half past four and the hospital entrance is in sight, but there's a queue of cars, stuck behind an ambulance, not moving fast enough, not moving at all. Jack flings open the car door, leaps out, yells a hurried 'Thank you' and runs like mad.

There she is! Molly, sitting on a bench seat by the entrance, between a nurse reading a newspaper and a heavily pregnant woman in a dressing gown and slippers, puffing away on a cigarette. Their weekend case is on the ground by Molly's feet, and that carrier thing she bought for lugging her cupcakes about. She's holding her phone in her hand, looking at the screen, and he has an awful feeling it's him she's looking for on it. A call, a text, anything...

'Mol!' he shouts as he runs towards her, out of breath, his tie flapping around his neck.

She looks up, but her expression gives nothing away. 'You made it then? At last.' She puts her phone back in her handbag. 'Where the hell were you, Jack? You know the appointment was at four, don't you? And it's...' She makes a point of looking at her watch.

The nurse gets up from the seat, folds her paper and walks back into the building behind them, and Jack thumps down in her place. 'I know, I know. I should have been here, but you'll never believe what happened...'

'I'm not sure I want to hear it, Jack. It'll just be an excuse, won't it? Something about work and how important this project is, and how you lost track of time. I've heard all this stuff before. But this was important too. Don't you get that?'

'Of course I do. And I'm sorry, Mol. So sorry. It's not too late though, is it? Can't we go back inside, ask to have the scan again? So I can see whatever it is that you've seen?'

'It's the NHS, Jack. Do you think they have the time or the

resources to let you waltz in there and expect, or demand, that they do it all again? And why? Because you couldn't be bothered to get there the first time?'

He feels deflated. He has no idea what to do next.

'So, did you? See if it's a boy or a girl?'

'Do you really care one way or the other?'

'Yes!' He picks up her hand. It's cold. She doesn't pull it away, which has to be a good sign. 'Tell me, Mol. Please.'

'I made cakes,' she says, not answering his question, tipping her head towards the carrier thing on the ground. 'Pink middles, blue middles, covering both possibilities. Once we knew what we're having, I was going to get rid of the wrong ones, and take the right ones with us on the train. I thought we could hand them round, to the whole family at dinner tonight, let them all find out together. I hadn't expected to have to give you one too. That you'd be as much in the dark as the rest of them. What happened to us being a couple, Jack? To sharing moments like these?'

'I am so, so sorry. What else can I do? And if eating one of your cakes is the only way I have of finding out, then come on, hand one over. I love your cakes. You know I do. So, I'll eat the whole lot if I have to. So long as there are no lumps of molten glass inside them. Or cyanide!' He thinks he sees a hint of a smile on her face at the mention of the poison. 'I just want to know what we're having.'

He lets go of her hand, leans down and picks up the carrier. 'Hang on. It's so light. This thing can't be full of cake. What did you do? Throw them away in a fit of anger or something?'

'No. I got rid of them.'

'What? All of them? What happened to taking some home tonight? How are we going to let the family know if it's a boy or a girl now?'

'We're not.'

He gazes at her, confused. 'Why not?'

'Because we can't tell them something we don't know ourselves, that's why.'

'But...'

'I don't know what we're having, Jack. They did all the measurements and things, and the baby is doing fine. Everything in the right place, the right size, but when they got to the bit where they asked me if I wanted to know the sex... well, I said no.'

'So you don't...?'

'I have no idea, Jack. It's something I wanted us to find out together. Still do.'

'But you said they won't repeat the scan.'

'They won't, no. But there are private places that will do it for us. It will cost a bit, but everyone says the scan pictures are fantastic, really detailed, much better than the basic one we would have seen today. Here, look, I was just looking them up on Google when you – finally – turned up.' She takes her phone out and flicks to the website, places it in his hand.

'Oh.' He doesn't know what else to say. He slips one arm across her shoulders and pulls her in close, kisses her cheek. 'I thought you'd be so mad at me. You'd have every right.'

'I know. And I was. I am. But... well, this baby needs a daddy. And, despite everything, I need you too. So, what do you say? Shall we? Book a scan and meet our baby? Together?'

'Yes. Yes, please.'

'And you'll be there this time? No work, no excuses?'

'I will. I absolutely will. And, thank you.'

'What for?'

'For putting up with me being an idiot these last few weeks. Burying myself in work, burying my stupid head in the sand. But there are reasons I was so rattled by it all... well, excuses probably, not reasons. But, you know, a pregnancy I hadn't expected, hadn't planned...'

'It surprised me too.'

'I know it did. But there are things I've never told you, things that happened when I was a kid, but I will. This evening, on the train, I'll tell you, I promise. Because they don't mean a thing anymore. And I do love you, Mol. And this baby too. You know that, don't you?'

'I suppose so. Fool that I am.' She shakes her head and snuggles into him. 'Come on, we've got a train to catch.'

He stands up and lifts their bag in one hand, the empty cake carrier in the other. 'What did happen to the cakes?'

'I gave them to the hospital. For the nurses to share, or to give to the patients after their scans. And left a few of my business cards too. Angela, that's the woman who did the scan, said she thought they were a great idea, something so many of their patients would love.'

'You are becoming a real little businesswoman, aren't you?'

'I'm trying. But maybe not so little these days.' She puts her hand on her rounded belly and, in a sudden rush of love, Jack kneels down on the cold concrete and kisses it. 'Our own little secret centre!' he says, a sudden sense of wonder running through him as he imagines the tiny person lying just beneath her skin, his son or daughter slowly growing inside her.

She laughs and runs her fingers through his hair.

'Am I forgiven?' he says, wobbling back onto his feet.

'You're on probation. In fact, if you're good, I might even give you a dog biscuit!'

He has no idea what she's talking about, but Syd's words ring in his ears. Him in the doghouse. Woof, woof! How could she possibly know?

'A new gingerbread recipe. They're shaped like dogs. I made

them for Sian, but I can spare a couple. Something for you to nibble on the train.'

'I'd rather nibble you,' he says, nuzzling her ear and making her laugh again.

He doesn't see her feel for the scan picture in her pocket. She does not take it out to show him. A beautiful image of their tiny baby girl. He's not the only one to have secrets and this is hers, for now.

Chapter 42

Carly

The ambulance moves forward at last and manages to squeeze past whatever had been obstructing its path. I can see them now. Jack and Molly, outside the entrance, him down on his knees for some reason, as if he's proposing. Or begging.

'Well, that's that then,' Syd says, as the car moves past them and all I can do is peer over my shoulder as we drive away and they disappear from view. 'Nothing else we can do, but hope he sorts things out.'

'He will.'

'And is that what you want, Carls? Jack playing happy families with his wife and child?'

I don't have to think about my answer. 'Yes. Whatever I felt for Jack, or thought I felt, it's gone. Finished. And he'll be a much better dad, and hopefully a better husband too, now he's realised that's what he wants.'

'That's good, because he was never good enough for you. Or available enough! So, tell me about you and that daft brother of mine. Things going well? He seems pretty smitten.'

'Does he?' I am ridiculously pleased to hear that, because I have to confess I'm pretty smitten too. 'I like him, Syd. I don't know him very well yet, but I really like what I've seen so far.'

'Oh, don't tell me what you've seen so far, Carls. Which bits my brother has had out on display. Not an image I want to have in my head before I eat my dinner!'

'You know what I meant.'

'When are you two getting together next, then?'

'I don't know. I have a funeral to go to, with Mum, next week. And Suze wants me to go shopping with her for bridesmaid dresses. And there's work...'

'Sounds like you're making up reasons to be busy. Don't you want to go out with my brother?'

'Of course I do, but... well, he won't be here for long, will he? I don't want to get too attached and then have him leave.'

'Like Jack did?'

'Yeah, I suppose so.'

'Daz isn't Jack, Carls. And he's not going back to Australia with Mum and Dad. He's decided to stay. Didn't he tell you? A few months at least, and if he can get a visa sorted and find a job, he's thinking of staying on longer term.'

'Is he?'

'Yeah. Great news, eh?' Syd stops the car in a layby and just looks at me.

'What? Why are we stopping?'

'This is meant to be your driving lesson, remember? We've wasted a good half of it chasing about sorting out Jack's horribly messy love life, but there's still time left for you. And I won't charge you for the full hour, don't worry.'

'Maybe we should send Jack a bill.' I laugh. 'For the taxi fare?'

'No, I think we can let him off this time. A mission of mercy.

For a mate. Now, come on, swap over. You're in the driving seat now, Carly.'

And, as I sit behind the wheel, take a look in the rear-view mirror, put my foot down and move cautiously ahead, I think maybe, finally, I am.

THE END

Also by Vivien Brown

A Part of Me

Thought-provoking and absorbing, this novel explores the meaning of family, the nature of guilt and regret, and the conflicts raised by the miracles of modern medicine.

BUY NOW

Acknowledgements

I really enjoyed writing this book, stepping back from my usual more serious themes, bringing in a lot more humour and simply writing about the ups and downs of love, lust and having babies. Okay, so it's a one-man-and-two-women triangle, so not quite a straightforward 'happy ever after' romance, but both women really do love Jack and, although they can't both have him, I have made sure they all get the ending they deserve!

My thanks, first of all, must go to the wonderfully supportive staff at Bloodhound, especially to Ian Skewis for his gentle and insightful editing, and to Tara Lyons, who has that magic touch that manages to turn a manuscript into a real book, even replacing the boring rows of asterisks between scenes with perfect little hearts. Genius!

I could not have written all the 'twins' scenes without having had twins myself. The juggling and feeding of two babies, the regularity of one waking up just as the other goes to sleep, the friendship and advice that comes from other mothers in the same boat when it so often feels that nobody else really understands... so I give thanks, as always, to the Humana Wellington IVF team for making my twins a reality all those years ago, turning the hopes and dreams into the beginnings of the family I have today. No gender-revealing scans back then, so I had no idea what I was getting until the night my daughters arrived, within five minutes of each other. Secret centres to the end!

Other writers play a huge part in any author's life, so a huge thanks must go to the members of the Society of Women Writers and Journalists, the Romantic Novelists' Association, and Phrase Writers, for being my 'tribe' and sharing the rocky road that leads so many of us, hopefully and eventually, to publication. And to the Swanwick Writers' Summer School where, as a regular course leader, I have had the privilege of passing on so much of what I have learned in thirty years as a writer to those who follow on.

And lastly, my readers. I couldn't keep doing what I do without you. For the support, the reviews, and simply for choosing my book out of the thousands you could have picked... Thank you.

About the Author

Vivien Brown was born and grew up in Middlesex and still lives there today, with her husband and two cats. Following an early career in banking and accountancy, the lure of working with words instead of numbers became too strong to resist and she went on to spend the happiest years of her working life reading with the under-fives in children's centres and libraries while writing short stories for women's magazines in her spare time. She went on to train as an adult education creative writing tutor and started writing novels, specialising in women's fiction with domestic drama and family relationships at its heart.

She is a past winner of the annual Mail on Sunday 'Best Opening to a Novel' competition and reached the shortlist again three years later, and was wined and dined on both occasions alongside the famous judges, Fay Weldon, John Mortimer, Sue Townsend and James Herbert, all incredibly friendly and supportive but sadly no longer with us.

Vivien is a fellow and honorary secretary of the Society of Women Writers and Journalists (SWWJ) where she oversees writing competitions and social media, and is a member of the Romantic Novelists' Association and a reader for its New Writers Scheme. She is also a regular tutor at the annual Swanwick Writers' Summer School.

Away from writing, Vivien loves playing with her grandchildren, watching and occasionally taking part in TV quiz shows, is an avid reader and reviewer of women's fiction, and enjoys the challenge of both solving and compiling cryptic crosswords.

A note from the publisher

Thank you for reading this book. If you enjoyed it please do consider leaving a review on Amazon to help others find it too.

We hate typos. All of our books have been rigorously edited and proofread, but sometimes mistakes do slip through. If you have spotted a typo, please do let us know and we can get it amended within hours.

info@bloodhoundbooks.com

www.ingramcontent.com/pod-product-compliance
Lightning Source LLC
Chambersburg PA
CBHW061521210726
48287CB00006B/1770